BROKEN CROWN

BROKEN PEAK PACK
BOOK 5

BY JULES CRISARE

BROKEN PEAK PACK

Broken Hero
Broken Sage
Broken Mage
Broken Rebel
Broken Crown
Broken Witch

HIDDEN RUNAWAYS

Hidden Trouble

BLACK HILLS VENDETTA

Wolf's Retribution
Wolf's Revenge
Wolf's Reckoning *(coming to Kickstarter in 2024)*

BOX SETS

Broken Peak Pack eBook Bundle Volume 1
Broken Peak Pack eBook Bundle Volume 2
Broken Peak Pack Omnibus Collector's Edition *(Kickstarter Exclusive)*

SILVER SENTINEL NOVELS

Destined Heir
The Last Immortal Mystery Files *(coming to Kickstarter in 2023)*

SENTINELS OF THE SILVER ORB

BROKEN CROWN

BROKEN PEAK PACK
BOOK 5

BY JULES CRISARE

SILVER ORB BOOKS

BROKEN CROWN

Designed by J. Crisare

0123pbk

ISBN: 978-1-948603-27-0 (pbk.)

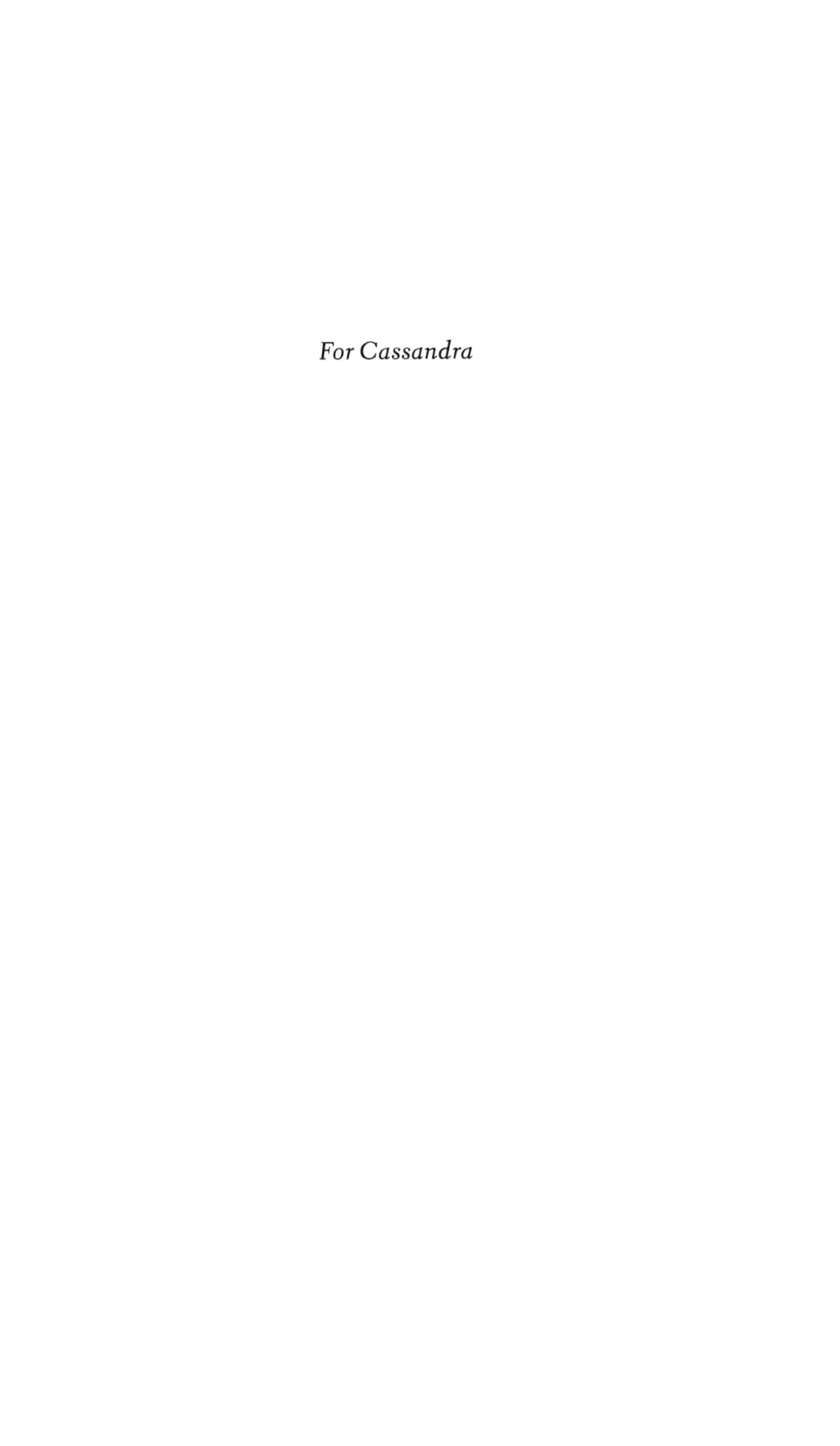

For Cassandra

PROLOGUE

A History of Shifters & the Role of the McCallisters
—from Edna McCallister's journal

IN THE beginning, the lesser shifters, supernaturals, and humans respected the Great Shifters. They also feared and resented the power of the dragon and griffin shifters. But as was the way with so many powerful entities, the Great Shifters were revered and sometimes worshiped.

The wolf shifters had the strength of numbers from living in packs, and this gave them more power among the lesser shifters. One pack among them was the strongest in all ways. They held themselves apart from the humans, supernaturals, the lesser shifters who weren't wolves, and even the Great Shifters.

When the Great Shifters came to realize their eventual fate, they set the pieces in place for a future when all shifters and supernaturals would need to unite to prevent the humans from eradicating them. A dragon and griffin shifter searched for the isolated pack.

As the two Great Shifters approached, the pack Alpha greeted them before they crossed into pack territory and questioned their presence. The Alpha's pack stayed out of the Great Shifters' way for a reason.

The Great Shifters asked the Alpha to walk with them while they explained.

The Great Shifters couldn't foresee the future, but they could read the present. Eventually the supernaturals would unite and destroy the Great Shifters. The costs would be enormous and the balance would be upended. Humans always feared what they didn't understand and many generations from them, the lesser shifters and supernaturals could no longer hide from the humans.

The Great Shifters couldn't change destiny, not even with their combined power, but they could set pieces in place that might alter destiny's shape. The Alpha's pack would provide two of these pieces, if the Alpha agreed.

Because of the pack's isolation, the wolf shifters were purebred, the only truly pure shifters left in the world besides the Great Shifters. The Alpha's descendants would be the perfect candidates. The Alpha's bloodline would need to remain pure in shifter blood, but the Historian would help with that. However, keeping the bloodline pure wouldn't be the greatest of costs. The Alpha would need to integrate his pack into human society and adapt to hiding in plain sight.

For in the future, when the Hero emerged, a descendant of the Alpha would step away from her role as Alpha and embrace the role of ruler of all the lesser shifters. She would stand shoulder to shoulder with the Hero and be known as the Crown.

CHAPTER ONE

ALLARD glared at the two cardinals munching happily at the giant bird feeder stuck in the middle of the yard. Another happy pairing the world loved throwing in his face. More than ever, during the past few months. It was like mother nature was giving him the finger at every turn. Even Finley, his packmate and best friend, had found love with his mate Maggie, a fierce little raccoon shifter who made all their lives more interesting since her arrival at Broken Peak.

But love wasn't in Allard's future. He'd be lucky if he got a happy mating out of the deal.

Wolf shifters liked to pretend they were as civilized as the humans they hid amongst. Unless, it came to the Alphas. For whatever reason, the wolf shifter packs arranged all the Alpha matings. If the Council didn't approve of the mating, then it didn't happen.

Some Alphas had negotiated matings before their pups were even born. Which was pretty much what happened with Allard, he hadn't been born yet when the most powerful and influential pack in the United States approached his father.

The first-born son of the Colorado Pack would mate the first-born daughter of the Chicago Pack. Among wolf shifters, the mating was considered a good one and would bring power and wealth to Colorado while increasing the number of those who would stand with the Chicago Pack without question. Although, it wasn't as if the packs battled like they did centuries ago.

Allard had hoped that when he left Colorado for West Virginia, the Lyalls would either find another first-born son to mate with their daughter or accept Allard's younger brother. Except that hadn't happened.

The Lyalls had remained silent about Allard's exodus and hadn't even complained to the Council about his apparent voiding of the mating agreement. It might have had something to do with Lennon Lyall bonding with a human female and not wanting to rustle any feathers before the dust fully settled.

Allard expected them to encourage any potential matings with their daughter to distract from a full-blooded wolf shifter diluting their line with a human, but neither Everest nor Mia appeared to care about the gossip. Not that Allard cared much either, but Danielle had been keeping an eye out for any news or gossip on the net for him.

On the plus side, he hadn't heard from his father with orders to return home. The respite wouldn't last much longer and then Allard would have to explain to his packmates, his friends, that he'd lied since the first day he showed up on Bray's doorstep.

Okay, so lying was a big word, and it wasn't so much he lied as he never corrected anyone's assumptions. Mac, the old coyote shifter who made it his business to know everything, knew. And Bray, Allard's Alpha, probably knew. But Vixen, Bray's mate, and the rest of the pack didn't know that Allard wasn't kicked out of a pack and didn't have a crappy childhood. He was the first-born son of the Alpha of the biggest and second most powerful pack in the United States.

Allard could have had everything he wanted if he stayed in Colorado, except for the mate of his choosing

He told himself he ran because he needed a break from political bullshit and not because he hoped to get out of the pairing. While it was mostly true, deep down that he hoped the Lyalls would break the mating because Allard was irresponsible and not reputable enough for their daughter, the crown princess of the Chicago Pack.

Yeah, that didn't happen.

The light tinkling of a giggle followed by the deep growl of a protective male came from the edge of the woods. Maggie and Finley. The two had been inseparable, even more so, now that they had both accepted they were bonded mates. Under most circumstances, Allard would have been happy for his friend. But it wasn't most circumstances.

"Allard?" A soft female voice called his name.

He snapped his head around and found Eleanor, Jackson's petite human mate and the adoptive mother of his pup.

Jackson liked to say Eleanor resembled Snow White with her dark hair and pale skin. Tonight she embraced the fairy tale look dressed in a pastel pink sweater and matching pleated skirt. She even held her hair away from her face with a matching pink ribbon. For a moment, Allard wondered if she deliberately picked her clothing to tease her mate, or if her clothes happened to be within easy reach when she got dressed.

Eleanor stepped down off the porch and took a few steps before coming to a stop a good fifteen feet away. "You've been out here alone for a while. Is everything all right?"

Allard turned away from her and stuck his hands in the pockets of his jeans. What could he say to her that she'd accept as the truth? Nothing. Eleanor was a mom and had all the magic most moms had in sussing out the truth in a pile of half-truths and almost lies.

"Depends on what you consider all right."

He should have popped in his ear buds and headed for the woods as soon as he walked out the front door. Or better yet, shift and go for a run.

"Allard, what's wrong? Did something happen?"

"Nothing's wrong. But, yeah, I guess you could say something happened." Allard pulled his hands free of his pockets and pressed his palms to his cheeks. "Granted, it happened over thirty years ago, but it still happened and I can't unhappen it."

"Problems?" Bray asked from behind.

How had the older wolf sneaked up on him? With his hands planted on his hips and his head tilted back, Allard kept his eyes closed. He could walk away and avoid the uncomfortable conversation that was long past due. Tell Bray he would talk with him in the morning. Or he could...

"Rip it off quick like a band-aid."

"Christ, Bray. No wonder Danielle's convinced y'all can read minds."

"Hm?"

Allard lowered his chin to his chest and released a noise similar to the sighs Bray used to give the pack before Vixen's arrival.

"Vixen says the phrase enough, and there's not much it doesn't apply it to." Bray supplied an explanation, but it didn't discount the whole mind reading conspiracy Danielle loved to chat about. "But it sounds like things aren't okay, so, I'll repeat my question. Problems?"

Putting the conversation off until the morning wasn't a viable option. "Where do you want me to start?"

Bray crossed his arms over his massive chest. "Under normal circumstances, I'd say from the beginning, but I think we both know that's not necessary. Unless, of course, Eleanor wants to hear the entire history of shitty pack politics. So let's go with what's changed in the last few days."

"Shit." Allard lowered his gaze to the ground, not wanting to look his Alpha in the eyes. "How long have you known?"

"Since you showed up on my doorstep with a not-so ratty bag in hand with more clothes in it than the rest of the boys had combined." Bray tilted his head toward the porch. "Come on, let's not stand in the yard. We might not get the most privacy, but Jackson will be happier if Eleanor is in the circle of the porch light and there's no way anyone except Vi will be able to pull her away from this."

"Where is Vixen?" If Allard had to tell the story, he only wanted to have to tell it once.

"Off with Mac. Not sure what they have planned, but it involves the county sheriff and the town of War, and I want to stay the hell away from it."

While they walked to the porch, Allard gathered his thoughts. He'd put this conversation off long enough. He should have shared it with Bray years ago. On the brighter side, he wouldn't have to go into the details unless Eleanor asked questions, which she likely would.

Bray sat in one of the Adirondack chairs Vixen recently added to the porch. She claimed she was tired of watching everyone lean against the railing, but Allard suspected it had more to do with Danielle, Eleanor, and Maggie hogging the swing and Vixen not wanting to lean against the railing. Eleanor took over the swing, as expected.

Allard sat in the chair next to Bray's and looked down at his hands. "Why didn't you say something sooner?"

"I figured you'd tell me when you were ready."

"I should have told you as soon as I realized you wouldn't send me back, but by then..."

"By then you'd have to tell everyone you lied."

"I didn't lie. I just didn't correct their assumptions."

"Fair enough." Bray leaned forward and rested his elbows on his knees.

"I didn't mean to add another enemy to the list, Bray."

"I know. And I'm not worried about the Lyalls." Bray lifted his head and stared across the dark yard into the trees. "I can't say the same for your father. He thought he was gaining a Lyall when he agreed to the arrangement. If the Lyalls push for the mating, I'll be the one getting a Lyall and Everest's support."

"Dad might be a bit of an ass, but he's not stupid. He'll wait until we're mated, then call me back home."

"He'll have to send an army. You're Broken Peak Pack, Allard. You're my wolf. The moment you crossed my threshold and your father didn't protest it, you became mine. And now Vi's." Bray grinned at Allard. The same grin Vixen used when her griffin pushed toward the surface and wanted out to play. "We both know she isn't good at sharing."

Allard sucked in a breath. Vixen, especially her griffin, didn't take kindly to anyone who trespassed on what or who she considered hers. The last time had been just a week ago when the bat-shit insane leader of Maggie's Gaze came into pack territory and harmed Maggie. The griffin ripped out a raccoon shifter's spine, but Vixen broke the Gaze leader's neck with her bare hands. Allard wasn't sure he'd call Vixen's problem a sharing issue.

"Do you have a copy of the agreement?" Eleanor asked.

She'd been so quiet during Bray's and Allard's conversation, Allard almost forgot she was there.

Bray reached into the pocket of his shirt and pulled out a piece of paper folded over several times. He handed it across to Eleanor. "Mac gave it to me a few weeks after Allard arrived in case the Council came and questioned our intentions."

Eleanor snatched the paper from Bray's fingertips. The paper almost tore as she yanked it open. She didn't read it so much as scan the document. "This doesn't make sense." Eleanor peered up over the paper at Bray and Allard.

"What do you mean?" Allard asked.

"I've looked at a lot of these mating agreements since arriving. Mac has a trunk full of them. But every last one isn't about the individual, it's about the pack." She dragged her hand over the surface of the paper along a line of text. "This agreement is specifically between Allard and Delia, not the Colorado Alpha's heir and the Lyalls' daughter."

Bray narrowed his eyes as he peered out into the darkness. "This agreement has me wondering. Why you, Allard? Why not any other Alpha's son?"

Eleanor looked up from the piece of paper she'd been frowning over. "I can answer that. You're a pure-bSlooded wolf shifter, Allard. One of the few."

Allard shook his head in confusion. "What? How do you even know that when I don't?"

"Mac has an enormous book filled with family trees that go way back. Apparently you came from the last pure pack." Eleanor finally put the paper down in her lap and looked directly into Allard's eyes. "The Lyalls came from the same pack. Difference is they came directly from the Alpha of that pack, your line came from the second in command, or at least that's what I think his role was. He might have been an advisor or counselor."

"That's a nice history lesson, but it still doesn't explain why me and not my brother or my father's heir."

"Your brother isn't a pure-blooded shifter. None of your siblings are."

Allard's eyes widened. The only way he couldn't be a pure-blooded shifter was if his mother wasn't faithful to his father, but his father would have known Allard wasn't his blooded son.

"You have a separate branch."

Bray shrugged and shook his head, staring at Eleanor with the same confused look on Allard's face.

"Eleanor…" Allard pinched the bridge of his nose and closed his eyes tight. "What do you mean by separate branch?"

Sheesh, it was worse than pulling straight answers out of Maggie when she was caught pilfering something shiny from the packmates.

"It looks like your father is a pure-blooded shifter, but your mother isn't."

"He loves my mom. They weren't an arranged mating, more of a 'oh look, we both come from strong packs, let's make an agreement so it looks like we're following tradition' kind of thing."

"Right, which is all fine and dandy, but if you're part of the pure-blooded line, you keep that going, right? Find a pure-blooded female, your father does whatever, and then your mom raised you as hers." Eleanor smiled at Allard and reached for his hand, squeezing it tightly. "And you know you don't have to have blood relations to love a child. You're your mom's son, no matter the circumstances."

Bray growled low and stood up from his chair to peer across the yard into the woods. "Visitors."

Allard sniffed at the air. Two visitors. One a female wolf shifter, and the other one smelled close to human, but not quite.

CHAPTER TWO

VIXEN strolled out of the woods from the direction of Mac's cabin, the older coyote shifter who had adopted the combination role of grandfather and wise old man to the Broken Peak Pack. The blond haired female Alpha paused and studied the furthest border of the yard before continuing to the porch. Her dark gray clothing hid her well in the shadows and even made it difficult to spot her movements once she appeared in the open yard and under the light of the moon.

Bray leaped to his feet and jogged down the porch steps and across the short distance to Vixen.

That was the type of mating Allard wanted. He didn't need a female who could break a man's neck or deliver an undercut to the jaw when injured and incapacitated by bullet wounds. But he wanted the same intimacy Bray and Vixen shared.

Envy crept its way into Allard's thoughts.

Vixen was right where she was supposed to be. And so were Eleanor, Danielle, and Maggie. He wished Delia was supposed to be here too, but fate hadn't been kind to him, and he wasn't expecting any miracles.

When he pushed up from the chair and stood at the top of the porch steps, Vixen was already walking away from Bray and heading toward Allard.

"We'll have a come to Jesus moment later about why you think you can't trust me, but for now I want to know how you're doing."

He tucked his hands into his pockets and shrugged. "As well as usual."

He didn't lie. Since arriving at Broken Peak over ten years ago, he'd been expecting his arranged mating to come to light. He'd learned to live with the anxiety instead of letting it overwhelm him.

Vixen tilted her head to the side and studied him with as much softness as she was capable of. "We're going to have to share this with the others."

He nodded. "Yep, I know. I was just hoping it would have worked itself out in any other way when the inevitable talk happened."

"They'll understand. It's not like they all didn't come with their own baggage. Even Eleanor had enough baggage to fill the back of the borrowed SUV she drove up in."

He glanced over his shoulder at Eleanor and grinned. Jackson hadn't been exactly ready to be a father, but he stepped up, and so did the rest of the pack.

"El!" Jackson yelled out from inside the Lodge. "Your son needs a bath. He got into the tunnels under the house again and is covered in what I hope is just dirt, but since Maggie's raccoon likes to hide down there, I'm not willing to put any money down on it."

"My son?" Eleanor rolled her eyes and stood. She looked down at the mating arrangement in her hand, then back at Allard. "Mind if I keep this for a while. It's subtle, but I think there are some other differences. I'd like to compare it to the agreements Mac has stashed away."

"Sure. Not like I have any use for it right now."

Eleanor tip-toed behind Allard and back into the Lodge before Vixen or Bray could comment. No one could accuse Jackson's mate of not being smart.

"Sit back down, Allard. We're not done yet."

Allard ignored Vixen's command and stared across the treeless expanse. "I didn't think we were, but we might have to postpone it for a bit."

"Mac and Roose are running interference to buy us a few more minutes." Vixen waved away his concern and climbed up the porch steps. She crossed to the swing and settled into the spot coveted by all the females in the pack. "Sit down."

Soon all three were settled on the porch, all watching the woods in anticipation of the owners of the unfamiliar scents making their appearance.

"If life were simple, we'd all be bored, Allard. We wouldn't know what to do with ourselves," Bray said.

"This isn't really a life or death matter though."

"No, but things will get interesting. I'm not sure how long we have before they figure out Mac is taking them the long way, which includes lots of big circles," Vixen added.

"Are you banking on our new visitors not being country wise, Vi?" Bray asked with a chuckle.

"Yes. Yes, I am." Vixen preened happily from her perch on the swing.

"I think I need to go to the Council." Allard looked down at his hands and folded them in his lap. "If I plead my case to them, explain that it's not a suitable match since I'm no longer going to be the Alpha of the Colorado Pack, they might nullify the agreement."

"This is out of the Council's hands," Vixen said. "Besides, as I'm sure Eleanor explained in great detail, the match wasn't made because of your status as heir."

"I don't see how the Council can abstain," he responded. "All the official packs agree to the Council as the de facto governing board, and in return they keep the packs as safe as possible. Broken Peak is an official pack and unless we want to be excommunicated, we have to obey the Council's decisions."

"Yeah, normally we do. But I think what Vi's getting at is that there's a higher power at work and the Council is no longer the top dog."

Allard whistled low. "The Council's not going to like that."

"They don't have to like it to agree to it. The Council was established long ago with the understanding that they're guardians and would have to surrender their power, eventually."

"Is this more of the mumbo jumbo stuff you and Mac have decided is some great destiny set in place thousands of years ago? Because if it is, I don't think the Council is going to welcome that as a reason for the shift in power."

"It's a moot point, Allard," Vixen ended the circular conversation. "With the Lyalls' son claiming his mate, their role has ended. They might continue as a mouthpiece, delivering the edicts of the Heir, but their days of deciding the fates of the wolf shifter packs are over."

Allard looked over at Bray and asked, "do you have any idea what she's talking about?"

"It's the mumbo jumbo stuff you all laugh about."

"You laughed too." Allard didn't want to be the only one standing out on his own when Vixen, the biggest believer in the mumbo jumbo, was sitting so close.

"Yeah, but Maggie's arrival and then the Lyall's son claiming the supposed human with Everest Lyall's complete approval, it's looking less like mumbo jumbo," Bray explained his change of heart.

"Are you saying you're buying this prophecy crap?"

Vixen growled softly.

"It's not crap. And don't think of it as a prophecy. It's like a chess game that's been playing out for centuries."

"Eons," Vixen corrected Bray.

"Fine, eons," Bray continued, "and each century a piece on the board moved. Until now, all the pieces are where they're supposed to be."

"Okay, let's say I agree with that premise. Why are they supposed to be where they are?"

Bray shrugged.

"Mac and I never shared the entry about me, Allard. About my griffin. You all believe there's never been griffins before, but ask yourself how likely is it for a new shifter species to just appear?"

"I haven't heard of it, but shifters have stayed well-hidden over the centuries. New shifters, who are just as good at hiding in plain sight too, are a possibility."

"We'd recognize an unfamiliar scent, Allard. We all recognized Vi wasn't human, but we couldn't figure out what she was."

"According to Danielle, new species are being discovered every day. She's convinced BigFoot exists."

"She was also sure that we were wolf aliens who wore human skins."

"Yeah, she's not exactly the best way to support your argument, Bray. Danielle's brilliant with computers and organizing ops, but she's always had one foot firmly planted in the land of conspiracies, especially cryptids." Vixen laughed softly and tucked her feet beneath her. "But, Bray's argument isn't less valid. What if griffins existed thousands of years ago? And what if they could read the signs and knew that there'd eventually be a war they might not be able to win?"

"Depends how smart they were." Allard grudgingly accepted Vixen's point.

"Assume they aren't just smart, but powerful too. And that they aren't the only ones, like what if dragons existed too?"

"No. Nope. Not going there. Griffins I can see, they're small enough, but dragons? Dragons don't just fly, they breathe fire and are probably ten times the size of a griffin."

"Doesn't mean they didn't exist."

"There'd be bones. Or fossils."

"No one's found griffin fossils." Bray had definitely turned on them.

Allard covered his face with his hands and sighed. "If you all are trying to distract me, you're doing a brilliant job of it."

"We aren't. I promise." Vixen spoke softly. "Going back to your original question, why do the pieces need to be where they're supposed to be. What if these griffin and dragon shifters not only read their present situation, but could see what might eventually happen?"

"Oh? They could read the future too? That's a new one."

"No, not read the future. Just read the humans and shifters and others and understand that once they destroyed one enemy, there would have to be another. Humans don't like things that are different."

"Humans just want a shifter back in their employment," Allard responded.

He was done listening to the mystical crap. None of it would fix his current situation. Placing his hands on the arms of the chair, he pushed to his feet and climbed down the porch steps.

"I'm not finished, Allard."

Vixen's voice halted him in his tracks. He couldn't take another step, even if he wanted to.

"If the journal entries aren't just the ramblings of a senile old shifter, then it's likely a war is coming. Similar to the one the great shifters faced. Except this one will include all the shifters, and possibly others, against humans. Whether or not you want it, you are a piece still in play on the board."

He might not have been able to move, but he could still speak. "The prophecy, or whatever it is, only names the females. No males are named."

"Except without Bray, I wouldn't have my griffin, or even be alive. Without Jackson, Eleanor would never have come to Broken Peak. Without Leighton, Danielle wouldn't have stayed, and without Finley, Maggie never would have approached us, much less stuck around."

"Vi," Bray chastised his mate, "you and I both know we'd have to kick Danielle out to get her to leave, and that might not even work."

"She would have been killed if Leighton and his wolf weren't around to keep her safe."

Vixen stared at the back of Allard's head. He didn't need to see it to know either. Her stare could be as forceful as her voice when she wanted it to be. And right then, she wanted it.

With a deep breath, she finally released him. "We aren't going to force anything on you that you don't want, Allard."

"I'd love to believe it, Vixen, I really would. But I'm not convinced by Edna's journals, and I don't think anyone else will be either." Allard headed toward the shadows of the woods for some time alone. What he'd been planning on doing before Eleanor had stopped him.

CHAPTER THREE

AS ALLARD strode into the forest, his wolf finally made an appearance, urging him back to the Lodge.

He did his best to ignore the wolf. The last thing he needed was to be surrounded by the judging eyes of his packmates and the knowing smiles of their mates.

"Wha'cha doing out here? Hiding?" Roose, the giant bear shifter and friend of the Broken Peak Pack fell into step with Allard.

"Avoiding," Allard said.

"The visitors?" Roose asked. "Or your Alphas?"

"Can it be both?"

Allard laid out everything to Roose, starting with where Allard came from, and ending with why the last place he wanted to be was at the Lodge with his packmates.

Roose scratched at his beard. "Well, the way I see it, you being in the woods won't change anything," he said. "Vixen and Mac believe everything Edna wrote, and they're convinced there's a reason for everything that's happened around here. Including your arrival. You could have gone anywhere, but you came here, right?"

"This is the place for last chances. And my father would have found me and dragged me back if I went anywhere else.

"Yeah, Bray's a scary fucker when he wants to be. But you could have found other places to hide. So why here?"

"I don't know. I guess I heard my dad talk about it before. Or someone else mentioned it."

"You don't remember?"

"Never really considered it."

"You can't remember how you heard about Broken Peak or the pack here, but this was the first place you came to." Roose added. "This is probably the safest place, despite our recent troubles. Your father can't reach you here, the Council can't touch you, and even the Lyalls won't cross Bray."

Allard sighed hard and pinched the bridge of his nose while counting to five. Great, Roose was a believer too.

"I just meant that you came here for a reason. And maybe it had nothing to do with you." Roose said. "You're tied to the Lyalls' daughter, right? If you had stayed, she'd be in Colorado now. If you had found another place to hide, then she'd be stuck back in Chicago, waiting until your father uncovered your location and dragged you home."

Allard wasn't ready to admit it, but Roose made sense. More sense than anyone who let the ramblings of an old crazy woman dictate their future had a right to be.

Every time the girls talked about the journals, Allard humored them. Which was better than the others, who tuned them out and nodded at the right times.

"You think I need to head back to the Lodge and wait with the others?"

"I didn't say that," Roose said. "But ask yourself if you want this Lyall female's first impression to be Finley and Tevin, or Vixen?"

"How do you know Delia is here?"

Roose laughed. "Do you think Vixen and Mac would let anyone else wander into the territory as freely?"

"Fair point."

"She's here for a reason, and I'm guessing that reason is you. You really want her to have to wait to see you? It's not as though this meeting is on the best of terms either. You might want to make her introduction to the pack a little easier than say Eleanor or Danielle's."

"Maggie's was at least funny."

"Maggie is funny. She's a weird little female." Roose chuckled. "Speaking of which, make sure you ask Vixen more about Maggie. Edna shared an interesting story about Maggie's ancestors and whether or not it's true, it explains almost everything that confuses the shit out of us."

After Roose switched topics, they continued walking along in silence.

Roose was right. Allard couldn't let Delia walk into the pack alone. Their meeting might not be under the best of circumstances, but she deserved better. He needed to get back and wait with Vixen and Bray. Or maybe he should intercept Mac before the old coyote led them to the Lodge.

A heavy hand landed on his shoulder, jerking him out of his thoughts. "Yeah?"

"Let her come on her own terms. She's here for a reason. I think we all know it has to do with the mating, but none of us know what her message will be, and it'll be better if she can deliver it according to her timeline and not yours." Roose squeezed his shoulder, and Allard's knees practically buckled under the weight of his hand. "Plus, I don't think her dad's one of those guys you want to offend and I'm sure she has him on speed dial."

"Assuming he knows she's here."

"He knows. Trust me. A father will always know where his daughter is. Even if they don't want to be found."

Again, Roose was right. The old bear had no reason to be as right as he was all the time. He lived alone, Drank Mac's moonshine by the barrel full, and avoided anything that had to do with the outside world.

"I should head back."

"Yeah." Roose peeled away from Allard, leaving him alone in the woods.

Allard slipped his ear buds into place and scrolled through the music Danielle, Leighton's mate and the pack's resident technical genius, helped load onto his phone, to find the perfect playlist. Preferably one without love songs. The last thing Allard needed a reminder of, was something he'd never experience. Especially as he headed to face whatever message Delia came herself to deliver.

Seven Nation Army's guitar riff welcomed him, and Allard closed his eyes as the drum beat joined the recognizable chords.

Five minutes. Five more minutes of wandering alone in the woods without the watchful and curious gazes of his packmates before he'd head back to the Lodge.

With his eyes closed, he tilted his face toward the rising moon.

How horrible was Delia, for her parents not to even entertain another mate when Allard fell off the grid?

Not that it mattered, but after watching most of the males in the Broken Peak Pack and his Alpha find their own mates, Allard allowed hope to seep in where it had no business belonging. Vixen, Eleanor, Danielle, and Maggie bulldozed their way into the pack and strengthened it. And better. They turned the Broken Peak Pack into everything Allard imagined a pack should be. A place filled with love and laughter. All sense of duty came from the need to keep the pack strong and safe and not from a family obligation.

Seven Nation Army came to an abrupt end. He should have paid closer attention to the playlist. If he had, the immediate lyrics from a man singing about his perfect love wouldn't have invaded his ears.

Allard bit back the scream threatening to break free. The universe wasn't playing fair. Ripping the earbuds from his ears, he gripped the phone in his hand and hurled it into the woods.

The phone smacked into a tree. Or a rock from the sound of the impact.

"Shit."

Danielle was gonna kill him. And he'd deserve it, too. Allard wasn't like the others. He didn't lose control. He didn't allow his emotions to get the better of him. Ever.

"Fuck me."

He trotted across the yard to where he thought the phone might have landed.

"Shit, shit, shit."

No flashlight. He could have used the phone's flashlight. Except, you know, he didn't have his phone.

"Fuck."

He didn't think the day, well night, could suck any more than it did, but quickly pushed that thought away. No reason to tempt fate. The way everything had played out, Allard wouldn't be surprised if his father didn't come strolling down the path to drag Allard back to Colorado.

It was bad enough they had some shady government operatives after them, but there was no telling if the crazy raccoon shifter cults would heed Vixen's warning and stay away or ignore it and launch attacks. Now Allard might add to the pack's growing list of enemies by two. The Lyalls were more powerful financially, but it didn't mean they couldn't field a small army if necessary. And Allard's father wasn't lacking in the enforcer department either.

Allard crouched and patted the dead leaves in hopes his fingers might brush against his fallen phone.

"Fuck!" He tilted his head back and screamed at the darkening sky.

Arranged matings sucked. They made packs stronger and also prevented all-out wars between packs, but they still sucked. Allard didn't buy into the whole fated mates idea, but he did believe in love. And he trusted his wolf's instinct. Even in matters of the heart.

And wouldn't that be perfectly fitting to the perfectly crappy day.

CHAPTER FOUR

DELIA Lyall's perfect life had taken a hard turn to the left and was currently pulling a Thelma and Louise.

Fate had to have it out for her. It was the only explanation.

She gripped the steering wheel of her car and stared at the road in front of her.

Geneva, her best friend and now sister-in-law sat next to her in silence. Geneva gave up on her attempts to calm Delia down six hours into the drive, but that was three and a half hours ago and Geneva was getting impatient.

She wondered why Geneva insisted on accompanying her. It wasn't as though she wasn't capable of driving half way across the country on her own.

Probably because her brother believed Delia would be better behaved with Geneva there. He promised to stall her parents from sending anyone after her only if she agreed to let Geneva ride shotgun for the trip.

Not that Delia minded.

Geneva had been her partner in crime since she was in grade school. Together they had gotten into and out of more trouble than most parents would consider healthy. They even got themselves kicked out of the library. Not for being loud, but for using the bathroom to clean off the dirt they got covered in when they took a detour to visit the slow-moving river that ran through the town they grew up in.

Too bad Delia had crossed the line from polite socialite to pissed off she-wolf.

She wasn't happy with the arranged mating. But she was less happy with her arranged mate.

Her irresponsible, moronic, coward of an arranged mate.

"Delia?" Geneva asked.

"What?" She ground out. Her fingers tightening around the leather wrapping the steering was the only thing keeping her from snapping at her friend. Sure, it would have been mostly undeserved, but it might have made her feel a little better. And Geneva, a lot worse.

Only one of them needed to be pissy because of someone treating them like shit. And as angry as Delia was, her best friend didn't deserve to be on the receiving end.

Allard did.

Allard, the stupid idiot who made the past year and half miserable just by not being anywhere he was supposed to be.

"What's the end game here? Once we get to where you're hell-bent on going, what do you want to have happen?"

To castrate and castigate the bastard who's single handedly made the last year and a half of my life a living hell. Except she didn't think his packmates would let her get close enough to castrate him.

Although, they had to sleep sometime…

"I don't know Neva. The best-case scenario would be we hold a mating then go our separate ways and live our own lives until we have to fulfill some obligation."

"I don't think that's going to happen, Del." Geneva pressed closer to the car door, as if she expected a full-blown tantrum from Delia.

Delia turned off the two-lane highway and onto a dirt road that came to an abrupt end at a wall of trees less than fifty feet from the road.

"Why are we turning here? Is this a driveway? There isn't a more direct route we could take?" Geneva released a shotgun of questions while staring into the trees with a combination of dread and fear.

"Because this is where I'm going. No. Yes." Delia replied just as quickly.

She was used to her friend's nervous habits, especially when she was outdoors. Catered picnics were as close as Geneva ever got to communing with nature.

She didn't wait for the expected protests and excuses from her friend and jumped out of her car onto the gravel covered ground. Before Geneva opened her mouth, she slammed the car door shut. With a deep breath, she scented the air. The woods welcomed her, even if they were filled with the scent of countless shifters.

Wolves, a bear, a coyote, some mountain lions, something she couldn't quite identify, and, was that a raccoon?

What was a raccoon doing away from a Gaze? The nearest Gaze was hours from here. Unless the raccoons established a new Gaze and the Council didn't know about it yet? That seemed unlikely.

Plus, from everything she'd overheard from her parents, she didn't think the Broken Peak Pack would tolerate a Gaze anywhere close to their territory.

"Took you long enough." An old man, who fit all the stereotypes of a backwoods moonshiner, stepped out of the woods.

A long beard covered the bottom portion of the old man's face and wrinkles formed a road map from the corners of his eyes to the corners of his mouth.

He smiled. A lot.

His thick gray hair stuck out in all directions, like he'd given up trying to pull a brush through it years ago.

"You're Delia and I'm Mac. Vixen sent me out to greet you, but really it's to stall you."

So this was the coyote shifter. And if he knew Vixen, the recent and unknown Alpha female of Broken Peak, then he was probably aware of the reason for Delia's arrival onto pack territory.

"Yes, Delia Lyall, and Geneva is still in the car." Delia glanced over her shoulder to confirm that Geneva was in fact still sitting in the passenger seat. "She doesn't do nature."

"We have one of those living here too." Mac chuckled and combed his fingers through his hair. "She's the Moon Child?"

"What?" As far as Delia understood, no one outside of her immediate family knew what Geneva was. And Delia had been the last to find out too.

"Your family isn't the only one with records," Mac answered. "Vixen suggested I walk you around in circles, but I'm betting you're too smart for that."

This was so unexpected. The coyote shifter greeting them. His knowledge about Geneva. And most of all, admitting why he was there to begin with. Mac's behavior didn't mesh with what she knew about coyotes.

"So, why are you here, Delia Lyall of the Chicago Pack?" Mac asked.

"Because your pack–"

"Not my pack." Mac raised his hand holding his palm out towards her. "I just hang around the outskirts and interfere with their business. My life gets a little boring."

"Fine. Because the Broken Peak Pack is harboring my mate. And frankly, I'm tired of Alphas throwing their unmated sons at me, hoping my father will agree to a meeting."

"Bray and Vixen aren't harboring Allard, Delia." Mac planted his hands on his hips and watched a car drive down the highway. "This isn't a good place to talk. Come on, there's a nice patch of grass deeper in the woods with some tree stumps we can sit on and won't have to worry about curious gawkers."

They both turned and peered through the windshield of Delia's car. Geneva hadn't budged from her spot in the front seat.

"We can't just leave her here."

"It's not a tough hike, she'll do fine," Mac said.

Delia shook her head in resignation. As much as she wanted to demand they bring Allard to her, it would not happen. And the only way she'd get deeper into pack territory was with Mac's help.

The old shifter bumped his shoulder against hers. "It won't be that bad Delia, plus, I know Vixen wants to talk to you."

"I'm not worried about that." Delia nodded to her friend still in the car. "That's what I'm dreading."

"Well then, let's get your friend and get on our way. It'll just get darker the more we stand around gibbering away."

Mac loped around the front of the car and opened the passenger door before Geneva could lock it.

"Let's go, Neva. Mac here promises it won't be too bad. And he knows about you. You could probably ask him a few questions to make the walking easier." Delia wasn't above bribing her friend to get her to do something she'd normally kick and scream to get out of.

"If I trip and fall and break a leg, Lennon won't be happy."

"You aren't going to break a leg."

Delia left off the bit about not tripping and falling since her friend had the grace of a newborn deer and spent most of her time stumbling over invisible grains of sand when walking down the street. Visible branches and roots might pose a problem.

Geneva stepped out of the car, carefully placing her feet on the gravel as if it might wrap itself around her ankles and pulled her down.

"Oh, for Pete's sake, it's not that bad, Neva."

Before Geneva came up with a reason to stay in the car, Delia spun on her heel and threaded her arm through Mac's. "Come on. If we start walking, she'll have to follow."

She huffed that last bit under her breath, so Geneva wouldn't hear.

Mac chuckled and led the way to an unseen trailhead.

For five minutes, they walked along the trail listening to Geneva's complaints.

Friends in Broken Peak might be difficult to come by, and Delia didn't want to annoy Mac. Years in Chicago society had taught her how to spot an ally a mile away. And Mac was an ally. To distract him from the whining coming behind them, Delia debated the best question to ask.

"Has he found his true mate? Is that why he's hiding away here?"

"Allard? Nah, he came to Broken Peak for the same reason all the other boys came. It's a last chance for shifters who don't have any other choices."

"So, he came here to get out of the mating?"

"I'm not sure why he came. Don't think he knows either. But nope, lass, he hasn't found a mate. Yet."

Delia could have sworn Mac giggled with his last word, but she had to be wrong. Coyote shifters didn't giggle. Especially the old codger ones like Mac.

"So if he hasn't found a mate, why hasn't he returned to fulfill the agreement? It's not like I'm chopped liver."

"Maybe he wasn't supposed to return and you're the one who's supposed to be here."

The old shifter wasn't making any sense. Delia hadn't heard of any shifters with dementia, but she hadn't spent much time with coyotes. Nonsense might have been a trait of coyote shifters.

A loud 'oomph' followed by some mild cursing came from behind them.

Delia didn't look back. "You okay, Neva?"

"Yeah. But that root moved, I swear. It wasn't right in front of me a moment ago."

"The root didn't move."

"Maybe it did." Mac grinned over at Delia with what could only be described as a twinkle in his eye. "I imagine the moon's pretty happy to have you here. She might be excited enough to jostle the earth around."

"You know, believing in shifters was one of those 'saw it with my own eyes' things. It was either accept shifters or accept I was mad as a hatter. I don't have to believe in this Daughter or Girl of the Moon crap, though."

Delia glanced over at Mac, worried he might be upset with Geneva's casual reference to what apparently a bunch of wolf shifters had built their entire lives around.

Instead of glowering or being angry, he was cackling. Well, he was actually laughing, but it sounded more like a cackle.

"You and the boys will get along just fine. And most of the others felt the same way too. Until Eleanor and Vixen sat down with them and the journals."

"Eleanor?" Delia had only heard rumors of Vixen joining the pack. As far as she knew, there were no other females living in the territory.

"Jackson's mate. You'll meet them both, eventually. But without her, we probably wouldn't be as far as we are with understanding a crazy old shifter's ramblings." Mac looked behind him at Geneva.

He was checking on her or maybe he just wanted to see the supposed Child of the Moon, assuming he believed in that stuff. But either way, Delia swore his eyes glowed. And not the normal shifter glow that happened when they were emotional. This was a full-on white glow.

Thankfully, Geneva was looking at the ground or she would have run back to the car and definitely broken a leg. And then Delia would have to deal with an angry Lennon on top of a selfish, no good, moronic, soon to be castrated, wolf.

Mac took a sharp right and led them into a clearing, just like he described.

"Go ahead and sit. It will be awhile yet."

"Okay?" Delia eyed the broken stump for all of thirty seconds before surrendering to the urge to sit on it instead of the cold ground.

"You know the moment my ass hits it, it's going to roll." Geneva wasn't as forgiving of the fallen log.

"No, it won't."

Both Mac and Delia spoke at the same time, but for different reasons.

"Broken Peak is strong. It's one of those weird places where things just come together in weird ways. The magic that's running through you won't let you get hurt. It needs you alive and well, before it's done with you."

Geneva held her hand up. "Gonna stop you right there. I don't want to hear about that. This is Delia's mission or whatever. I just came along to keep her company on the drive and to keep her brother from going straight to her parents to stop her."

Mac raised a questioning brow at her.

"I can go longer without sex than Lennon can. If he wants any nookie when I get back, he won't have told Mia and Everest where Delia went. But he insisted he wanted to come too. Which would have been fine, but then he would have felt a need to beat the crap out of this Allard for hurting his sis-"

"Neva!"

"What?"

She looked over at Delia with the most fake innocent expression Delia had ever seen.

"I don't need to hear about your and my brother's sex life." Delia grumbled. "And neither does Mac."

The old shifter was back to his cackling.

At least Geneva entertained him, instead of annoyed him.

"I'm sure Vixen will make arrangements for your departure. Probably first thing in the morning."

"We'll both be leaving in the morning. Allard just needs to sign the papers, Bray will have to officiate, and then we can go our separate ways."

"You have this planned out already, do you?"

"Sure. I even have an explanation. He needs to stay in Broken Peak for some secret shifter reason, but I have family obligations at home. Then once every three months or so, we meet in some city somewhere, be seen by as many people as possible, then return to our own lives."

"Vixen and Bray won't force a mating on him. Or you."

"But they have to."

This time Mac laughed, and it wasn't a cackle. It was a full-bodied, tear-inducing laugh that left him gasping for breath.

"I think you'll find that Vixen is a firm believer in not having to do anything at all." Mac wiped away a tear. "Those boys aren't going to know what hit them. Roose and I are gonna have to make a batch of popcorn for this."

CHAPTER FIVE

MAC studied Delia with a knowing grin and raised eyebrows.

She looked away, finding his stare unsettling. "It's the best solution all around. We mate in name only, I get the freedom of not having to deal with unwanted potential matches, and Allard gets to keep doing whatever it is he's doing here."

"Sure. Or it backfires on you and you get dragged to Colorado to get Allard to come home."

"I won't let that happen. My father won't let that happen."

"It's not safe to underestimate anyone, especially an Alpha hungry for more power."

"Delia, can I suggest something?"

"You haven't been?"

Mac rolled his eyes and ignored her question. "I can help you. I might not be able to get you what you want. Well, no, I definitely can't get that.

No way will Bray and Vixen go along with your plan. But I can still help you."

"Why would you do that?"

"Because that's what I do, Delia. That's what I'm supposed to do." He stretched his legs out in front of him and tilted his head back to the sky. "You might not believe it, but I really am on your side."

"But..." She bit down on her thumb and stared at the bare dirt beneath her feet. "You say this mating won't happen, but without it my life is on perpetual hold. There's nothing you can do to help."

Unless Mac had some inside track with the Council and could convince them to nullify the agreement, there wasn't anything he could do.

"Who says the mating has to be fake?" Geneva asked. "What happens if you take one look at Allard and that bonding slash mating thing kicks in."

"It doesn't work that way. It never has."

Mac chuckled, as though he knew something they didn't. He probably knew a lot they didn't, but not regarding this agreement. Everest Lyall wrote it up, and it was ironclad.

She swore to herself when she decided to drive halfway across the country, that she wouldn't leave Broken Peak without a mate. It might have been a mate in name only, but she didn't care about that.

Now look at where she was. No where closer to her goal. If anything, she was further away. If even half of what Mac said was true, no way was she going to walk out of Broken Peak as a mated female.

She felt helpless. Her father turned away all the potential mates, but for how long would he be able to keep it up and demand respect from the other packs. If he couldn't enforce a legally binding, at least according to pack laws, mating agreement, the other packs would see it as a weakness.

Mac handed her a folded piece of paper.

She opened it and studied the words written on the page. It was a copy of the mating agreement. She had examined the copy in her father's safe enough to know it word for word.

"I already know what it says."

"You might know the words on the page, but I don't think you know what it says. Or why your father let you hop in a car and drive ten hours to a little town in West Virginia."

"My dad doesn't know I left the city."

"He does. Roose said a dad always knows."

"Roose?"

"Bear shifter. You'll meet him, eventually." Mac answered before continuing as though her interruption never happened. "I'm guessing Allard's studied the same document, looking for a way out. Just like you. Except neither of you stopped to ask why you specifically and why not just daughters and sons?"

She needed to get away and clear her head.

Mac made it seem like so much more than a contract, but it wasn't.

Arranged matings happened all the time with the children of Alphas. Her mom explained it to her when she was a little girl and informed her family she was going to mate Danny, a young shifter who attended grade school with her.

She hadn't really understood the meaning behind the words until she was older, but she always knew she wouldn't mate for love. Her obligation wasn't just to her family, but to her pack. The mating would strengthen her pack. It would help the pack.

At least that's what she told herself to make it more palatable. And now Mac was yanking all of that away from her and she hadn't even spoken with Allard.

Stupid wolf shifter.

Castration wasn't enough.

Allard made her life a disaster, and she was slowly realizing there wasn't any way to apply a quick fix.

It would have been so much nicer if everything had gone according to her intended plan.

Delia glanced up and found both Geneva and Mac staring at her.

"What?" She brushed her fingers across her cheek. "Is there something on my face?"

"You were lost in your thoughts. So lost you didn't hear the whole Daughter of the Moon saga, which if it were a book or movie would be kinda cool. But since it's my life, it's less cool." Geneva supplied an explanation. "We also chatted about our current options."

"Oh."

"I'm going to fly back in the morning. There's no reason for me to stay, but I think you should."

"No. If Allard doesn't agree, he doesn't agree, and I'll head back to Chicago with you."

"What's waiting for you in Chicago, Del? More of those accidental meetings with someone's creepy ass son?" Geneva made finger quotes around the word accidental. "You admitted it before we even left the city, Allard is kind of off limits if he's here. You could be too."

"I can't. I have things I need to get back to. And the longer Dad has to ignore valid requests for a mating, the weaker we seem because it means he couldn't enforce a simple arranged mating."

"It's not an option, Del."

"What! Why?"

"Oh, come on, Delia, Mac here, who doesn't know your father, figured it out and has been dropping clues this whole time, but you're so focused on that stupid arranged mating and dragging Allard back into the dark ages, you missed it." Geneva stood and planted her hands on her hips in an approximation of an angry pose.

It was an approximation because Geneva never got angry. Ever. Not even when Delia's brother did stupid things. Which he did. A lot.

"Everyone knew your plan. You can't do sneaky. You never have been able to. The only reason I'm here is so you didn't have to drive alone. Your dad is sending the plane out to pick me up and drop off some of your things."

"What are you talking about?" Delia jumped to her feet and paced the clearing.

"How did you learn where Allard was?"

"I overheard Dad and Mom talking."

"And despite the whole scenting things and knowing when strangers are near, which is both really cool and a little freaky, only Mac greeted you?"

That nugget was a bit of a question. Why had Mac been the only one to greet them?

Shifter tradition demanded the Alpha pair greeted any strangers in their territory. Broken Peak Pack might not have been the most traditional of packs, but Delia figured they didn't just let anyone wander onto the land.

"It was a set up, Delia. From the beginning. If you're here, you're safe from any upstart packs thinking they can grab you. Or worse." Geneva rolled her eyes at Delia. "But if any of us had suggested it, you would have refused and then we'd have a much bigger mess on our hands because when you don't get your way, you get pissy."

"I do not."

"I love you, Del, you know that, but you get pissy and the rest of us are miserable because of how pissy you are."

Delia turned away from Geneva and glared at her from the corner of her eyes. "Don't... Don't say anything else."

"See." She waved a hand in Delia's general direction while looking at Mac. "Pissy."

Delia turned her back on both of them and pressed her hands against her stomach. It didn't help with the pit slowly growing in her stomach or settle the rolling waves of nausea. Humiliation crept in right behind the nausea. She was being sent to Broken Peak, the last-chance pack, and everyone knew it.

Everyone except her.

God, she was stupid. So stupid. How had she missed so much?

"If it makes you feel any better, I packed for you."

Delia closed her eyes. It would be a long time before she forgave her supposed best friend.

"This probably won't help, but your dad only reached out to me and I spoke with Vixen. None of the others know anything at all. And we aren't planning on sharing it either." Mac's words softened the blow.

But not by much.

"Bray doesn't even know. And your father isn't sending you here as a punishment. He's sending you here to keep you safe."

"Del?" Geneva reached out and placed a hand on her friend's shoulder. "This isn't permanent. Things are getting weird in Chicago. They're getting weird all over the country, really. And this is the only place your dad could feel secure in knowing you'd be safe."

"What do you mean by weird and safe?" Delia still didn't look at Geneva.

"Just weird things. People asking strange questions, who shouldn't be asking questions. And... well, you know how I feel about the whole prophecy, or whatever the hell it is, but there are others who are true believers. And not in the 'how can we use this for good' kind of way, but in the 'I want to be a major player in it' kind of way and willing to do whatever it takes."

"Come on. Let's head to the Lodge. We've given enough time for Allard to settle down from his panic and Bray enough time to explain some other things to the rest of his pack. If we wait out here any longer, we're going to be facing an impatient Vixen. And that's not something any of us want to see."

"What's the lodge?" Geneva asked.

Delia had wanted to ask the same question, but was still angry, and yes, as Geneva said, pissy.

"It's where Delia's going to be staying." Mac pushed to his feet with a groan. "And you'll be staying for the night. But knowing Vixen, she'll have you out the door before the sun's even up as a precaution."

"Why does Geneva need to have precautions?" Delia's curiosity overcame her pissyness.

"Because you're not the only one who might be a target. We don't know who else has copies of the documents we have." He started for the woods. "It's better to be safe than sorry."

Delia didn't look at Geneva as she fell into step behind Mac. If she looked at her friend, Delia would get over her anger before she was ready, which would likely be as soon as they arrived at the lodge.

Who named their house something like the lodge, anyway?

CHAPTER SIX

DELIA wanted a drink. Correct that, needed a drink.

Too bad she'd left the bottle of wine she brought with her to celebrate her fake mating in the car.

She also wanted to vent to her best friend, but that was currently off the table, since Geneva was in cahoots with her entire family. Who, apparently, felt they needed to orchestrate Delia's life with no input from her.

Unable to actually pick up the phone, Delia imagined the conversation in her head. God knows, they had enough of these conversations when some guy did them wrong. It was just a matter of changing the names and adjusting the adjectives to fit the situation.

"What'd he do now?" Imaginary Geneva asked.

"Besides running off, shirking his duty, being a stupid butt coward pants, oh, and let's not forget, being a complete and total pain in my ass?"

Nope. Wasn't the same. She needed the genuine deal. But Geneva was still being punished for colluding with her family to get Delia to voluntarily head out to the middle of nowhere and believe it was all her own idea.

Crap.

Delia was just going to have to get over it. If she didn't, she wouldn't have anyone to vent to. It wasn't as if she could trust this Eleanor person not to go running back to Vixen or Allard and share all her rantings.

Delia sniffed and brushed the back of her hand across her wet cheeks. When had she started crying? She rubbed the heels of her palm against her eyes, hopefully erasing any of the telltale signs of the tears.

"Del?" Geneva asked. "You okay?"

"As okay as can be expected."

That was the good thing about Geneva and Delia's relationship, they never had to utter the words 'I'm sorry'. Their friendship survived minor tiffs and major spats. It even survived a month of silent treatment from both girls. But Geneva was Delia's best friend and Delia was Geneva's best friend. Nothing would change that.

Not even a manipulating, overbearing, interfering family. Especially now that Geneva was technically family.

"It can't be all bad," Geneva said. "Remember that time your dad tried to send you to summer camp where they didn't even have running water, and your mom put a stop to that pretty quick? This place must at least have running water if she signed off on it."

Quickly translated, what Geneva actually said, was 'I'm sorry, and as a peace offering, I'm reminding you about some good times.'

Delia didn't want to laugh. Nope. Not laughing.

Except...

God, Delia must've been eleven or twelve years old and Lennon was fourteen or fifteen. Their mother had read their dad the riot act. It had gone on for hours, and of course Lennon and Delia took advantage of their mom's distraction. The two of them had gotten into so much trouble separately and together, that their mother was still finding reminders of that fateful weekend.

At last count, Mia Lyall discovered all but three of the broken plates they had used to play disc golf in their backyard. Lennon had tried to blame the broken dishware on the caterers, but Mia wasn't buying it. Thankfully, she was still pissed at her mate and wasn't willing to dilute her anger.

Geneva had been there too. But then, Geneva had always been there. And she probably always would be. No, not probably. Definitely.

"Yeah, but they probably won't have 1000 thread count sheets." Delia replied.

But what she really said was, 'yeah I'm sorry too. Let's just forget either of us said anything at all and go back to the way it was, before I learned just how conniving my mother could be.'

"Delia?" Mac asked. "I think I might have an idea…"

By the time they reached the edge of the woods that bordered the expanse of lawn in front of the Lodge, Mac was grinning like a cat who got into the cream, if he'd been an actual cat.

Three figures lounged in the chairs on the front porch waiting for Mac and the two females. The cool night air was still, but the moon was high in the sky surrounded by a vast field of stars.

Whatever those great shifters planned all those years ago was finally coming to fruition, and the moon couldn't be happier.

Now, if Roose had just done his part, then Delia and Allard's meeting might not be all that bad.

Vixen had opted for reverse psychology. She insisted Allard would recognize Delia for what she was if everyone took a step back and didn't interfere.

Of course, it could all go pear-shaped, as Vixen liked to say. Which was why, Mac had come up with a Plan B. One that Vixen didn't know about. Sure, she'd be pissed that Mac hadn't shared it with her, but some things were better left secret.

In the end, it didn't matter whose plan worked as long as Delia and Allard spent enough time together to realize they didn't need the formality of an arranged mating to follow their fates.

Roose and Mac were definitely going to grab some popcorn and sit back to watch the fireworks.

At least the next few weeks in Broken Peak wouldn't be boring.

DELIA SMOOTHED BACK HER WAYWARD wisps of hair and brushed the dirt from her clothes, but it probably wouldn't be enough. The plan she worked out in her mind before leaving Chicago, included changing clothes and primping in front of the mirror before she made her grand entrance.

Lacking a mirror, she turned to her friend.

"How bad is it?"

"Well, you don't look like the Princess of the Chicago Pack. But somehow, I'm thinking, that wasn't your goal."

"Can we fix it?" Delia asked.

"Um… Well… No. No I can't. To be fair though, I don't think anyone could." Geneva shook her head from side to side. "But on the brighter side, your Valentino skinny jeans and boots look fantastic with that gray Valentino wool sweater and Max Mara teddy bear coat."

Delia rolled her eyes upwards and bounced her head from side to side for a few moments before flicking her hand down, as if waving away the compliment. "These old things?"

Both Geneva and Delia broke out in a fit of giggles. In Chicago, some women use 'this old thing' and other variations as code for, 'thank God you noticed, I spent a fortune on this outfit'.

The January evening was warmer than a January night in Chicago, but still cool and the coat was doing a brilliant job keeping Delia warm, but Geneva had a point, even if she didn't say it outright. Most, if not all of Delia's clothing was going to be terribly out of place in Broken Peak.

The vast yard at the edge of the woods was bare, except for the almost brown grass. The animals living in the forest fell silent with their approach.

Three figures on the porch sat up, but didn't stand. She eyed them curiously. In her life, she was used to being approached and not the one who did the approaching.

With a slight shake of her head, she sighed loud enough for Mac and Geneva to hear.

"Well Dorothy, I don't think you're in Kansas anymore." Geneva bumped Delia's arm with her elbow.

"No shit," Delia said with another sigh.

"Sorry." Except Geneva's tone sounded anything other than sorry. "If Scott can't be with us in person, then he can be with us in spirit."

Scott was both Delia and Geneva's friend from middle school. He'd been officially declared their 'no' friend. The one person in their lives who told them no whenever a bad idea came to light.

Accidentally on purpose forget to wear panties? No.

Drive to the airport to pick up your ex-boyfriend, who took you months to get over, as a surprise? No.

Pick up the phone and call half the people on your contact list after a night of over indulging in that great wine you discovered at Binny's? Not only no, but Scott confiscated their phones as well.

If anyone would appreciate the mess Delia found herself in the middle of, it was Scott. And the only reason she hadn't brought him along was because he didn't know about shifters. He probably had suspicions about her family, but unless those suspicions bordered on the supernatural, he was wrong.

"Speaking of which..." Delia dug in her back pocket for her phone. When she looked at the screen, the words no service greeted her. "What the—I'm supposed to get service everywhere. Even Antarctica."

"Danielle will get you set up the new phone when she goes through your contacts," Mac said.

Wait, Danielle? There was a third female living with the pack? How could the rest of shifter society be so out of the loop? Last chance bachelor packs might, under rare circumstances, have an Alpha female, but as a rule no other females lived within a 100-mile radius of them.

Delia shook her head in defeat. "Nothing makes sense here."

"It will after a few days, you just need to give Broken Peak and Vixen a little time."

"Not to be a buzz kill or anything, but don't you think it's kind of rude to just stand here? It's not like we're invisible and they can't see us."

Once again, Geneva made a fair point. Except Delia hadn't decided yet on whether she cared if the shifters living at Broken Peak thought she was rude.

"Now or never?" Delia asked.

"I think it's more of a now or now situation," Geneva said.

Worry crept into her mind. Of course, if she was being honest, it made a permanent camp in her thoughts when Geneva admitted her family's duplicity. As she stepped out of the woods, and walked across the hard ground, her wolf reminded her she might hate Allard. If she couldn't stand him, she doubted she'd be able to stand the rest of his pack.

In which case everything was moot, because she'd be damned if she had to stay longer than absolutely necessary.

Worst-case scenario, she still had her car and could drive off into the proverbial sunset if she had to.

A striking female came down off the front porch and headed across the yard to meet Delia and the others.

At least she assumed it was to meet them.

With the way events had been developing, it was an equal possibility that the female would challenge Delia for trespassing or welcome Delia to the territory.

CHAPTER SEVEN

"DELIA Lyall, I'm Vixen," the female said as she drew closer. "Bray, my mate, will do the formalities when I introduce you. But until then, welcome to Broken Peak Pack. I'm going to tell you the same thing said to me when I first arrived, and I've said to the others. You are safe here. No one will cause you any harm."

She didn't need to tap her wolf to confirm the veracity of Vixen's words. The Alpha female spoke with such conviction, Delia didn't think it was possible to not believe her.

"Thank you." Delia wasn't positive thanks were necessary, but she wasn't sure what else to say.

"Her car?" Vixen asked while still looking at Delia.

Somehow, Delia didn't think Vixen was asking her. Her suspicions were confirmed when Mac answered.

"Up by the road still. Figured I could stall longer if we walked down instead of driving."

"What? We could've stayed in the car and driven down?" The revelation perplexed Geneva. "I had to contend with roots and branches, and wayward pebbles and we didn't have to walk. That's so not fair."

"You still would've had to walk. It might've been shorter, but the ground is more uneven." Mac said, clearly amused by Geneva's outburst.

"Have Roose bring it down to the garage, and I'll have a few of the boys go down and pick up their belongings." Vixen said before turning her full attention onto Delia. "You probably have a lot of questions and there's a lot more to explain. I'll do my best to answer what I can before the welcome wagon invades."

"Boys?" Delia questioned.

"They aren't really boys. All are full-grown males, except for Foster, but don't call him a boy, or a pup. He prefers to believe that he's all grown up since turning four."

Delia stepped back and almost fell over a blade of grass with Vixen's revelation. That last bit of information about a pup was news to Delia. The last she heard about Broken Peak Pack was that it was a last resort pack for problem wolves. In fact, her father had often threatened Lennon with being sent to Broken Peak when he did something stupid during his adolescence. "There's a pup here?"

"And two human women and another female shifter, and me."

Why hadn't the packs heard about all the changes? News about the females, humans, pups, and whatever animal Vixen was, hadn't hit the packs yet or Delia would have heard about. Wolf shifters gossiped worse than Gladys Kravitz.

She pondered her next words. "The last anyone heard, Broken Peak was a bachelor pack."

"Things change." Vixen grinned at Mac. "I figured you would have filled her in about some of the latest happenings. You're failing at your job, old man."

"A., who said I hadn't, and B., not a man."

"Yeah, but old male doesn't have quite the same ring."

If Mac's gossip about the females in the pack hadn't piqued Delia's curiosity, Vixen's further reveal definitely had.

"The boys aren't going to know what hit them." Vixen stared at Delia for a moment before shaking her head slowly from side to side. "I was hoping we have more time, but Allard's pacing the porch and probably annoying the hell out of Bray."

Delia glanced over Vixen's shoulder, and sure enough one male was pounding his feet from one end of the porch to the other.

She also noticed several faces pressed up against the window. They must be the welcome wagon.

"Well, let's do this." Vixen wrapped her arm around Delia's shoulder. "I promise they won't bite, well most of them won't bite. Foster's going through a biting phase."

"Geneva, why don't you come with me? I can show you some things you should probably look at before heading back to Chicago." Mac held his arm out for Geneva to take. "Then I promise to bring you right back here so you and your friend can have a sleepover party, or whatever it is you females do, before heading out in the morning."

Clever Coyote. Separating Delia and Geneva might not have been his goal, but it would probably make Delia's introduction to Allard less confrontational.

Delia glanced over at Geneva, who didn't seem at all bothered with the invitation. In fact, she gave Delia an encouraging nod.

"When I get back, you can share all the juicy details I missed." Geneva threaded her arm through Mac's. "Lead the way."

"I find in times like these it's easier to just rip it off like a band-aid." Vixen squeezed Delia's shoulder. "Before we introduce you to Allard, I want you to know, neither Bray or I will force either you or Allard to mate. If it works out, great, if it doesn't, that's great too."

Delia rubbed her palm against the side of her face. Vixen might be the Alpha of Broken Peak Pack, but Delia was the daughter of purebreds, the last remaining line of pure shifters, if she believed the histories the families kept locked away. "I was under the impression my arrival at Broken Peak was a matter of safety."

Vixen grinned, except it wasn't a nice cheery smile that made someone want to smile back. Vixen's grin was ferocious. Almost hungry for violence. "There's a lot more, but Allard's growing more impatient every minute we stand here talking instead of walking."

Delia narrowed her eyes, crossed her arms over her chest, and tapped her toe. "If I'm at the center of all this, don't you think I have a right to know?"

"Who said you were the center of it?"

The Alpha female of Broken Peak Pack brushed away Delia's suggestion that she should know more with a wave of her hand and spun away on her heel before continuing across the yard.

Delia might have been stubborn, but she wasn't stupid and there was no way she'd be able to out stubborn Vixen. Vexing would have been a better name for Delia's temporary new Alpha, something else that bothered Delia. Vixen was as much an Alpha as Mia and Delia. It was easier accepting her fate in an arranged mating when she knew she was more powerful than her mate's mother, but Vixen felt a hundred times more powerful than Delia, her mother, and her father combined.

"Come on." Vixen didn't bother looking over her shoulder at Delia.

Great. What other option was there now except to trot after Vixen like the obedient wolf she was?

Vixen strode in front of her with the easy gait of someone comfortable with themselves and secure in the knowledge she was the most powerful one in the room. Which was more than likely true. Too bad it didn't ease any of Delia's confusion regarding Vixen's creature. Raptor shifters might have been known for their strength and power, but an entire convocation couldn't take on a pack the size of Colorado and win, much less a single raptor shifter.

As she approached the massive log cabin, no wonder they called it the lodge, the two males moved to stand at the top of the steps and Delia saw just how large they were.

She always believed her brother and father to be larger than most males, even the enforcers in her father's pack didn't have quite the same size as her father. But the two males standing there made her father look positively tiny.

"Allard, Bray," Vixen called to the males. "I see the peanut gallery peering through the window."

The larger of the two males crossed his arms over his chest and closed one eye as he apprised Vixen. "I did what I could to keep them from coming outside. In the end we compromised. They agreed to look out the window and claim I was ignorant of their spying to keep you from getting angry with me."

"You did your Alpha thing any time they got close to the door, didn't you?"

"It's not as strong as yours, but it gets the job done."

Vixen shook her head and Delia glanced over at the movement. The Alpha female of Broken Peak Pack was grinning widely. Not quite the hungry grin from earlier, but it also didn't look normal. As though Vixen's face wasn't used to smiling, much less grinning.

This pack was weird.

"That bad?"

"Eleanor and Danielle are arguing over who gets to be the maid of honor and Maggie may or may not be, but probably is, concocting a plan to lock them in the cellar so she can be the maid of honor, even though she has no clue what one is." Bray paused in his speech and glanced over at the male standing beside him. "Delia overhearing that conversation would be cruel. Even by your standards."

Vixen lifted a shoulder in an approximation of a shrug. "That's fair."

"I assume this is Delia Lyall."

"Who else would it be?"

"With the way you and Mac are, I wasn't sure."

Vixen bent her head to the side, not quite agreeing with Bray's assessment, but neither did she disagree.

"Delia, this is my mate Bray, Alpha of Broken Peak, and the male next to him is Allard." Vixen turned her head slightly and gave Delia a sly look out of the corner of her eyes. "But I'm assuming you already knew that."

Bray nodded at Delia, simultaneously acknowledging her presence, but dismissing her at the same time. Bray was the kind of Alpha her father respected. No wonder he agreed to send her to the outskirts of civilization. "Your father entrusted us with your safety and we vow to do everything in our power never to lose that trust."

Delia wanted to roll her eyes at the formal announcement, but bit her lip. Even if she was the only representative of her family present, she understood the necessity behind the formality. With his promise, Bray and his pack justified any violence against the Colorado pack, or any other pack, who figured it would be simple to grab Delia from Broken Peak.

"My father is honored to entrust me to your safety and is certain of your word." Delia returned the expected response. Even if Broken Peak didn't appear to follow all the social norms of structured packs, they were still a pack recognized by the shifter community, and Delia wanted to respect that.

"Allard, you have at least ten, but likely not more than fifteen minutes to talk privately with Delia. Maggie's gotten way too good at evading me as of late."

"Haven't you been training her to do just that?" Bray asked.

"Yes, but not with me. With others. I need to remind her we only use our powers for good."

"Good as defined by you?" Bray pulled his lips between his teeth, as though he was fighting back a smile.

Vixen stared at Bray for a few seconds before lifting her chin and up the steps toward the front door. "Plan on ten minutes, Allard."

Despite finding herself in the middle of everything unfamiliar and surrounded by oddities, Delia wanted to smile. Growing up, Delia's mother had used that exact expression on her father. When Delia finally asked her mom about it, Mia had explained it was her way of letting her mate know that she heard him, but was choosing to ignore him.

Delia's father had a different explanation for her. Her mother used it when she didn't want to admit he was right.

Delia decided it was a combination of both.

That slight gesture between mates, so close to one she'd seen between her parents, settled some of Delia's nerves. It wasn't as good as having a Lou's down the street, but it would do. And she could always have Lou's shipped out here. They might ship their frozen pizzas to the middle of nowhere for a good customer.

"I'll see if we can't distract Maggie and give you two fifteen minutes." Bray followed Vixen.

"Delia."

Whoa.

Allard's voice was all low and growly. Nice and rough and totally unexpected from the refined voice she expected. "Allard."

Allard stepped down and moved closer to her.

Double whoa. Yeah, Allard was big. Delia had already come to that conclusion. What she hadn't realized was that Allard was one of those sexy guys who didn't know it, or maybe he did. Except he didn't bother to do anything to make himself sexier.

Worn jeans hugged his legs, not because the jeans were tight, but because his legs were just that muscular. And the worn flannel shirt, unbuttoned at the collar, was just snug enough to showcase his broad shoulders.

She wasn't sure what she expected exactly. After Allard ran off to the boondocks, his image stopped appearing in the social pages. But the male standing in front of her, with cheekbones that could cut glass, and a jawline only found on the photoshopped cover of a magazine, wasn't even a glimmer in her imagination.

All things considered, being mated to Allard wouldn't be as bad as it could be. At the very least, if his personality turned out to be lacking, she could wear a pair of ear plugs and spend her time staring at him.

"I'm not sure what to say." There was his gravelly growl again.

Delia pushed her hair behind her ear and looked past his shoulder, anything not to stare at his face. "I know Vixen said we didn't have to mate, but I think you of all people should know what will happen if we don't complete the agreement."

"There are plenty of loopholes. And you might not know or trust Vixen yet, but I do, and if she says she won't force the terms of the agreement, then she won't. And she won't let my father, his pack, or the Council force the terms either."

"Allard, you haven't been out of pack politics that long." Delia swallowed the small lump in her throat, blinked back her tears, and turned to the male who she needed to convince to be her mate. "You know as well as I do that if I don't mate you, your father will try to get the Council to transfer the terms of the agreement to your brother. And they'll do it. The Council can't have a binding agreement between packs broken. We might as well make the best of it."

"You might want to read that agreement again. Besides, the Council doesn't have enough teeth to win a war against Vixen." Allard shoved his hands deep into his pockets and rocked back on his heels. "So, no, Delia. I'm not prepared to mate you. Or at least I won't until it's not because of some damn agreement made between our fathers before we were even born."

Allard turned his back to Delia, a brave move considering she had a dominant wolf inside her and was born an Alpha. But Delia wasn't considering pouncing on his back, she was too busy staring at his broad shoulders and the pleasant way his waist narrowed so his jeans hung just right on his hips and showcased one of the best asses she'd seen.

Wait.

What had he said about mating? Not the part about him not thinking he'd mate her, but that he wouldn't do it because of an agreement.

Did that mean he'd want to mate her for other reasons?

CHAPTER EIGHT

ALLARD turned away from the lithe redhead decked out head to toe in designer clothes. It didn't matter what anyone said. Hell, they'd probably have to add a room just to accommodate her clothes. She didn't belong at Broken Peak.

When she approached the porch with Vixen, Delia wore a smile that hinted at a delightful sense of humor despite her current situation. With her hair pulled back in a ponytail and no make up on her face that Allard could tell, Delia looked like a teenager.

And those freckles. They covered her cheeks and nose and even with the lack of any real light, they stood out against her fair skin.

But then Allard looked down and holy hell. Her tight sweater didn't just hint, but showcased the most perfect set of breasts Allard had ever seen in his entire life. And that damn coat, it tried to hide them, but failed miserably. It couldn't even hide the gentle swell of her hips.

And those boots… They were as tight as her jeans, except for where the boots flared over her knees before reaching her lower thighs. Allard didn't realize he had a thing for thigh-high boots, but he decided right then and there he wouldn't mind seeing her in those boots and nothing else.

A small whimper came from her lips when he turned away. He knew better than to turn around, but he couldn't help himself.

She planted her hands on her hips, pushing her jacket wide open so it framed and displayed her breasts, as if her jacket realized what a masterpiece they were.

She coughed, and he looked up to meet her gaze, where he should have been looking to begin with.

The sweet innocence he saw in her when she neared the porch was gone. In its place stood a determined female who practically shouted with her body language that he needed to stay away.

And that's exactly what he planned on doing.

The last shifter he needed to have any attraction to, no matter how small, was Delia Lyall.

Shit.

Roose's words had dug their way into his thoughts and buried themselves down deep.

They didn't have to mate, not with Bray and Vixen running interference, so it was probably best to convince her of that and send her on her way. Far away from the Broken Peak Pack where Allard wouldn't consider using that fucking arranged mating to get her into his bed.

What the fuck?

Now he was thinking about Delia in his bed.

What the hell was wrong with him?

This wasn't just Roose's fault, Bray's words had probably planted the seeds that allowed Roose's words to take root.

Why couldn't she be anyone else? Hell, that other female she was with would have been better. He didn't want to see that female naked.

How the hell was he going to survive a day, much less the few weeks she'd probably end up staying, with Delia under the same roof?

The front door cracked open and Vixen stuck her head out. "How are things going?"

"Fine." Delia answered with a sexy growl.

Shit.

Allard knew what fine meant, and it wasn't good.

And that growl... It didn't belong to the crown princess of the Chicago pack. She should have sounded refined and elegant, like she had when she was lecturing him about the mating agreement.

Another part of his body, namely his cock, disagreed. It seemed quite happy with that growl. Allard was tempted to adjust himself, but didn't want to draw Delia's attention to his semi-hard cock.

"Allard! Duck and cover, man! That's not a good word! Ever!" Jackson's shout, followed by an oomph of air leaving his lungs as Eleanor probably elbowed him in the stomach, came from inside.

Vixen ignored the shout. "We have a new development Bray and I want to talk with you about before you two decide whatever it is you want to do."

Allard didn't like the sound of that and from the soft growl coming from Delia, neither did she.

"Bray's rounding everyone up and sending them to the kitchen so we can have some privacy." Vixen didn't wait for a response as she held the front door open. "Come on inside. Both of you."

She wasn't giving them a choice. Allard had heard this tone before and it never boded well for anyone involved.

Allard's jaw tightened. He held his hand out to Delia, allowing her to go first. He told himself he was just being polite, but he really just wanted to see if he could catch a glimpse of her ass.

Delia didn't exactly stomp past him in those magnificent boots, but her steps were loud enough against the wood of the porch. Vixen raised a questioning eyebrow at Allard as Delia sauntered past and into the Lodge.

His jaw clenched hard enough for his molars to grind together. He followed Delia inside and took the chair furthest away from the one she was already sitting in.

Bray sat on the couch and Vixen joined him.

No one spoke for several minutes before Allard couldn't stand the silence any longer. "So what was it that Eleanor brought up?"

"Before I go on, we need to have an agreement." From her perch, Vixen smiled beatifically at the two of them. "No matter what happens, it doesn't leave the Lodge. That means, no calling home and telling your friends and family, Delia. And Allard, I don't think you're still talking to anyone in your father's pack, but the same goes for you."

The finality in Vixen's tone reassured him she meant business and if either of them blabbed, Vixen would come up with a suitable consequence. He had experienced her consequences before and didn't need a reminder of how harsh she could be.

He glanced over at Delia. If she questioned the directive whatever Vixen had to say would remain with Vixen.

Delia's reaction surprised him. Instead of protesting and coming up with excuses about why it wasn't fair, she nodded slowly. "That's fair enough. However, if I learn something that could put my pack at risk, I have a duty and obligation to report it to my father."

"Your father and I have an open line of communication since he informed us of your departure from the city. I assure you, any information we learn that could potentially impact your father's pack will be shared." Bray promised.

That was new information. Everest and Bray had spoken? Why hadn't Bray said anything sooner?

Allard didn't have to look too closely to find an answer. Both he and his wolf were runners. If he knew Delia was coming, he would've packed a bag and left Broken Peak before she had even crossed the state line into Indiana.

Vixen stared at Allard expectantly.

What was she—oh, that's right, she needed him to agree.

"Yeah, sure, no talking to anyone else about this." Not that he had anyone outside of Broken Peak who'd he'd want to share anything with.

"Good. Is there anything else we need to know before continuing?" Vixen didn't spare Allard a chastising glare. When neither Allard or Delia offered anything new, Vixen continued. "Allard, why don't you share with Delia why you came to Broken Peak. I think she's under the assumption you were running away from the mating."

Allard rolled his eyes at the impromptu counseling session. It wasn't anyone's business why he left his father's pack and was prepared to say as much when his wolf intervened. The beast was normally quiet, so when he pushed his opinion on Allard, he usually listened.

Which was how he spent the next ten minutes explaining it wasn't the mating that caused him to run, but not wanting to be his father's pawn. What he hadn't counted on was Everest Lyall not being open to replacing Allard with one of his brothers.

Delia sat in her chair with her feet flat on the ground and her hands clasped together on her lap. "You have an obligation to your pack, Allard. Mating me was part of your duty to your pack, not as a ploy by your father."

"Broken Peak is my pack now." How dare she question his integrity? His obligation was to the Broken Peak Pack and his duty was to do what Vixen and Bray needed to keep the pack safe and healthy.

Delia didn't flinch or back down. With her spine impossibly straight and her shoulders thrown back, she turned in her chair so she could look at Allard without turning her head.

The anger that flashed in her eyes shouldn't have turned him on, but Delia Lyall was anything but a typical female.

"You don't get to pick and choose your duty, Allard. You're an Alpha, whether or not you want to be one. And shifters need Alphas if they're going to survive. Without packs to keep wolf shifters protected, we might already be locked away inside a government lab somewhere."

"Who says there aren't any now?" As soon as Allard said the words, he wished he could take them back. He wasn't sure what Vixen and Bray wanted to share with Everest and the knowledge that the government had been targeting Broken Peak, specifically Foster, might not be information they wanted to get out.

Delia rolled her eyes. "Oh, please. There's no way that wouldn't have gotten out by now if it was true."

Allard avoided looking at his Alphas. He didn't need to see the look of disappointment on their faces to know it was there. But educating Delia about duty and obligation didn't have to happen then. It could wait for later. He leaned back in his chair, crossed his arms over his chest, and stretched his legs out in front of him.

Bray pinched the bridge of his nose and stared at the floor while Vixen pressed her thumb and middle finger against the corners of her eyes. It was like they had simultaneous headaches.

They probably did.

Vixen took a deep breath and let it out slowly. She was probably counting. "Delia, would you like to explain to Allard why you're here.

And not the part about the mating, but what ultimately became the catalyst for you to get in a car and drive here from Chicago?"

Delia stared at Vixen with a deadly glint in her eye. Allard couldn't tell if the death stare was because that was the last thing she wanted to share or that Vixen might actually know the real reason for her arrival. He imagined her delivering that stare to him when he did something to piss her off and a shiver ran down his spine.

Thirty seconds later, Allard counted, Delia shared her story. Starting with the subtle attempts at matchmaking and ending with an attempt to kidnap her.

What the actual fuck?

She didn't actually say the word kidnap. But a small group of enforcers pulling up to her as she walked down the street and trying to force her into the car is the definition of kidnapping.

"Does your father know?" Allard growled out his question between clenched teeth. How had he thought it was okay to let her drive off by herself? Well, not completely by herself. She drove with her friend, a not-human by the scent of her, but Allard didn't think she had a griffin inside her like Vixen.

"No. Of course not. He didn't need the details."

Vixen sat back on the couch and leaned into Bray. "That's not the only time something like that has happened though, has it?"

"No." Delia shook her head. "The other attempts were more subtle and carried less of a threat."

"What makes you think that mating me and going back to Chicago is going to stop them from trying to grab you?" Allard was pissed and so was his wolf. Or his wolf was pissed and pushing those emotions onto Allard.

Delia's head bounced between facing Allard and facing Vixen.

She had thought a mating would stop them.

Shit. Just how sheltered was she?

Just as quickly as she revealed her ignorance a wall shuttered down. She pushed her shoulders back and tossed her head so her ponytail swung around like a whip.

She might have been innocent as fuck, but she had a spark. Delia lifted her chin at Allard, daring him to vocalize his anger.

"All I had was this arrangement. I will not come begging for help from you."

"Why not?" Where the hell had that come from? Why not? Allard had hundreds of reasons why not and he was sure Delia had thousands more.

"Can I suggest we put the bickering on hold? Bray and I will offer our proposal, you can decide if you both agree to it, and then you can go back to bickering when Bray and I don't have front row seats."

Bray chuckled, "Oh, this is going to be interesting."

"So, it would seem the Council has learned about Delia's arrival. They contacted Bray and asked to visit." Vixen ignored Bray's comment.

Allard's eyes widened at the news. No way would the Council insist on visiting Broken Peak. That was part of the deal, Bray took on the fuck ups and the Council left them to their own devices. He closed his eyes and released a loud breath that might have been a sigh. "So why the sudden change of heart about interfering with your pack, Bray?"

"I don't think it's interfering. Well, Vixen doesn't believe they are," Bray said. "Eleanor believes it's more about you two being pure-blooded shifters and born Alphas and I'm inclined to agree."

"They claimed they only wanted to verify the mating so they could share the information with anyone concerned about the status of the agreement," Vixen said. "But if we don't allow them to visit, it will bring questions we might not want to answer just yet."

"So what's the proposal?" Delia asked.

"You're here for the time being, Delia, and this is Allard's pack. We stand by not forcing you to mate, but you two can at least pretend to be mated while we allow the Council to visit. You'll need to sell it and Foster has a big mouth, so if you two can fake it for a few weeks and not kill one another, it would be best."

"And the rest of the pack?" Allard knew what was coming next, and he hated it. He'd already lived one lie with them, he wasn't sure adding a second would help with any of their relationships.

Bray pressed and rubbed his palm against his cheek. "Except for Eleanor, they're going to have to buy into the mating as well."

"How is that even going to work?" Delia asked.

"Well, whether or not you believe in the mumbo jumbo crap," Vixen paused and glared at Allard, "I don't think anyone in this pack would deny the concept of a fated mate."

"You want us to convince everyone, including the Council, that we're actually fated mates?"

"Right now it's the best option we have." Bray said the words with the biggest shit-eating grin Allard had ever seen.

"You both have to agree. We'll leave you to decide if this will work or not." Vixen stood from the couch and Bray followed suit.

"Wait, what about the others, how come you don't think they haven't crept up the hallway to overhear all this?" Allard asked.

"Eleanor was the one to propose it and has been keeping them distracted. She's also been planting the idea that the Broken Peak Pack is special and brings fated mates together." Vixen smirked and walked from the room arm in arm with Bray.

CHAPTER NINE

DELIA wanted to jump from her seat and pace the room, but Allard's intense gaze held her in place.

She blinked under his steady blue stare. "Well…"

Allard remained silent, but his gaze never strayed from her.

"It's a bad idea, right?" Surely he had to agree that pretending to be happily mated was the worst idea on the face of the planet.

"And your idea of mating in name only is a good idea?"

Sure, now he had an opinion.

Delia popped up and walked to the large picture window that looked out across the front yard. She wasn't sure what Allard was thinking and wasn't prepared to jump through hoops trying to decipher the meaning behind his words.

When she first walked in, she hadn't taken the time to look around the room. The large room was filled with comfortable furniture.

Couches and chairs formed a circle. Enough seating space for a small pack. And their mates. The closest thing to a room like this at the Lyalls', was at their cottage in northern Wisconsin. And that house was private, never visited by anyone except immediate family and close friends.

The closer she looked at Broken Peak, the more the pack looked like her family, even though she hadn't yet met the other pack members.

And then there were the Alphas. Delia couldn't ever imagine her father sitting down with a pack member and giving them a choice. When Geneva discovered the shifter world, Delia's father hadn't given her a choice. Geneva had been told that she would go to work for her father, and he'd expected her to obey. Just like any other pack member.

Broken Peak was weird.

"It will never work." Delia turned and stood behind the couch, pressing her hands down on the soft leather while looking across the room at Allard.

The male didn't have the first understanding of what duty and obligation meant. How could he maintain the facade of being fated mates if he couldn't accept the facade of being the heir to a large pack?

"You're right. It won't." Allard stood and stormed out of the room.

"Well, then…" Delia looked around the room again. This time taking in the braided rugs covering the hardwood floors and the picture frames lining the mantel over the fireplace.

She walked across the floor to take a closer look. Each picture caught an intimate moment of the pack. From couples to the entire pack. There was even a funny picture with all the males in the pack dressed like The Village People standing in front of a small cabin.

"It was Halloween. We wanted Foster to have as normal of a childhood as possible. Even if it meant trick-or-treating at two cabins over and over."

A soft voice came from behind Delia and she glanced over her shoulder and the newcomer. The petite dark-haired woman smiled up at Delia.

"I'm Eleanor. It's nice to meet you." She held her hand out to Delia.

"Delia. But then I think you already knew that." Delia took Eleanor's hand and shook it.

"You know, he's usually not so hot-headed. Of all the males in the pack, Allard is the most level-headed."

Delia blinked. Level and headed were the last two words she'd use to describe Allard.

"I know you think this won't work. I'm pretty sure Vixen doesn't think it will work either. But I'm not willing to give up on this plan just yet."

Great. Just what Delia needed, someone intent on pushing this stupid plan forward. She swallowed back the 'hell no' she wanted to scream out at the top of her lungs. The mere act of biting her tongue made her stomach churn. "There's probably a good reason Vixen doesn't think this will work."

"Allard might be the most level-headed and probably the most laid back of the males, but he can also steam roll over his packmates. They don't even realize it's happening."

"And that's a selling point?"

"Yep. He can't steamroll over you and that just might be the glue that will keep this plan together."

Delia narrowed her eyes at the human, not trusting the mischievous look she saw in Eleanor's eyes. "That's not a good enough reason."

"No. But you also understand packs. Danielle and I had no clue about pack life and Maggie's life made her view on packs pretty weird."

"And that's important, why?"

"Your experience will make it easier to know what you need to do in order to keep the Council happy." Eleanor gave Delia a helpless shrug.

"They've already tried to kidnap you, Vixen shared that with me. Who says they won't try again? If you're mated into this pack, Vixen can use protection as a justification for punishing and teaching a lesson to anyone considering trying to take anyone in the pack."

The flood of words from Eleanor sent a fresh wave of nausea through Delia. There really was only one viable option. She'd like to believe her father was strong enough to protect her, but if he had been, then the enforcers would never have tried to force her into their car.

She held up a hand, stopping Eleanor from saying anything more. "I get it."

"You aren't alone here, Delia. I know you think you are, but you aren't. You have a pack and the allies of the pack standing behind you no matter where you go. It will just make things easier if you and Allard are, in appearance, mated. And the fated mates spin--"

"The fated mates spin makes the narrative romantic and not just political."

Eleanor smiled and nodded.

They were on the same page.

"Fine. I'll do it. But I'm not going to be able to convince Allard."

"Between Vixen and Bray and me, we'll get him to come around." She looked over her shoulder and down the long hallway that the Alphas and later Allard disappeared to. "It's probably best if you stay here though, okay?"

"You don't want me meeting the others unless I'm standing next to Allard."

"Yeah, they're a curious bunch and won't be happy until they get to ask you the list of questions Danielle is probably writing up as we speak."

CHAPTER TEN

ALLARD slipped down the hallway and instead of turning right, which would lead to the bedrooms, he turned left. The first place Vixen would look for him was his bedroom. The only safe hiding place he could think of, short of shifting and running off to the woods, was the laundry room.

He'd be surprised if any of his pack, except for Eleanor, knew where the room that held multiple washers and dryers was located. It took opening a few doors before he found the right room, but it was blissfully silent. He left the light off and shut the door behind him.

There weren't any chairs in the room, so Allard sat on the floor and leaned against the back wall.

The solitude lasted for all of three minutes before Bray opened the door. He flipped on the light and closed the door behind him.

"Allard." Bray said nothing else. Like he expected Allard to want to fill in the silence.

It wouldn't work. Allard's father was good at that trick, so was Vixen, hell, even Eleanor could get Jackson to talk, just by not saying anything.

"Bray."

"I'm supposed to share with you that the proposal is still on the table. Whatever you said to her, Eleanor fixed. If you can keep from saying something stupid again."

The door was blocked by Bray's massive body, but if it wasn't, Allard would have charged out of the room and opted for that other option. Shifting and running through the woods.

"Who says I said something stupid?"

"Even if you didn't, you did. It's easier for all of us if you accept you are going to say a lot of stupid things around Delia. Trust me."

"She's the one who thinks this plan won't work."

"Except she needs this plan to work more than anyone else. I'm pretty sure Eleanor is reminding her of that little fact right now." Bray crossed his arms over his chest and leaned back against the door.

Allard knew eventually he would have to agree to his Alphas' proposal, the same way he knew the sun would rise in the morning. He didn't want to concede to it just yet, but he didn't know how long he could sit in the dark and brood before Vixen found him.

Not long he guessed.

"Do I need to remind you that even if she needs this more, you need it too. Because right now all the options lead us down a path to all-out war." Bray raised his eyebrow. "I'll admit, Vixen wouldn't be disappointed with any of those options, but she'd prefer they were on her timeline and not based on the decision of the five shifters who make up the Council or some power-hungry Alpha."

"So what you're really saying is I don't have a choice?"

"You always have a choice. Yes, we're pushing this fake mating, but if you're adamant that you don't want this, we'll support your decision."

Bray was right. Allard knew that no matter what happened, at the end of the day, Vixen and Bray would stand behind him. And now it was Allard's time to stand behind his pack. He had others to consider rather than just his own self.

"Fine, I'll do it. What do I need to do?"

"Good. I know you can pull this off, Allard. That the both of you can pull this off."

Allard wished he had as much faith in himself as his Alpha.

CHAPTER ELEVEN

TEN minutes after Eleanor had left her alone, Delia was still standing alone at the top of the hallway.

The sound of the boisterous pack carried up from what she assumed was the kitchen. Delia was tempted to disobey Eleanor's suggestion and venture down the hallway. Curiosity had always been one of her bigger faults. A closed door was just an invitation to find a window to see what was inside.

The lighted hallway beckoned and Delia succumbed. Just a few steps. Only to the first door which happened to be open.

Delia peeked inside. A large bed took up most of the room. Two armchairs, looking no less comfortable than the furniture in the front room, sat in the small alcove next to the window.

She smiled at the homey and welcoming sight in front of her. The room clearly belonged to the Alphas, but it didn't appear to be off limits to the rest of the pack. The small pile of toy cars by the chairs confirmed her assumptions.

Liking the pack and Broken Peak wasn't part of the bargain, but Delia was finding it more and more difficult to maintain her distance.

She couldn't see any more doorways in that main hall and wondered where the rest of the bedrooms were. Her curiosity drove her down a few more steps. And that was when she realized the hallway slanted down. The house wasn't just built against the mountain, it was built into it.

The chatter grew louder as she moved down the hall, but she couldn't make out any words.

A few more quiet steps and the words became more clear.

"She's a wolf shifter."

"From a huge pack."

"Why's she here?"

"Allard."

Before she got caught where she shouldn't be, Delia hurried back to the big room in the house's front. The last thing she needed was for the pack to catch her eavesdropping. Her brother and parents might tolerate it, but this new pack might not be so forgiving.

Plus, it wasn't like she was going to learn anything she didn't know.

Bray and Allard found her sitting in a chair, just like a good little wolf shifter guest should be doing.

"Delia?" Bray asked.

"Yeah?"

"You ready?"

"Do I have a choice?"

Allard smiled at her. The broody glower was gone from his face and in its place was amusement. "I said the same thing."

Okay then.

Delia stood and slipped her coat off, letting it drop to the chair. If she and Allard were supposed to be fated mates, wearing a coat wouldn't help with the roles they were going to have to play. And play convincingly to boot.

"I'm gonna head on down, you two can follow whenever you're ready." Bray left them alone once more.

Delia stuck her fingers in her front pockets and tilted her head to better study Allard.

He hadn't changed his clothes from earlier, but for the first time she noticed the way the worn fabric stretched over the muscles in his arms and across his chest.

His dark hair was long enough to brush his collar, but not long enough to cover his face or hide his blue eyes. Bright blue eyes that Delia wouldn't mind spending a few hours staring into.

"So…" Delia finally broke from her staring fest. "What's the story then?"

"Exactly what Bray and Vixen suggested."

"Yeah, but love at first sight? Even someone with the worst eyesight in the world could see that we aren't each other's favorite."

"Yeah, but from what both Jackson and Leighton said, their wolves practically claimed their mates at first sight. And Finley didn't even need to see his mate, he just visited her camper and knew she was for him. We can just use our wolves as the reason."

"You ever think about whether you had a true mate somewhere waiting for you?" Delia asked.

"I envied my friends for having a chance at one, but I tried not to think about it much." Allard almost smiled, or it was just a smirk. "You?"

"Didn't think about it much either. But then my wolf has been remarkably silent ever since I got in the car and started driving. She usually makes a point of sharing her opinion with me."

"Mine too."

Delia's eyes opened wide. "Really? Is that normal?"

Allard shook his head. "But don't tell Eleanor that or she'll go digging in her books to see if it's significant."

"There are books about us?" Delia hadn't heard of any kind of written shifter record, except for the few documents handed down through the generations within families.

"Well, journals. You met Mac earlier, one of his ancestors kept journals and if you can weed out the mutterings of a crazy old shifter, there're some hints of truth."

Delia pulled her bottom lip between her teeth. "There's a lot going on here that the rest of the shifter community doesn't know anything about."

"Is that supposed to be a question?" The guarded look was back on Allard's face.

Delia could have kicked herself. It was going to be difficult enough faking being mated, but if Allard was offended by whenever she spoke, it would be damn near impossible.

"We can still back out of this. It's obvious that we won't be able to pull off being fated mates to the Council." Delia sighed.

Although she had no idea what she'd do if Allard agreed and walked away. Sticking around for a few weeks until her father and the Alphas of Broken Peak Pack were convinced everything was safe, was going to be miserable.

Or she could walk right out the front door, find Geneva, and get the hell back to Chicago.

Instead of walking away, like he'd done every other time, well, okay, one time before, Allard surprised her. He didn't move from his spot. The glower didn't move either.

"My wolf likes you."

She rolled her eyes and threw herself into a chair. "Yeah, well, I don't know why. But I don't think you like me, and if we're being fair, I'm not sure I like you either. So what your wolf likes doesn't matter." The last thing she wanted was to be stuck with someone who glowered all the time.

Although, the Alpha of the enforcers who tried to take her from the street always smiled when she'd seen him. So a glower wasn't such a big negative.

"Bray and Vixen like you too." He ignored her words.

"And I like them too." Or at least she thought she did. Delia wasn't really prepared to say she didn't like the Alphas of the pack where she was supposed to be staying for a while. Somehow that didn't seem like a good choice.

"Eleanor and Mac like you too."

"Okay." She had no clue what Allard was trying to say.

"My wolf, he's been content here, but not quite happy. Like something's been missing since we got here."

Delia counted back the years. Had it been almost ten years since Allard disappeared from Colorado? That was a long time to be living with a wolf who wasn't satisfied.

"That must be hard." When she had gone away to college, her wolf practically pined away until she got back to Chicago. And Delia had only stayed away for a few months at a time. More than a year and her wolf would have driven her crazy. "Look, none of this is what I expected. My parents tried to make things as normal as possible, but the arranged mating has loomed over my head since I can remember. It's like a cage that's holding me back instead of keeping me safe. And now, I'm still stuck in a cage, it just has different bars on it."

"Yeah, I was in the same cage too, remember?"

"Yeah, but you got free for a few years." She picked at a stray thread poking out of her sweater.

"My wolf wasn't the happiest though and didn't make my time here feel very free."

"Yeah, so you said." She knew he was making an attempt at being friendly, or at least less broody, but she still didn't trust that he wasn't just going to walk away.

"I stopped listening to my wolf."

What? Oh shit. That was bad. It didn't matter how annoying her wolf was being, she never shut her out. "But you still shift, right?" She'd heard stories before, in some extreme cases, where shifters had refused to let their animals run and eventually gone mad. The stories made it worse than when shifters turned feral from giving their animals control for too long.

"Yeah. Bray forced it and eventually my wolf and I found a compromise. When my wolf's out, I lock myself away. And when my wolf's inside, he's locked away."

"Oh." Delia should have said so many other things, like why it was a bad idea to lock away his wolf, but lecturing him seemed like a bad idea of colossal proportions. She looked down at her fingers, still fiddling with the loose strand of yarn.

Allard surprised her. One moment he was across the room and the next he was standing in front of her chair. Her wolf was usually much better at tracking everyone's movements.

He reached down and lifted her chin with his fingertips until he was looking into her eyes. His skin was rough, like he worked hard with his hands. Nothing like any of the other males she had met over the years. Even her father and brother had smooth hands.

"Hey. Don't feel bad for me. Okay? It was both my and my wolf's choice. We weren't unhappy. Just not happy."

"Who said I was feeling bad for you?" Delia smiled slightly. Allard didn't deserve a full-blown smile. Not yet at least.

Allard rolled his eyes then pulled his hand away. "You don't have a very good poker face."

"What? Yes I do. My mother raised me since I was young to never reveal my emotions. Unless I want to. I can play and win poker with the best of them." The slight smile grew into something much larger.

"So, you went to college?"

"Yeah, I studied European history, of all things. It's not like I really need a college degree or anything, but I wanted one."

"You left Colorado just after graduating high school, didn't you?"

"Eh, that was the story they let out, but actually, I dropped out." Allard glanced towards the empty hallway, as if checking to see if anyone was lingering close to the doorway. "None of the males here have much of an education beyond high school. Eleanor and Danielle have degrees, but Maggie's education doesn't really count as education. Eleanor will probably recruit you to help with teaching Foster. The pup is a curious little fucker, but doesn't much like sitting down and learning things when it's not on his own terms. She's subscribing to a bribery program to get him to pay attention."

This was the most that he'd said to her since walking onto the pack's territory that didn't include a veiled insult. Her heart beat a fraction faster than before.

Or maybe it was her wolf's doing.

He turned his attention back on her and his bright blue eyes flashed to a brilliant gold for a moment before returning to their natural shade.

Whoa. His wolf wasn't locked away as much as Allard believed.

His intense stare drilled into her, but instead of riling up her temper, it riled up something else. Namely the little fluttering feelings she got in her belly. The last time she experienced those butterflies, she'd had her first kiss. It was also about the same time her mother sat her down for a long lecture about her obligation and duty to the pack.

"We can make this work, Delia. It's important for Bray and Vixen. I don't quite understand why right now, but I'm not going to do anything to ruin it." He crouched down in front of her so she didn't have to lean her head back to look at him. "So, what do you say? Wanna give this fated mate thing a go?"

Delia shook her head in defeat. "Didn't we already agree to this when your Alphas took the divide-and-conquer approach?"

"We might have said we'd do it, but…"

"But now you're willing to buy into it?"

"We both are, right?" He took her hands in his and pulled her up to her feet.

She could have fought against him. Kept her body firmly planted in the chair until he had to physically pick her up. But that wouldn't have been good for anyone, so she let him pull her up. She didn't even let go of his hands when she was fully standing.

Or when he tugged her along to the hallway and led her past the door she had peeked into earlier.

Or when he led her into the kitchen filled with all the pack members she'd heard about, but hadn't yet met.

Delia stepped back, but Allard's hand stopped her from getting too far away.

The kitchen was as large as the front room, except somehow it was even more comfortable looking. Like the pack spent most of their time in the kitchen and not just because of meals.

The long counter against one wall held a large farmhouse sink, a massive stove and oven, and what looked like an industrial fridge. It also had a professional grade espresso maker. The kind usually found in the coffee stores on every other block across the country.

Who would have thought Delia could get a good latte in the middle of nowhere?

A large island with stools along one side sat closer to the counter by the wall than the center of the room, but still had enough space to move between the counter and island comfortably.

But it was the massive table taking up almost half of the room that grabbed her attention.

Well not the table as much as the people sitting around the table.

CHAPTER TWELVE

ALLARD tugged Delia closer to him until she was half hidden behind his back. She leaned around him, peering into the room, and right at a male whose scowl could give Allard's glower a run for his money.

"Um… does Bray teach you all how to kill with a look?"

Allard followed Delia's gaze. "That's Leighton. He always looks that way."

"Not always!" A curvy little human with turquoise colored hair protested.

"And that's Danielle, Leighton's mate."

The male looked torn between wanting to kill Delia and wanting to make his mate happy. She assumed any harm done to her wouldn't make his mate happy, which was probably why he was still scowling.

"Don't worry, he'll warm up, eventually. Although he still hasn't warmed up to Tevin, and Tevin's been around for years." Allard chuckled, and the sound warmed her. "Eleanor, you've met. Jackson, her mate, is the one looming behind her and Foster, their son, is the one climbing Jackson."

Delia took in the names and faces, relying on some tricks her mother had taught her to remember who was who. A smile, a wave, and repeating their names as she said hello. Thankfully her mother also taught Delia how not to sound like a broken record.

"Tevin and the fuzzball in his hand is Hampstead, Danielle's hamster." Allard made his way around the table, naming the remaining members of the pack. "And finally, there's Finley and his mate Maggie."

Delia repeated the same routine, smile, wave, and a hello accompanied by their name. She was on a roll until she came to Maggie.

Maggie was the raccoon she scented earlier.

The pack didn't have a gaze close by. They counted a raccoon shifter as one of their own.

Holy hell.

The Council wouldn't care how well Allard and Delia pulled off their fake mating, they'd be more concerned about the raccoon shifter.

"And you've already met Bray and Vixen." The Alpha pair stood behind the island.

"We have some stew on the stove if you're hungry, Delia?" Bray asked. "Or I could make you a sandwich?"

"Stew is perfect, thank you." Delia stepped around Allard and walked further into the kitchen.

But she didn't get very far. Allard kept his hand on hers and tugged her back to him. Once she was tucked against his side, he stepped into the room with her and brought her to the table.

"So mates, huh?" Maggie asked. "Let me ask you a question. Have you decided on who your bride's maids will be and who gets to be the maid of honor? And if you haven't, what sort of tribute are you asking for?"

"Um, yes. Funny isn't it, believing we're just part of an arranged mating for all this time then coming here and learning it's something more?" Delia fell into the role of Allard's mate. It was that or try to figure out what Maggie meant by tribute. "As for the rest, that's more of a human tradition than wolf shifter tradition."

Maggie's eyes widened, and she leaned across the table, practically climbing over it. "You know about human traditions?"

Okay, the raccoon shifter was just weird. There wasn't any other way to explain her behavior.

"Maggie, let Delia breathe a little." Allard pulled a chair out for Delia and waited until she sat down before taking the seat next to her.

"But…" Maggie narrowed her eyes at Allard, attempting to send a scowling glower his way, but failing and looking more like a pouting toddler than ferocious raccoon shifter.

Allard just looked back at Maggie and raised his eyebrows at her.

Whatever else he did, Delia didn't catch, but it must have annoyed Maggie because she blew out her breath at him.

Everyone around the table stared at Maggie for several moments. So did Delia. She knew better than to gape, but she couldn't help herself. Maggie was just so unusual.

"Was there a spark that time?" Maggie sat back in her chair and looked around at everyone. "Did anyone see something this time?"

"Um, no?" Danielle answered for all of them, then leaned in close to Eleanor and spoke softly, but not softly enough for the rest of the shifters in the room. "We don't want to know, right?"

"Probably for the best." Eleanor nodded.

Bray set a large bowl filled with a thick stew full of hearty chunks of meat and large vegetable pieces in front of Delia, then handed her a spoon. "It's shiny. If we don't hold on to things, they might find their way into Maggie's pockets."

"I resent that!" The tiny raccoon shifter cried out.

"You were supposed to." Finley, the almost boyish faced shifter with a striking set of sparkling turquoise eyes, grabbed Maggie by her waist and pulled her into his lap. "Come on, Pocket. You'll have plenty of time to spook Delia out. You don't have to do it all in one night."

The gesture was sweet and almost romantic, but Delia figured it was less about romance and more about keeping Maggie under control.

Turned out, Maggie wasn't the craziest one of the bunch, as Delia learned a few seconds later when Danielle focused her attention on Delia.

"So, when can we expect the whole bonding claiming thing to happen? And then how long after until there are pups. Broken Peak has a lot of things, but we're slacking in the children department. We have Foster, and sometimes Maggie depending on her mood for the day, but we need more shifter babies."

Delia almost choked on her stew. Babies? The last thing either of them needed to worry about during their fake mating, was a baby.

Except she couldn't say that. At least not if she wanted to sell their mating as real.

"I don't know what you know about shifters, so I apologize for telling you something you might already know, but shifters are a little different from humans and wolf shifters even more so. For whatever reason, we're most fertile during the first few months of the year." She looked out the corner of her eyes at Allard and gave him a coy grin, hoping he'd play along with her. "So, it's possible sooner rather than later."

Allard's arm slipped around the back of her chair and he squeezed her shoulder. Not hard enough to bruise, but hard enough to let her know he was not amused.

Well, tough. He'd figure out soon enough that Delia needed to keep herself entertained if she expected to survive their little farce with her mind still intact.

He leaned in and brushed his lips against her ear. "Careful, Red."

She smirked, but hid it well with a spoonful of stew slipped between her lips.

Maggie's eyes grew even wider, which Delia didn't think was possible, but apparently it was. "Mating season?" Her words came out with a heavy breath and she twisted her head around to direct an accusing glare at Finley. "Why didn't you tell me about that?"

"Remember the deal, Red." The laughter from the others in the room kept anyone from hearing Allard's words.

"Just friends," she murmured under her breath.

His words reminded her that the last thing she needed to be considering was romance, love, or even sex. Especially not with a male who looked like Allard being so close. Strong. Sexy. Handsome. Probably a great fighter from the looks of him. Exactly what she didn't need to be thinking about.

Just like she didn't need to be thinking about what it would be like to feel his body pressed against hers. In bed. Without clothes on.

Yeah those thoughts had to go away. And fast.

For a minute she wondered if Geneva was nice enough to pack her vibrator. If not, she supposed she could order one online. If they could deliver to the middle of nowhere, no one needed to pick up the package for her and then question her about what she ordered.

Her cheeks heated with a blush.

Why couldn't Allard be soft like all the other sons of Alphas she'd met over the years? It would be so much easier for her.

CHAPTER THIRTEEN

ALLARD leaned back in his chair and looked around the kitchen at his packmates.

"At least none of us will have to double up rooms. When Bray said we were going to have a guest, I figured I'd get stuck with you and your snoring, Allard." Tevin leaned forward, resting his elbows on the table.

"Well, actually Tevin…" Vixen snickered from her perch behind the island where she could keep an eye on the entire kitchen.

"What? They're mates, right? And not a stupid contract mating, but real mates, that's what you said."

"We have one more guest coming, just for the night. You'll have to double up with Foster, but she'll be leaving early in the morning, so you can move back to your own room as soon as she leaves."

Tevin's jaw dropped. "What the hell?"

Eleanor glared at Tevin. "Language."

"Oh please, the pup has heard it all. Hell is minor compared to everything else he hears." Tevin was pissed.

Of all the members of the pack, Tevin probably had the worst childhood. No one really knew his history, but he came to the pack at a younger age than the others. He also had an issue with marking things.

When he was a kid, his wolf would run around peeing on everything. Then anything his wolf didn't mark, he would use a sharpie to sign his name on it. They still had some dishes with the name Tevin scrawled across them. He still wrote his name on things, but it wasn't nearly as bad.

Having to room up with Foster, even for one night, was going to drive Tevin insane.

Allard almost offered to sleep with Foster so Delia could spend the night with her friend, but then the little minx leaned back, and consequently against his arm that was still resting on the back of her chair. The thought of her sleeping anywhere but next to him felt wrong.

While Tevin pissed and moaned, Delia reached into her sweater and pulled a necklace out. The thin gold chain held a small green colored stone. Could be an emerald, but Allard wasn't certain. She lifted the chain close to her chin and ran the small pendant back and forth a few times before dropping it so it hung over her turtleneck.

Whether she intended it, the gesture with her necklace drew attention to her chest. The turtleneck sweater might have covered her from the neck down, but it didn't hide the perfect swell of her breasts.

And they were perfect. She had to have a bra that made them look the way they did because Allard had never seen a pair of breasts like hers before.

Then she had to go and take another bite of stew. Instead of staring at her breasts, he was focused on her mouth. Specifically on her lips as they wrapped around the spoon. Thoughts of her mouth wrapped around other things invaded his thoughts and Allard bit back a groan.

He wasn't sure how much more he could handle.

Thankfully, he didn't have to worry for long because Foster, who had been quietly playing with some of his toy cars on the table, sent one across the way, directly at the bowl in front of Delia.

The car, despite being small, had enough force to jostle the bowl and stew sploshed over the sides onto the table and Delia's lap.

Eleanor, horrified at the sight of the stew dripping into Delia's lap, jumped from the table and grabbed a handful of napkins. Before she could even swipe them across Delia's lap, Allard had them in hand and was prepared to do the honors himself.

Except Delia intervened. She pulled the napkins from Allard and blotted at the stain, all while attempting to put Eleanor at ease and laughing at the situation.

"That'll teach me not to put a napkin in my lap. My mother would be giving me her patented 'I told you so' look if she was here." Delia smiled across the table and winked at Foster.

Allard had to give her credit. Not for blotting the stain off her jeans on her own, he would have been quite happy to do that for her. Instead of getting angry, which he half expected considering the way she dressed and the family she was from, she rolled with the accident as though it was no big deal.

Fuck, he needed to get his mind free of all these thoughts about her.

Once the Council was satisfied the mating was real, they'd go back to the way things were before Delia arrived at Broken Peak.

The last thing he needed was to be thinking about how comfortably she fit into the pack despite meeting all them for the first time less than fifteen minutes ago. Or how amazing her breasts were. Or the shape of her lips. Or how great she smelled.

Wait....

How great she smelled?

Where the hell had that nugget come from?

Probably the same place that rated her breasts perfect and her mouth fuckable.

He looked down at his lap and groaned.

Yep. If the state of his cock was anything to go by, it had taken over control of his brain.

And his wolf wasn't helping matters either.

The beast had been silent, but had crept closer to the surface. He wasn't interested in the goings-on of the pack. The wolf only cared about Delia and what she was doing.

No wonder Alphas had been throwing their sons at Delia. How the hell had Everest Lyall convinced himself that Delia would be safe. Her father should have done something a lot sooner.

He shook his head in what would likely be another failed attempt to get Delia out of his thoughts.

Sure, they had to fake the mating well enough to convince his packmates and whichever members of the Council that came to verify Delia and Allard were indeed mated, but they didn't have to convince each other.

As if she could read his mind, Delia reached over and placed her hand on Allard's thigh and left it there.

And then Danielle had to ruin it for him.

"Hey, if you're here and you're Allard's mate, then you have to be in the journals too." The feisty human looked between Eleanor and Delia. "Well, is she there? Who is she? Have you looked? We should look and see."

"What?" Delia snatched her hand from his leg and looked around the room before settling her gaze on Allard as though he could answer her questions. "What does she mean by me being in journals."

"I'm not the one to ask." Allard groaned silently. Of course, she'd look to him instead of the others, like Vixen and Bray, who were basically to blame for Allard's current predicament. "I haven't read any of the journals. That's Eleanor's domain."

"And mine." Maggie jumped in.

"And Maggie's." It wasn't, but they'd learned that it was usually easier to agree with her than argue. Besides, she liked to steal things as a way to punish those who she felt offended her sensibilities. "You'll have to ask Eleanor or Vixen, not me."

"Or me." Maggie jumped in. Again.

But this time, Allard ignored her. He was too busy staring at Delia's gorgeous green eyes. How come he only noticed now, that they matched the color of the gemstone on her necklace?

He wanted her hand back on his leg. Or anywhere else on him for that matter.

Which was wrong on so many levels.

Allard had to focus. They just had to convince the Council and life could go back to normal.

And it wasn't like it would be difficult to play the protective mate in front of them. Always having a reason to touch her. Feel her perfect breasts pressed against him.

He just needed to remember that as soon as the Council left, they'd go back to the way things were before she waltzed right into their lives.

CHAPTER FOURTEEN

DELIA blinked hard. Several times. She opened her mouth to say something, then closed it only to open it again. She must have resembled a fish pulled out of the water and gasping while flopping around.

Except she wasn't flopping. Which was a good thing.

The journals had been mentioned before, but always as part of the discussion of their arranged mating. Yet Danielle, the sweet, if slightly impolite, human mate to the male who looked like a serial killer, or at least what Delia imagined a serial killer might look like, brought up the journals like they were something so much more.

Come to think of it, hadn't Mac mentioned the Muse when he walked Geneva and Delia down from where she parked.

Speaking of parking. What about her car?

Random thoughts poured into her mind and careened off each other, like that old chaotic children's game Popcorn where you tried to capture the same colored marbles.

Allard bent his head forward and kissed her.

Holy crap.

Not good. In fact, it bordered on moronic.

Except, it was good. Really good.

His soft lips pressed against hers and his nose rubbed hers as he tilted his head.

Then her wolf perked up. She'd been curious before, but mostly quiet and staying in the background. Now that the male next to her, the one who she was supposed to be pretending was her true mate, was kissing her, her wolf pushed her way closer to the surface.

The distinctly male scent coming from Allard tickled her nose and sent the fluttering in her belly into a tizzy.

She wanted more.

Her wolf wanted more.

Her fingers itched to run across his broad chest and shoulders and her arms wanted to wrap themselves around his neck so he couldn't pull away.

A giggle broke into her wandering thoughts and reminded her of where she was. Sitting around a table in a kitchen surrounded by Allard's packmates, and hers too, at least for the time being.

One good thing came from the kiss. Her thoughts were now solely focused on one thing and one thing only.

Allard. What it would feel like to have his heavy weight on top of her. What it would be like with him behind her. He was a born Alpha and naturally dominant. Did that transfer to the bedroom? And who said they even needed a bedroom?

A blush shot up from her chest to her cheeks and forehead. The bane of being a redhead with freckles was the obvious blushing. Try as she might, she'd never been able to control the flushes.

She hoped everyone in the room believed the blush came from embarrassment and not the arousal that had built within her.

Except she was surrounded by shifters. If her arousal wasn't obvious to them, it was definitely obvious to Allard.

Pulling away from Allard, she leaned back in her chair.

This was so not good.

Not good at all.

His gaze caught hers and instead of the cool detachment she expected to find, his hungry gaze met her stare.

His eyes flared gold. Too quickly for anyone else to catch, but she saw his desire. The same desire she felt.

Shit.

This was not supposed to be happening.

The arranged mating was off the table and everything that was happening was supposed to be fake. They were supposed to be playing at being mated and Delia needed to remember that.

Allard's expression shuttered, and the wall returned.

They weren't going to convince anyone of anything if Allard shifted from hot to cold in a matter of seconds.

One deep breath later, a quick glance to Foster, and she reached out and pressed her hand against his cheek. "That should wait until there are less impressionable eyes around."

Allard blinked, and the glower was gone. The wall still remained in place, but at least he wasn't scowling at her. "I'll hold you to that promise, Red."

Finley snorted out a loud laugh, not even bothering to hide it behind a cough. "Trust me, the pup has seen it all. He doesn't know the meaning behind a closed door and locks might only buy a few extra minutes before he barges in."

Finley's words caused another blush to rush across her cheeks.

Even if she understood this was all an act, her body wasn't receiving the message.

Neither was her wolf if the satisfied growl was anything to go by.

Allard's lips stretched into a satisfied grin. And her body went into overdrive with the fluttering again.

Nope.

Not happening.

Not with this male.

CHAPTER FIFTEEN

IT FELT as though someone had punched Allard right in the chest. Hard. Even taking a breath was difficult. Mostly because all the blood rushed from his brain to his cock and he couldn't remember how to breathe.

Kiss more. His wolf practically howled.

Eleanor set a glass full of Mac's moonshine in front of him and he was yanked back to the kitchen, away from the fantasy of kneeling behind Delia with her hair wrapped around his hand to better hold her in place while he slammed into her.

Across the kitchen, standing behind the island still, Vixen and Bray gave him twin smug smiles. Like they knew something he didn't.

He avoided looking at his Alphas and instead looked down at the moonshine. Drinking some of the moonshine wasn't exactly a smart move considering his brain was already shorting out, but it wasn't like it could make matters worse.

A quick glance next to him, and he noticed Delia had her own glass of moonshine. As did the rest of the pack.

When had that happened?

Probably while he was busy deciding the best way to find an excuse to kiss Delia again.

Delia lifted the glass and sniffed its contents. "What is this?"

"Mac makes it. If you were human, it would knock you on your ass, but since you're a shifter, it will give you a healthy buzz." Finley answered before Allard could.

She sniffed again. "He makes it? Like in a bathtub?"

"Not a bad assumption, considering his original still had a bathtub. But no, Vixen ordered him some better equipment." Allard responded.

"Safer." Vixen corrected. "I wasn't sure the alcohol content would be high enough to kill off all the bacteria thriving in his old still."

Delia's eyes widened. "It smells like it could strip layers of paint off the walls of a 100-year-old house."

"That's why he adds fruit to it. It hides the flavor." Danielle sipped her drink. The last time she downed a glassful, she insisted hamburgers had some magical quality to them.

"Consider it a kind of initiation to the pack." Tevin raised his glass to her, but his gaze focused below her neck.

Allard rumbled out a soft growl. It wasn't what he wanted to do or what his wolf wanted him to do, which was jump across the table and yank Tevin's head up so he was looking anywhere but at Delia's breasts.

Tevin looked up at the sound of the growl, but he ducked away, as if he knew Allard's next move would involve fighting. Not that any of the males in the pack shied away from a good brawl, but Tevin learned pretty quickly that the mated males of the pack took the fighting to a whole new level when it involved some perceived offense to their mates.

A warm hand settled on his leg. Delia. She rubbed her palm across the top of his thigh, easing both him and his wolf.

Fuck him.

Why was it so easy for her to relax his wolf? The same beast who kept himself hidden away most the time because Allard was tired of fighting with him.

And why the hell was he thinking about Delia as a mate. She wasn't. She was his fake mate.

Fake mate. Fake mate. Fake mate!

He repeated the words over and over like a mantra. Not that it helped much with his wolf snickering in the back of his mind.

His arm shot out and wrapped around Delia's shoulders.

Fuck him twice over. Now other parts of his body were acting on their own volition.

What the hell happened to his brain?

"When in Rome." Delia lifted the moonshine to her lips and drank.

Before she finished the entire glass, Allard pulled it away from her mouth by wrapping his free hand around her fingers. Yeah, there were probably better ways to stop her from drinking it all, but most of them didn't allow for him to touch her.

She closed her eyes and the tip of her pink tongue poked out and ran across her lips.

A shudder ran through Allard. Right from the top of his spine down to his cock. Which somehow managed to get harder than it was before.

Great, no way he'd be able to get up from the table anytime soon. Not without everyone seeing how hard he was.

When she finally opened her eyes, her nostrils flared, as if she was taking in all the surrounding scents. "Oh."

"Strong?" Maggie leaned forward in her chair and pulled out a notebook. Where the hell had she been hiding that? Or the pencil that appeared in her hand. She licked the tip of the pencil and set it against the paper. "I'm researching his moonshine. This is the triple berry blend. On a scale of one to ten, how would you rate the likelihood of you tipping over. One being your feet are firmly on the ground and ten being the world is spinning and you want to get off."

Allard pinched the bridge of his nose and shook his head.

Screw being embarrassed by his erection, Maggie was doing a fine job embarrassing the entire pack.

"Somewhere between a one and two, leaning closer to a two." Delia turned to Allard and whispered in his ear. "It's probably closer to a five, so we might have to sit here for a while."

He laughed. He couldn't help himself. Burying his nose in her hair, he murmured in her ear. "Red, we can sit here for as long as you like."

"Also, don't let me have any more. I have a feeling this stuff can make the tightest tongues wag." She camouflaged her whispering by nuzzling against his neck.

"Fair point." He pressed a kiss to the top of her head while pushing both their glasses away.

The last thing either of them needed was to share their secret around either Maggie or Foster. The others might keep their mouths shut, but the little raccoon shifter and the pup were notorious for blabbing things out to anyone close by looking halfway interested.

When the sound of the front door opening, then closing, carried down the hallway into the kitchen, all the shifters turned their faces to the noise.

Danielle and Eleanor only followed after they noticed the others looking towards the kitchen door.

Mac was returning with Roose and the not quite human.

"It's just me, don't shoot!" Mac called out.

"We know it's you, you old coot." Bray grumbled back.

"Well yeah, but in case you forgot." The old coyote shifter stepped into the kitchen with Geneva in tow. "Oh, you got the triple berry out, how is it?"

Maggie looked down at her notebook, prepared to read back her litany of notes when Finley placed his hand on the book and pressed it down with a gentle shake of his head.

"Neva, you're back." Delia turned around in her chair and knelt on the seat so she could better see her friend.

Allard reached out and placed his hand on the middle of her back, holding her steady. Yep, Delia was closer to a five than a two on Maggie's moonshine scale.

"I'm back..." Geneva looked around the table, her gaze pausing momentarily on Allard and his nearness to Delia. Her brows furrowed at the sight, but she said nothing.

Roose cleared his throat and lifted the bags in his hands for everyone to see. "Where do you want these?"

"There's fine, I'll bring them back to my room when we head there."

Geneva's eyes nearly bugged out of her head, but Eleanor jumped to her feet and covered up the best she could.

"Hi, I'm Eleanor, this is my mate, Jackson, and our son, Foster." After she introduced her family, she introduced everyone else in the room.

It was an effective distraction to keep Geneva from blurting something out that would ruin Delia and Allard's chance of convincing everyone they were fated mates.

By the time Geneva finished learning everyone's names, Allard got Delia sitting back in the chair. Considering she hadn't completely metabolized the moonshine, he counted it as a win. Geneva sat down next to Delia, Roose joined the Alphas behind the island, and Mac squeezed in between Maggie and Jackson.

"Here, try this." Delia pushed her glass of moonshine in front of Geneva and grinned in anticipation. "I might have to send you home with a bottle of it for Scott. He considers himself a professional drinker, but this might drop him back down to amateur status."

Thankfully, Geneva just sampled the drink before setting it back down on the table on the side away from Delia.

Maggie, pencil and notebook in hand, watched Geneva with a look that bordered on being creepy. Before she opened her mouth, Finley covered it with his hand.

Eleanor turned to Jackson, "Let's get Foster to bed."

And by let's, she meant him. Eleanor had said similar things to everyone else in the pack at some point and they were all adept at reading between her lines.

"Sure." Jackson didn't fight it. He scooped the pup up under an arm and strode out of the kitchen. "Say good night, pup."

"Good night, pup!" Foster giggled like he'd said the funniest thing and waved goodbye to everyone.

Allard thought with Foster out of the way, things would get easier, but they didn't, they got harder.

First, Geneva stared at Delia for at least five minutes, before finally holding up a hand and shaking her head back and forth. "I don't want to know, so I won't ask."

When the words came pouring out of Geneva's mouth, Vixen, Bray, Eleanor, and even Mac, opened their mouths at the same time.

"I'm hungry. Is anyone else hungry?" Vixen asked.

"So, what movie do you have planned for the next movie night, Danielle?" Came from Mac.

"We need to do a pack run. When Jackson comes back, we should head outside." Bray suggested.

"Maggie, remind me to tell you about another entry I found in one of Edna's journals. It looks like some kind of corroboration to the Rebel's entry." Eleanor blurted out.

Maggie's eyes pinged between everyone speaking, as though her brain couldn't settle on who she wanted to listen to.

Which was good. It meant she was less likely to pay attention to Geneva.

Unfortunately the tactic wasn't as successful with Danielle. The brilliant woman narrowed her gaze on Geneva, even as she answered Mac's question. "Well, according to Eleanor's latest directive, we need to keep it Disney centric, so I'm going with *Chitty Chitty Bang Bang*."

CHAPTER SIXTEEN

ACROSS the room, Vixen pushed away from the island and circled around until she stood by the table. "Why don't we head back to the front room so we can all interrogate Geneva and Delia to our heart's content without help from the boys." She said. "Danielle, why don't you grab a few bottles of wine and Eleanor, can you grab some glasses?"

"Why *Chitty Chitty Bang Bang*?" Geneva asked as she pushed her chair away from the table and stood.

"Child Catcher and Disney," Danielle answered.

"Ah, in that case, might I suggest *Return to Oz*?" Delia said. Her older brother loved to find movies that would give her nightmares, but still pass their mother's strict appropriate movie protocol. Disney movies from the 80s strayed into the land of the weirdly terrifying.

Danielle's eyes widened and a wide smile slowly appeared on her face. "Delia, you're my new best friend."

"Nope. She's mine. I did some research and maids of honors are always the best friends. I'm her maid of honor, so I'm her best friend. Proctor ipso hoc factor ergo."

"Pocket, I think it's propter and not proctor." Finley gently pushed Maggie to her feet and sent her toward Vixen.

"Not to mention it's post hoc ergo propter hoc." Eleanor offered from the cabinet where she was gathering wine glasses.

"How were you researching maid of honor, Maggie?" Danielle asked.

"Um, well, see, I'd tell you, but that would be gasconading, and I don't do that."

Danielle held her hand out, palm up. "Give it up."

"Why? See, I knew I shouldn't have said anything, I made you frumious." Maggie reached into her pocket and pulled out a large yellow cased phone, like the ones seen in movies about military teams on secret missions, and gave it to Danielle.

"You know you don't have to use your words-of-the-day all the time, right?" Vixen wrapped her arm around Maggie's shoulders and walked her out of the kitchen.

It might have sounded like a suggestion, but Vixen delivered an order. If Delia planned on staying in Vixen's good graces, it would be better not to argue, even if she didn't want to move away from Allard's arm. Delia stood to follow the Alpha female from the room.

As she turned, Allard grabbed her arm and tugged down so her face was close to his. He tapped his finger against his lips. "Before you go."

Delia lifted an eyebrow. So, he wanted to give his packmates a show. She could do that. Or it was the moonshine telling her to play it up. She placed her hands on his shoulders and slid them around his neck. The muscles under her fingers twitched, and she bent down to kiss him.

The kiss was a hundred times better than the one before.

His lips opened and the tip of his tongue brushed against her lips until she parted them for him.

He tasted like the moonshine they'd had earlier. And more. Like pine and a strong male.

Whatever it was, his taste gave her a better buzz than the moonshine had. Or it was just the moonshine.

What did it matter?

The only thing she cared about at that moment was getting more from him.

He must have had similar thoughts because next thing she knew, he pulled her into his lap, held her head just where he wanted it, and deepened the kiss.

He wasn't going to stop, and she didn't have plans on stopping either.

At least until someone coughed.

Delia yanked away from Allard and jumped from his lap to her feet.

What had they done?

For a second time?

Didn't she learn her lesson from the first kiss?

Apparently not.

Allard stared back at her. She imagined her eyes looked the same, filled with regret, but it didn't make the sight feel any better.

Whatever was going on between them, she'd need to be the one to keep things from getting out of hand. Except, they were supposed to be mates. They were supposed to kiss like that. Just not with all the bells and whistles that came with his kiss.

She fell back into her role and blew Allard a kiss. "Later."

He winked back at her. The look of regret gone and the emotionless wall to its place.

When Delia turned toward the door, Geneva was staring at her with a perplexed look. The smile, hidden from the rest of the pack, Delia gave her friend was one they'd exchanged before. She just hoped Geneva would recognize it. It was the, just pretend everything's normal, I'll explain it all later, smile.

Except what she really wanted to be doing later was kissing Allard.

CHAPTER SEVENTEEN

ALLARD'S head swiveled to follow Delia's hasty retreat. He just kissed the fuck out of her, enough for her to know better than try to stand and walk, but she was practically running away from him.

He was a powder keg, waiting to explode, and Delia was the flame dancing dangerously close.

The glass of moonshine found itself into his hand and to his mouth. He set down the empty glass and looked around for the jug.

The males left in the kitchen stared.

Leighton pushed the jug toward Allard. "This what you're looking for?"

"He doesn't need that if what we saw is a prelude for tonight." Finley said with barely a straight face.

Allard glared at his friend.

"Gotta say, I didn't expect you to find a mate." Tevin said. "And whatever you got for her, it's bad."

Tevin pushed away from the table and stared at them all for a few moments before he reached for the salt and poured some into the palm of his hand then threw a pinch over his shoulder. Next he spit on the ground. And finally, he knocked on the wooden table.

Roose stared at Tevin before shaking his head in resignation. "What the hell was that for?"

"Figured it would stop whatever y'all have caught."

"Don't add me to that list." Roose stared down Tevin until the young male finally turned away.

Movement from his Alpha caught Allard's attention. When he looked at Bray, the male nodded toward the hallway the females had disappeared down.

Bray wasn't telling Allard to follow Delia, even if that was what he wanted to do. His Alpha wanted to have a little chat, away from the curious little fuckers. There was probably a better time for a conversation, except telling Bray that their talk could wait would have gone down faster than a lead balloon.

Allard stood and stepped out of the kitchen. Instead of turning left to the bedrooms, or heading straight to reach Delia, he followed the hallway to the right that led to the offices.

Bray and Mac came along behind him, offering some excuse about having to contact Everest Lyall to keep the others from asking too many questions.

He hurried down the hallway before turning left into Bray's office. Not that it was much of an office, just a desk, a few chairs, and some filing cabinets. At some point Vixen had added some bulletin boards and a white board to stop Bray from tacking papers and receipts to the wall, but Bray just stuck the papers into the wall next to the boards.

Bray came in right behind him.

"Where's Mac?" Allard looked around Bray's shoulder.

"Bringing Gareth in the back way."

"Gareth? He's coming? Since when are cats concerned about wolves?"

"Since they live next to a small pack of them. Especially since one of that pack happens to be the son of an Alpha of a large pack and is also supposed to be mated to the daughter of the most powerful Alpha."

"Since you put it that way..."

"How much more crap can you drag to the Peak, Bray? You're worse than a fucking cat. Which, I don't need to remind you, is why I moved away from the clans to begin with." Gareth walked into the office and sat down in one of the old chairs Vixen relegated to Bray's office.

Mac stepped into the small office, which suddenly seemed smaller with four large males, all dominant, crowded into it.

Bray rapped his knuckles against his desk. "Let's get this over with. I don't trust the others being left to their own devices for long, even with Roose there to keep them in line." He leaned back in the old office chair and stretched his legs out in front of him. In a room filled with dominants, Bray wore the mantle of Alpha with a comfortable ease.

"You and Delia look to be getting on pretty well." Mac grinned behind his bushy gray beard.

"What did you find out?" Bray gave Mac a pointed glare.

Apparently Delia and Allard's interactions weren't on the agenda.

"Well, Geneva accepted her role faster than the others, but that's probably because she was thrown into an impossible world, so something like having a witch for an ancestor fits right into her new reality."

"Witch?" Allard's eyes widened in surprise. "There are witches?"

"Case in point." Mac gestured toward Allard. "According to Edna, yes, there were and are witches, also wizards, and vampires."

Gareth combed his fingers through his short blond hair and snorted out a laugh. "His head is really going to spin when you tell him about the dragons."

How come it felt as if a pile of secrets was being dumped on him. Allard closed his eyes and took a deep breath. "I heard about the dragons. Not saying I believe it though."

"You should," Gareth grinned with glee at him. "Supposedly raccoon shifters came about because a dragon shifter gave a few of them his magic with the help of a wizard."

"It really does explain Maggie and her need to hoard things," Mac said.

"All raccoons hoard things." Allard offered a reason that didn't include dragon shifters for Maggie's habits.

Bray cleared his throat. "So, Allard's fake brother-in-law is the Heir?" He changed the subject without so much as a comment about dragon shifters or Maggie.

Apparently she wasn't on the agenda either.

"Looks that way." Mac agreed.

"Vixen's griffin is convinced Geneva has some magic in her. She recognized it as soon as you brought them into the yard." Bray added.

"That makes Delia the Crown for sure then?" Gareth looked between Mac and Bray, completely ignoring Allard.

Not that Allard minded all that much. The entire conversation was going over his head. Sure, he listened to Eleanor when she got excited about a new find in a journal, but he didn't pay close attention to what she said most of the time.

The females of the pack bought into the titles and roles things, the males in turn humored them.

If he kept his mouth shut, he might learn something.

"Everest Lyall agrees she's the Crown too," Bray said. "Safety might have been the excuse for pointing Delia in our direction, but it wasn't the reason."

"Their histories are different though." Mac leaned forward in his chair and rested his elbows on his knees.

"What do you mean?" Gareth asked.

"They don't have access to Edna's journals. At least not that I know about. But they've passed down a story from generation to generation about the Heir and the Crown?" Mac paused and looked up at Bray. "We need a copy of their records."

"I'll see what I can do." Bray didn't sound optimistic.

Allard might have spent his adult life with the Broken Peak Pack, but he grew up inside a traditional pack and was being groomed to lead it before he ran for the hills. Literally. He understood how Alphas operated. "Offer him access to Edna's journals, and he'll say yes."

The three males turned to Allard, as though they forgot he was in the room with them.

"All of them?" Bray asked.

"Give him everything that pertains to his kids and then whatever else you don't mind sharing. As long as he thinks he's getting more out of the deal, he'll agree."

"He's going to need your support eventually, Bray. He won't do anything to offend you." Gareth said.

For as wise as these males might be, they were ignorant about how the shifter world worked outside of their cloistered life.

"Unless he thinks Bray owing him a favor has more value than, say another Alpha from a large pack owing him, he'll balk." Allard looked at Bray, who didn't seem to understand his words. Allard tried to explain it. "Shifter society is a zero-sum game based on favors. The Alpha who owes the most favors is weakest, and the Alpha who is owed the most favors is the strongest. Bray doesn't owe anyone any favors that I know about, but no one owes you any favors. You owing Everest isn't worth more than giving him knowledge he doesn't have."

"I think you're underestimating just what the Broken Peak Pack is."

"No, Mac, I'm not, but the Alphas and Council members will." Allard looked between Bray and Mac before settling his gaze on Bray. "Shifter society is really close to politics. Vixen has an understanding, but she probably doesn't grasp the nuances. I'd ask the General about how it works."

The General was an older human who'd retired from the military, but was close to Vixen and came and went from Broken Peak as he pleased. Allard knew Bray had gone to the older man for advice from time to time, especially when he had questions about Vixen. If anyone could explain the game of favors to Bray, it was General Jessup.

Bray stared back at Allard for several minutes before finally nodding his head slowly. "Okay." He then turned to Gareth. "Want to share with Allard why you're making one of your rare appearances?"

"We learned there are a few males in town asking some questions about this area."

"Wolf shifters?"

Gareth nodded.

"How'd you learn about this?"

"We have a friend in town who passes on any information he thinks we might find interesting."

Allard looked at Bray, "My father?"

"Maybe. Or maybe it's one of the packs who thinks Delia is still available."

"Technically, she is."

"Yeah, but they don't know about the technical crap." Mac grumbled. "So, we think it might be a good idea for a few of you to head to War and visit a bar."

"Our friend in town will have your backs when you go." Gareth said.

"A few of us? Which few? And you know this can't possibly end good, right? Before some of us got mates, when we headed to town it always ended in fighting."

"Don't remind me." Bray glared at Allard. He'd had to go to town on more than one occasion to bail them out. "Make it a group outing. There's no way to keep Maggie or Danielle from going, not without Vixen getting pissed at me."

"I'm saying it now, so I don't get blamed for shit later on, but this is a bad idea."

"Leaving Maggie and Danielle out is a worse idea." Bray stated in the most matter-of-fact tone he'd ever used. "Plus, Gareth's friend will be more helpful than you realize."

Allard narrowed his eyes at Bray. Things weren't adding up the way he expected them to. What was he missing? "Just who is this friend?"

"Someone who Vixen trusts." Gareth said without further explanation.

Normally, that would have been enough, but for whatever reason, Allard needed more than Vixen's trust. "Bray?"

"Vixen's vetted him. Mac's vetted him. Hell, even the General's vetted him." Bray glanced over at Gareth before returning his gaze to Allard. "He's not human."

Bray's answer helped ease Allard, but he still felt like he was missing something. However, he didn't think anyone in the room was going to fill in the blank spaces just yet.

Gareth pushed up from the chair and looked down at Allard. "He has your back. That's all you need to know. Now, if you'll excuse me, I need to get back to the girls. The attention Broken Peak Pack is getting from the Council is making them nervous." He nodded once at Bray, then padded silently from the room, closing the door behind him.

"They're worried that if the Council is allowed here, the Chiefdom will insist on visiting." Mac spoke softly enough for Allard and Bray to have to lean in to hear him.

Gareth's clan fell under the rule of the Chiefdom, as all mountain lion clans did. Except while the Council guided the packs, the Chiefdom ruled the clans. Gareth's was somewhat different in that the Chiefdom believed Gareth was a bachelor living on his own. They didn't know his nieces lived under his protection, although they probably suspected.

Suddenly, with the realization of just how shitty some shifters' lives were, Allard felt guilty for complaining about an arranged mating.

"Well, this was revealing." Allard leaned back in his chair and studied the paper-filled wall behind Bray's desk.

"Don't share anything about our friend in War just yet," Mac said. Allard nodded.

"So, next is this mating thing. None of us have had official ceremonies, but then none of us came from families who'd need to have one."

"Does Delia know about a ceremony?"

Bray shook his head. "Not yet, but after the General gets back from delivering Geneva to the airport tomorrow morning and things have settled down a little, why don't we take care of it in the afternoon."

"I'll do the officiating part of it." Mac offered his services with a grin. "Then you all can head to town to celebrate."

"Vixen's debating rearranging the rooms again," Bray rolled his eyes at his mate's insistence that she could make things work with their limited bedrooms. "I told her we just need to expand already, but she doesn't trust anyone to come in and do the work and she sure as shit doesn't trust any of you fuck ups to do it instead. So, it looks like Delia will be moving into your room until Vixen figures out what she wants to do."

"My room isn't that big, and I have to share a bathroom with Maggie, Finley, and Tevin. I'm not sure Delia will be okay with that. Even for the short term."

"It's the best we can do." Bray's word ended the debate.

"What about security training?" Maggie was getting special training, and both Eleanor and Danielle had daily target practice so they could handle a gun if necessary. He didn't want everyone relying on Delia being a wolf shifter as her only means of protection.

"Not sure you have much to worry about. If what Everest claims is true, she fought off three enforcers on her own. Sure, she might have been in public, but it could have easily gone the other way," Mac said.

"Delia is smart. She'll do just fine." Bray agreed. "But just in case, I'll have Vixen look at supplementing any training she already has."

"You know, there's a story going around. Delia killed a male who showed up at her door and attacked her and his mate. Supposedly the family was moving the female back to Chicago because her mate was abusive. The rumor is the male attacked and killed his mate, but Delia ripped out his throat."

"Yeah?" His stomach roiled at Mac's words. Allard didn't like the thought of Delia fighting, even if her wolf was strong enough to kill a male.

Mac nodded. "Yep. And the next day, when she showed back up in Chicago. Not a single scratch. Your girl's strong."

"Not my girl," Allard groused.

"So you say." Bray smirked. "Either way, she can handle herself just fine."

"Shouldn't have to." Allard's grumbling continued. The fierce redhead with perfect breasts and a take no prisoners attitude shouldn't have to worry about fighting males.

"Do me a favor?" Bray asked and waited for Allard to look at him before continuing. "When you all go into town tomorrow night, grab one of those long-distance radio things Vixen has in the equipment room. I want to keep tabs on you."

"No argument from me." He wouldn't say the words, but he wanted to keep Delia safe.

Bray stood, effectively ending the impromptu meeting. "Good. Now, let's get back to the kitchen. It will be a fucking miracle if something hasn't caught fire."

CHAPTER EIGHTEEN

ALLARD reached the kitchen first, which was how he intercepted Foster before he could take off to the front room of the Lodge. Allard bent down and scooped Foster up into his arms. "Where you off to, pup?"

"Mommy." Foster said as if it was the most obvious reason for Foster to be up after his father had put him to bed.

A quick glance into the kitchen revealed Jackson sitting at the table with his back to the doorway. Except Allard knew Jackson was well aware of Foster's whereabouts. Which meant Jackson had likely given up on getting Foster to sleep.

"Okay then, let's go get your mom." Allard swung Foster around until the pup was clinging happily to his back.

Bray and Mac came up behind Allard and Bray paused to rub Foster's head before turning into the kitchen. "Don't think your dad was expecting you to get intercepted, Foster."

With the rest of the males happily ensconced in the kitchen, Allard headed for the front room. He needed to talk with Delia, so the pup gave him a nice excuse for getting her attention without having to pretend he couldn't spend more time apart from his newly discovered mate.

The females were all talking about nothing that made any sense to Allard. Something about sunscreens and moisturizers and why they were important. From the look on Maggie's face, she didn't quite understand it either, but was happy to be included. Vixen just seemed bored with the entire thing.

He pulled Foster around to his side to settle the pup on his hip and leaned against the doorway into the front room. Foster discovered the front pocket on Allard's shirt and slid one of his toy cars in and out of it. The pup was cute as hell, but usually caused a boatload of trouble. The good news was that the trouble he could find in the pack's territory wasn't anything life threatening.

Allard looked up and caught Delia watching them. It was as if all the worries and concerns in her life slipped away. He wasn't sure what the look meant, but he decided he wanted to see it on her face again soon.

He brought Foster into the room and stood next to Delia's chair. He reached down and placed his hand on the back of the chair. His fingers itched to brush across her shoulder, but he resisted the urge. If she flinched or pulled away from him in front of the others, they'd suspect something.

Foster bent forward and Allard shifted his stance, so the pup didn't fall into Delia's lap. In doing so, his hand slipped from the chair and to her shoulder.

Or that's what he told himself.

"Foster, what are you doing out of bed?" Eleanor popped out of her seat on the couch and crossed the floor to her son.

"I asked the same thing. He said Mommy."

Allard slid Foster to the ground so he could close the distance to his mom. He'd gotten too big over the past months for Eleanor to consider picking him up anymore and Allard hated seeing that sad look on her face when she couldn't handle a trade off from one set of arms to another.

"All right, let's try this again." Eleanor took Foster's hand and led him out of the front room and down the hallway.

When Allard looked back at Delia, she was watching him. He imagined she was waiting for a sign from him, or something. He tilted his head to the side and grinned at her.

"I'll let you get back to the girls' night thing, but can I borrow you for a second?"

"Of course." Delia returned his grin with a smile and stood to a chorus of 'aww's' from the other females.

The temptation to roll his eyes at the sound was huge, but he resisted. Barely.

His hand slipped into hers, as if it had a mind of its own. Which it probably did considering the trouble it had gotten him into earlier that night in the kitchen. The best place to talk was on the porch, but then the females would have their noses pressed against the window. The second best place was Vixen and Bray's room.

She followed him without needing to know where they were going or asking why. He rather liked that about her. Too bad every interaction with her hadn't been as simple.

Once inside the large bedroom, Allard flipped on the light and closed the door. "Hopefully Vixen will keep them from trying to listen in at the door."

"From the threats she sent Maggie's way whenever she got too personal, she'll succeed." Delia still hadn't released his hand.

"So, um, Mac and Bray think we need to do a ceremony. It's still fake and all, but some people have been asking questions and since ceremonies are important to most packs." He was rambling and stopped making sense after his first sentence. "Tomorrow afternoon, Mac wants to do the ceremony. Sign whatever and have the documents in hand to show everyone."

"Oh." She blinked up at him and her mouth formed a perfect circle.

Allard yanked his mind out of the gutter.

"The sooner the better. I had a feeling he'd do it tonight if he could."

"Okay. Tomorrow. I guess Geneva could stay a while longer?"

Allard shrugged. He wasn't sure what anyone would say about Geneva staying longer, except he worried if she was in on the secret, which Allard figured she would be, there was a better chance of someone learning the truth who didn't need to know.

"I'm sure Vixen and Bray will be okay with it. Also, at some point, you need to sit down with Vixen and go over some of our security protocol."

"You can't do it?"

"It's better for Vixen to handle it since that's her forte in the pack."

The smallest giggle escaped Delia's mouth.

Allard bent his head forward and lifted an eyebrow, questioning the noise without saying a word.

"Maggie's used the word forte at least twenty times already, except she pronounced it fort. No one seemed to have the heart to correct her."

"So you didn't either?" He was surprised. Delia seemed like the type who would have no problem correcting the little raccoon shifter.

"I think I prefer it to forte."

The tilt of her head so she looked up at him with her chin tucked down was so cute it sent a punch to his chest. His knees nearly buckled under the imaginary pressure. If her fingers hadn't tightened around his right hand at that moment, he might very well have found himself on his knees in front of her.

"She had a sheltered childhood, so she's making up for it with a word of the day calendar. Wait until she uses the word chagrin. For whatever reason, she thinks it's pronounced chargin. For about a week, we thought A Tale of Two Kitties was some obscure children's book until we figured out she meant A Tale of Two Cities."

The need to share these details about his packmates came out of the blue, but Allard wanted Delia to know all the details. Especially after she admitted to preferring the word fort to forte.

"All right. So mating ceremony and security whatever with Vixen. Is there anything else planned for tomorrow?"

"Yeah, we need to be seen together in public. We're gonna have to head to town after the ceremony."

"Why do we need to be seen in public? And just who's been asking questions that we need to have a ceremony?" The questions came right on top of each other, not giving him a chance to answer the first one before asking the second.

"We're not sure. Or at least they didn't tell me. It might be some wolves from my father's pack or it could be wolves from some other pack who's more interested in your current state of mating than they have a right to be." An image of the enforcers trying to take Delia from the street invaded his thoughts.

"Shit." Delia growled at his answer.

The noise sent a happy thrill through his wolf. When the other females in the pack growled, it was always cute, but not his mate. His mate had a growl that vibrated throughout the room.

Fuck! Not his mate!

His fake mate.

And of course she had a good growl, she was a wolf shifter and an Alpha.

"We'll figure it out tomorrow, after you've talked with Vixen," Allard told Delia. "We need to get you back to the others or they'll definitely be knocking on the door in a few minutes."

"Fine. Tomorrow."

"Wait. Is that a good fine or a bad fine?"

"Good. You'd know if it wasn't."

"I don't know the signs yet. Hell, Bray and Vixen have been mated the longest, and he doesn't know the signs yet either."

"It's a good sign to know."

"He knows most of them. Just not fine."

"Okay. Tomorrow." She gave him a teasing smile. "Better?"

"Yeah. For the next few weeks, let's just not use the word fine," Allard suggested.

"It's probably for the best." Delia agreed and for all intents and purposes appeared serious, but Allard was sure she was laughing at him.

They walked from the bedroom together and back to the front room, where all the females sat on the edge of their chairs and stared at them.

He squeezed her hand and gave her a gentle push towards the others. "Go spend time with your friend. I'll come and find you later."

CHAPTER NINETEEN

IN THE kitchen, Allard found his packmates still sitting around the table with Mac, and Bray standing with Roose by the island. The happy chatter about nothing in particular filled the room.

"Girls doing okay?" Finley asked, pulling the chair out next to him as an invitation to join.

"Looks like it," he sat down in the offered chair.

Finley wasn't really asking about the females of the pack, he was asking about Maggie.

"Delia really likes Maggie," he told Finley in a quiet voice.

"She's not trying to be polite?"

"She brought up Maggie while we were talking and not because I asked. She likes Maggie, Fin, I swear."

"I worry, you know. Her dad's a good guy, but her mother and her life in the Gaze? That's just crazy shit piled on top of more crazy shit." He rolled the nearly empty glass between his palms. "It's fine when it's just us, but what if someone who doesn't know her hears some of the shit she says? It will crush her if anyone laughs at her."

Allard nodded in sympathy. He hadn't realized it until Finley spoke the words, but Delia was in a similar position. Her childhood had been completely different from everyone else here. At some point she was going to say something that caused someone to look at her like she was crazy, and then what would happen? Knowing Delia, she wouldn't show her hurt, but it would probably crush her too.

"Don't worry too much," Allard advised. "She'll be fine."

The words might have been for Finley, but Allard said them for his own benefit as well.

"It'll be nice to have another female shifter around. I know Danielle and Elanor try, but there are things they can't always understand."

"Delia's good for that. Plus she's grown up around humans. She'll be a good intermediary between Maggie and the girls."

"So. Arranged mates, huh?" Finley skipped right past the segue and jumped directly to the heart of the matter. Allard would have been happy not having to answer at all. "Is that why you ran away? You didn't want to be mated?"

"It was a lot of things, Fin." He'd been thinking about why he came to Broken Peak since Roose posed the question earlier that night. "I'm not sure I was running away from anything. More like running to something."

"And she followed you here?"

"That might be what she believes, but I think it was a combination of a bunch of random things. That I was here was a happy coincidence."

"Yeah?" Finley looked like he wanted to say more. Instead of opening his mouth to speak, he finished the glass of moonshine in front of him.

Allard sighed. He'd never be able to keep the secret from his best friend. Right now there were so many lies being woven around each other, he wasn't sure who knew which lie was a lie. If he wasn't careful, he'd let the full story slip.

"Come with me to grab a few more jugs?" Allard stood up and headed to the pantry door on the back wall of the kitchen.

Bray noted his progress, and that Finley was right behind Allard, but Allard ignored the stare.

"You can't tell anyone, okay? Not even Maggie. Especially not Maggie." Allard said as he moved to the back shelves and pulled down a jug.

"Sure," Finley grabbed a second jug. He understood his mate struggled with keeping secrets and didn't seem offended by Allard's words.

"Alright. This is what's really happening."

Allard explained everything from the arranged mating to faking being fated mates for the Council, and even the bit about getting mated tomorrow and then everyone going out to town to make sure Delia and Allard were seen.

Finley stared at him with unblinking eyes.

"Well, shit."

"That about covers it."

"I never would have guessed. I thought it was the real thing. I saw the way you kissed her. And the way you looked at her."

Allard laughed. "We should be nominated for an acting award or something then."

"No, man. You can say whatever you want, but what went on in the kitchen between the two of you isn't acting. It might not be the real thing, but it's not completely fake."

"Mac knows, so do Bray and Vixen, obviously, I figure Roose probably knows too. And so does Gareth. Of the girls, only Eleanor knows. I guess it was partially her idea."

"You know you listed like half the shifters in Broken Peak, right? If you all wanted to keep this a big secret, I'm not sure you're going about it the right way."

"Gareth's nieces don't know. That's five. And Jackson, Leighton, Danielle, Maggie, and Foster don't know. Another five. So ten don't know, and six do. That's less than half." Allard didn't know why he needed to explain the numbers to Finley. He just did. "We're doing this to keep the territory safe. If the Council members leave and say we didn't fulfill the agreement, there's a good chance half the packs will send their enforcers here."

"Sure, I get that part. Just not the reason why has to be a big secret."

"Maggie and Foster will let it slip. Not intentionally, but they will. And if everyone else knows, chances are they'll let it slip in front of them at some point."

"True." Finley clapped his hand against Allard's shoulder. "Thanks for telling me."

"I didn't like you not knowing."

"Let's get back out there before Bray gets even more suspicious than he already is."

Finley walked out of the pantry and Allard followed.

The chatter was still going strong, mostly talking about the plans for the next few months. They hadn't seen many government agents lately, but they didn't know if that was because of the holidays or because of the latest message Vixen sent them — it included a box containing the remains of the man Maggie found.

Allard stretched as he sat down. He was tired and probably should be heading to bed, but he wanted to wait for Delia. He figured she'd want to spend a few hours with her friend, but if they were going to sell the mating, she'd need to sleep with him.

In his room.

In his bed.

Shit. He should go to bed before her.

Sleeping next to Delia was going to prove to be Allard's biggest challenge.

CHAPTER TWENTY

DELIA sat down at the corner of the couch, giving an apologetic smile to Geneva for leaving her friend alone in a room full of relative strangers.

Geneva grinned back, and then just as quickly returned to the conversation with Danielle, Maggie, and Eleanor. Vixen watched it all from her perch on a chair, but didn't appear interested in the current topic, which had gone from moisturizers to who was dating who and who was likely to get married in Hollywood.

Delia wasn't interested either. The hallway Allard disappeared down held her attention. Any second now, she half expected Allard to return with another excuse to speak with her. Except it didn't happen.

Not when the conversation shifted to the latest drama in the human world and not even when it shifted back to moisturizers.

Vixen's unwavering stare didn't move away from Delia, and eventually she couldn't handle the weight of it. She looked at the Alpha and raised an eyebrow, asking what the Alpha wanted without using words.

Despite Vixen not being a known entity in the shifter world, she could read body language. A curt nod toward the group of women and Delia understood the message.

Share your news.

She could do that.

Or at least she thought she could. Except coming up with the right words to explain that she was mating Allard tomorrow became an impossible task.

Finally, after what felt like an eternity, she blurted out the words tomorrow, mating, ceremony, and Allard in some random order.

Whatever she said must have been good enough because all conversation stopped and four heads pivoted to gape at her.

"Ceremony?"

"What?"

"We have ceremonies?"

"Are you sure?" The last question came from Geneva. "We'll have to see if we can delay the flight tomorrow morning then."

"If the flight plan is scheduled, we might not want to raise any attention by delaying it." Vixen didn't say no to Geneva staying longer, but the message was there.

Thankfully, Geneva ignored it. "The flight was tentatively scheduled. If we delayed it for days, I could see the concern, but delaying it by a few hours won't bring any undue attention."

"Besides, if you two are doing an actual official ceremony, then someone from Delia's family should be here." Eleanor added. "It would look more odd if none of her family was here."

"Maybe we should wait until her mother and father can get here then." Danielle, the sweet human who had spent several minutes complimenting Delia on her clothing when they first left the kitchen, suggested.

"No."

Delia, Geneva, and Vixen all spoke at once. Albeit for different reasons. Geneva didn't want there to be any conflict between Delia and her parents. Delia didn't want to face her parents just yet. And Vixen had her own reasons, but Delia wasn't about to question them.

"It will delay the mating, and Allard and I decided that since we're fated mates, we might as well get the formalities out of the way. Once Alphas are involved, the ceremony becomes a much bigger deal. This would be like Allard and me eloping."

Danielle sighed with a smile. "Elopements always seemed so romantic."

"What's loping?" Maggie asked.

"In human society, weddings can turn into a huge affair. Some couples prefer to elope, or run off to get married alone without all the chaos and stress a wedding might bring." Eleanor explained.

"Oh." Maggie looked between Eleanor and Delia. "But you aren't running off to get married are you? You're here and the ceremony is going to be here."

"Yeah, but her family is in Chicago."

"And she comes from a big pack."

"And that pack just got over a huge mating ceremony," Delia said. "At some point Allard and I will make our way back to Chicago and the pack can pay its respects, but technically, once I mate Allard, I'm not part of the Chicago pack any longer."

"So you'll officially be one of us!" Maggie cheered and fist pumped into the air.

The oddest things delighted the little raccoon shifter, and Delia found it refreshing. Unconditional joy and acceptance from someone she only just met was unheard of in Delia's life.

Well, previous life.

Even if everything was fake and even if her being part of Broken Peak was only temporary, Delia needed to start thinking of her stay here as permanent to convince everyone else it was all real.

"So, we'll hold a ceremony in the morning so Geneva can be here for it." Vixen accepted defeat gracefully.

Delia had witnessed a lot of Alpha females refusing to budge from what they wanted just on the principle that they were the Alpha. The more she witnessed in this pack the odder it seemed.

The Alphas didn't lead, they guided and suggested. The pack members all enjoyed one another's company. And there wasn't a single female wolf shifter in a wolf pack, except for Delia.

She still didn't know exactly what Vixen was? Possibly a raptor or a big cat? The scents coming from the Alpha female confused Delia. Just when she was convinced Vixen was an eagle, the cat scent came through.

Of course, that might have been because Delia had identified several scents belonging to cats, probably mountain lions considering the area, on her walk down to the Lodge.

Great.

Now she was capitalizing the word Lodge in her thoughts too.

This was just all so weird.

Not weird.

Her wolf had been nice and quiet, tucked away from her while her fate was being decided because of the actions of everyone else, but now wanted to offer an opinion?

Her wolf snorted.

Comfortable.

Why her wolf couldn't have made that same observation earlier, when she first arrived, Delia didn't know.

Ignored me.

Yeah, her wolf was probably right. Delia would have liked to think she would have listened to her wolf's suggestions, but whenever it came to Allard and the arranged mating, she ignored everyone's advice.

CHAPTER TWENTY-ONE

HAPPY shouts came from the front room and all the males in the kitchen turned toward the hallway.

While most of the mates were willing to let the girls have their own fun, Leighton tended to hover more often than not, eventually they migrated to wherever their mates happened to be spending time together.

Tonight was no exception.

Well, there was one exception. Allard was leading the group instead of following along behind them.

Finley pulled him back, just as they reached the front room, and tilted his head toward the females.

"Wait a sec." He whispered soft enough for no one else to pick up the words.

Allard shrugged. A few seconds more wasn't the end of the world. Besides, he had an unobstructed view into the room from their current position and could see the back of Delia's head. Her bright red hair became a beacon and something inside of him, possibly his wolf, settled as soon as his gaze landed on her.

As the other males filed into the room and found their mates, the remaining three unmated males, settled into open seats. Roose and Mac kept Tevin company. Like they understood the isolation of not having mates when surrounded by mated pairs.

"Maggie seems to really like Delia." Finley spoke soft enough for no one else to hear, which was surprisingly difficult considering most everyone in the room had over-sensitive hearing.

"Yeah." Allard agreed.

Delia smiled at Maggie as she spoke to her, probably explaining something Maggie didn't understand, and Maggie's attention was rapt. The raccoon shifter's eyes were wide open and her head bobbed up and down in time to Delia's words.

"Um, what's going to happen when Delia leaves? I hate to see her get attached only to lose it. Let's face it, she never really had any real females in her life, and while Vixen's great and all..."

"Yeah." Allard hadn't stopped to consider what would happen when Delia left. What it would mean for the pack or for him.

"She'll get over it, eventually, but it's something you should talk to Delia about? Maybe explain she should try to keep her distance from Maggie and Foster at least, and Danielle too so Maggie doesn't notice."

He pressed his thumb and middle finger against the outer corners of his eyes and rubbed at the slight ache that was slowly emerging with each of Finley's words.

"Or, you never know. Maybe she'll end up sticking around, right? I mean, it's not like any of the females showed up expecting to stay for very long."

"Except Danielle."

"Yeah, except Danielle. Which is probably a good thing. I'm not as worried about Leighton killing us all in our sleep anymore."

"And he hasn't had any more of those nightmares either." Allard added. Talking about Leighton was a hundred times better than talking about Delia eventually leaving the pack.

"He's still one step away from turning into a serial killer though." Finley cracked a smile and elbowed Allard in the ribs. "Like I said, maybe she'll end up sticking around."

"Nope." Even after he had explained everything to Finley, his friend was still convinced things weren't as fake as they really were. "All we're doing is finding a way to keep the status quo, so the Council doesn't get too involved in our lives here. They're already going to flip their shit once they realize we have human females here, plus a raccoon shifter. We don't need to add to things by appearing to tear up the arranged mating. Once things settle down in the packs, I'm sure Delia will take off."

Finley shook his head with a wide grin.

"Shit," Allard reached behind and pressed his hands to the back of his neck, rubbing the slowly growing ache that had moved from his forehead to his neck. "I'm gonna need more of Mac's moonshine if I have to put up with your crap." Allard grumbled. "Fuck, I don't need a drink, I need a good's night sleep. Delia's staying with me tonight and from the number of empty wine bottles I'm seeing in that room, sleep will probably be a way's off."

"Or you can be the good mate and let her have her last night with her best friend from home." Finley suggested with a knowing smile. "I'll make sure she gets settled, and knows where your room is, so go ahead and head to bed if you think it will make things easier."

"Actually, I might take you up on that offer. Today's been a long day and I'm tired as fuck. Maybe I'll just head to bed now." Allard yawned. "You'll explain it to her?"

"Sure." Finley's head bobbed up and down, and Allard didn't completely trust him.

"You're not gonna tell her what you said to me earlier, right? About the kissing and the looks? The last thing this pack needs is for her to run away in the middle of the night."

"Promise." He made a cross over his heart. "I swear, okay?"

Finley walked into the room and sat next to Maggie, pulling her into his lap. As promised, he leaned close to Delia and said something to her. Allard hoped it didn't include the words kissing and looking.

Before she turned around to look at him, Allard stepped back into the shadows. He could still see her, but she couldn't see him. Or at least she didn't behave like she could.

Allard stuck around for a few more minutes. When no one called to him or went to find him, he slipped down the hallway and headed toward his room.

A good night's sleep was what he needed if he expected to make it through all of tomorrow. And even though the thought of Delia sleeping anywhere except for his bed annoyed his wolf, having her there would have been too much of a distraction.

Once inside his bedroom, he found Delia's bags. Someone had delivered them. Bray probably sent Finley or Tevin to do the job when Allard sneaked up to the front room to share the news of the impending mating ceremony. He picked up the bags and carried them to the room Geneva was sleeping in. With everyone shifting beds, he couldn't remember where Vixen assigned the guests, but eventually found her bags in Foster's room but no Foster. So Foster must be in Tevin's room, or his parents' room.

Not that it mattered. Except it did. A little. Something inside of him settled at the thought of Delia in Foster's room and not Tevin's. It also eased his wolf.

Allard didn't want to dwell on why he cared where Delia slept and if he went straight to bed, that's all he would think about. Instead of returning to his room where he would just toss and turn in bed, he headed to the shared bathroom. He turned on the water and adjusted the temperature. He enjoyed a hot shower as much as the rest of them, but didn't enjoy the scalding heat it was usually set at. Stripping off his clothes, he left them in a pile on the floor, but the water took several more minutes to heat up.

He stared at his reflection in the mirror and wondered how Delia saw him. Did she see the male he turned into with the help of Bray, and Vixen, since her arrival? Or did she see the spoiled son of a power-hungry Alpha?

He had to hide his beginnings from his friends. They wouldn't understand the reasons for his complaints about a life of privilege, but Delia would understand. He wouldn't have to hide anything from her.

Steam finally rolled over the top of shower and slid down the mirror, hiding his view.

He could still say no to the fake mating ceremony and the story they concocted.

So could Delia.

If he did though, he'd have to leave Broken Peak. He couldn't bring any more trouble to the pack. And as long as Delia wasn't in pack territory, no one would have a reason to hang out in War.

They could walk away from everything and take their chances.

They didn't have to stay.

But Allard didn't want to leave Broken Peak. And the more he thought about it, he didn't want Delia to leave Broken Peak either.

With a sigh, he turned away from the mirror and stepped into the shower. He reached up and adjusted the shower so when he turned his back to the water, it would pound down on his neck.

Maybe it would help the ache. He bent his head down and let the water run down his back. The water pooled at his feet, slowly swirling as it made its way down toward the drain. He stared at the water to avoid looking at his hard cock.

Fuck. Just thinking about Delia staying in Broken Peak got his cock hard. He hadn't seen her in anything except jeans and a sweater, but imagining her perfect breasts under her sweater or the way her jeans hugged her ass did more for him than any other female, human or shifter, he'd spent time with.

His fist wrapped around the base of his cock. It would have been easy to take care of his erection. It wasn't like he hadn't done it count-less times before, but the idea of jerking off to Delia didn't settle well with him.

Eventually he gave up. Dealing with this new guilt about beating off to the thought of her was better than dealing with a hard cock all night. His fingers tightened around his shaft and his other hand cupped his heavy balls.

His cock jerked in response and he slid his hand along the smooth skin. Minutes later, his cock jerked again, and he came hard.

What the fuck?

He had more control than that.

The last time he came from just a touch was when he was a boy and had finally figured out that his dick was for more than just pissing.

The evidence disappeared down the drain.

He grabbed a bar of soap, one that didn't have Tevin's name written on it, and washed his body in record time. Once cleaned and rinsed he turned off the water and stepped out of the shower.

Too bad he couldn't clean his mind of the thoughts of Delia.

Grabbing a towel, he wrapped it around his waist without drying. The best thing he could do was get to bed and fall asleep as quickly as possible. Drying off would add seconds where his mind could wander back to Delia. He picked up his clothes, left the bathroom without looking to see if anyone was in the hallway and hurried to his bedroom like a coward.

CHAPTER TWENTY-TWO

DELIA shifted her attention from Maggie to Maggie and Finley when the male sat down next to his little mate.

"So," Finley said. "Allard's had a long day and tomorrow will be even longer. He headed to bed, but doesn't want to take time away from you with your friend. I told him I'd get you settled whenever you were ready to leave the party."

He spoke quietly enough for the others in the room to not catch all his words, for which Delia was grateful.

She turned and looked over her shoulder. Allard was still in the hallway, she could sense him, but she couldn't see him.

The lessons on decorum from her mother came back to her. "Thank you." She had hoped he would have at least said goodnight to her, but maybe the comfortableness she had been feeling around him was one-sided. "Tomorrow will be a long day. Let me get Geneva's attention and we'll head to bed."

"Sounds good. Maggie and I will wait for you in the hallway okay?"

Delia made her way around the chairs and couches to her friend. "Between driving here and everything that's happening tomorrow I think I'm ready to head to bed."

"Oh?" Geneva looked between Eleanor and Delia, caught between wanting to talk more about whatever their conversation was about and wanting to support her friend. In the end loyalty to her friend won out. "We can talk more in the morning right?"

Eleanor nodded, "of course."

"Okay then." Geneva jumped to her feet and threaded her arm through Delia's arm. "Come on, we'll get to have a sleepover like when we were younger. Except we won't have to worry about your mom peeking her head in your room and telling us to go to bed."

Maggie and Finley waited for them in the middle of the hallway, just like they promised.

"How long have you been friends?" Maggie asked.

Had the question come from anyone else, it might have been considered rude. But they'd learned Maggie's curiosity wasn't from being nosy, it was from her wanting to learn everything she could.

"Since we were in grade school, right?" Geneva said.

"We'd known each other for a while, but I think when we actually became close friends was in middle school? So eleven or twelve?"

"Wow? That means you've been friends for over ten years. That's a long time. I don't have any friends like that."

The four of them took their time walking down the hallway, slowing their pace so they could continue with a conversation that wasn't important to anyone except Maggie.

"This pack has been around for longer than ten years, right Finley?" Delia asked.

"Yep, but we all didn't arrive at the same time. Bray was here before Mac started dropping us off at his doorstep." Finley guided them to turn down the right passage when they came to the door that led to the kitchen.

"In smaller packs, the packmates usually end up being close friends. It even happens in the larger packs. Kids similar in age tend to grow up with one another. So give it another few years and you'll have friends for that long too." Delia winked at Maggie.

Finley stopped at one of the open doors and peered inside. "This looks like your room. Someone dropped your bags off too, Delia. Just a word of warning. It's Foster's room, so expect to find toy cars stuck in every nook and cranny. Oh, and the pup doesn't know the meaning of a closed door. Be sure to lock it or you'll get woken up at the ass crack of dawn."

"Good to know." Geneva stepped into the room and looked around.

"Oh and the bathroom is further down on the left. And Allard's room is three more doors down on the right." Finley grinned and wiggled his eyebrows at Delia. "I promised him to tell you where his room is. You know. Just in case."

"Thanks. I guess we'll see you tomorrow then." Delia fell back into the polite conversation she'd been trained in.

"Come on, Pocket." Finley pulled Maggie further down the hallway to another door. "We have an appointment we need to keep tonight."

"We do? What appointment? I don't remember anything about an appointment." Her voice faded off with a giggle as Finley tugged her into the room and closed the door behind them.

Delia stepped into the room and looked around. Two twin beds were pushed into the far corner of the room so they made an "L". A small dresser, littered with toys and pictures of the pack in frames sat against the wall with the door. And on the remaining wall with no bed, pictures drawn by the hand of a child had been taped up. There was also a small table, the perfect size for a child, with boxes of toys and crayons on the floor next to it.

"So, I'm going to go brush my teeth and do all that other fun stuff. Wanna join me?" Geneva asked.

"Hm? Yeah, sure." Delia located her duffel with her toiletries and grabbed the small bag.

When she stepped out of the room, she ran directly into Geneva, who had stopped in the middle of the hallway. Peering around her friend's shoulder she found the reason for the collision.

Allard, with a towel wrapped around his waist and gloriously bare everywhere else, hurried down the hallway before turning off to the bedroom Finley had pointed out to Delia.

"Whoa."

Whoa was right. Whatever muscles Delia had imagined hid beneath Allard's shirt didn't do justice to the real thing.

"You can never tell Lennon, I looked. Like never ever. Because we don't need your brother wanting to kill your mate."

She wanted to growl at her best friend, claw her eyes out, and more for daring to look at Allard. Not wanting to think too hard about where those feelings came from, Delia rolled her eyes and pushed past her friend.

"Come on. Apparently there's just this one bathroom so we need to hurry."

Geneva cleared her throat. "Del?"

"Yeah?"

"Um, you know you're making that weird growling noise Lennon makes, right?"

No, she didn't know.

What was wrong with her?

She'd never lost control like that. Delia raced down the hallway to the bathroom. The faster she could get ready for bed, the better off she'd be. Less time to think about all the things she shouldn't be feeling about Allard.

Teeth fully brushed and face washed, Delia left her friend behind in the bathroom.

Geneva hadn't said anything when she joined Delia, but that was probably only because she didn't want anyone to overhear their conversation.

Now, if only she could change into her pajamas and fall asleep before Geneva returned. It didn't seem likely, but a girl could hope. As soon as her head hit the pillow, Delia closed her eyes and pretended to be asleep.

"I know you're faking it." Geneva came into the bedroom and closed and locked the door behind her. She got changed for bed and cleaned up her things before finally turning off the light and crawling into the other bed. "And you know I'm not going to stop talking just because you aren't answering me back."

This was true. The silent treatment never worked on Geneva. Eventually Delia would give up and answer just to put a halt to Geneva's chatter.

"Wanna talk about it?"

"No."

"You don't have to be honest. I don't have that truth sensing trick you all have." Geneva flopped around on the bed until she got comfortable. "Which really sucks by the way."

When Delia still hadn't said anything after several minutes, Geneva gave up on taking the laid back approach and went for the full-frontal assault.

"Okay, so that's how it's going to be. I am going to assume this hissy fit is about you and Allard. Let's also say that because the mating is arranged and something beyond your control, you hate it. I get it. I'd hate it too. But, Del, you're kind of blind to a lot of things because you can't see it."

Delia turned to her side and faced the wall so her back faced the room. The move didn't please her wolf, but her wolf could deal.

"Del, you growled at me when I saw Allard in only a towel. And it was a glorious sight, I might add, but don't you dare tell Lennon I said that."

Geneva sat up in bed with a jerk and poked a finger on Delia's shoulder. Hard.

"See. Well, no, not see. Hear that? You're growling again. It's a wolf thing. You know how I know that? Lennon makes that same noise anytime he sees me so much as smile at a man. Any man. Even Scott, who has more interest in your brother's physique than my own." Geneva kept poking. "He doesn't make that noise when he catches you talking to a man, Del. Just me. So, I'm going to extrapolate that I could admire the bare chest of everyone who lives here, except for Allard's, and you wouldn't make that noise."

Delia heard the growling in her head. She assumed it was her wolf accepting Allard as her mate, fake or not, and doing what nature told her to do. She didn't realize she had been making that noise too.

Or her wolf was close enough to the surface that Geneva could hear it too?

No. Delia had too much control for that. She hadn't let her wolf take over since she was a young girl, seven or eight years old.

"So, this is what you're going to do. You're going to get up and walk down the hall and knock on Allard's door. And then you're going to let your wolves hang out and get to know one another. Or do whatever it is you werewolves do."

"Shifter."

"Hah!" Geneva stopped poking her. "I know that, but at least you're talking to me now. So it's a point for me."

Delia rolled over on her back and stared at the ceiling. "You really think I should go knock on his door?"

"Hell yes!" Geneva laid back down and pulled the covers over her. "If only so I can get some actual sleep without you tossing and turning all night."

Delia didn't want to admit it, but her friend had a point.

It didn't take long for her to jump out of bed, dig through one of her bags to find an oversized sweater, and head out the room and down the hallway. She was just pulling the sweater down over her head when she bumped into Allard.

Well, okay then, he had the same thought she did.

"You find your room okay?" He asked.

"Yeah. And the bathroom."

"You and Geneva have fun tonight?"

Delia smiled and nodded. She hadn't expected him to care whether she had a good time, especially since he had ran off without saying good night, but it was nice that he might care.

"We both did. Maggie's a hoot and everyone else was friendly and nice."

"Even Vixen?" Allard looked at her like it wasn't possible for Vixen to be nice or friendly.

"Especially Vixen. Most Alpha females wouldn't want to spend time with their pack like that. It makes it hard to take on an authority role."

"Yeah, well Vixen doesn't have any problem with being authoritative when it's needed."

Neither one of them spoke again. They just stood in the middle of the hallway and looked at each other. Finally, she gave up waiting for Allard to say anything.

"Night." She turned and went back to the room she was staying in for the night.

As she slipped back under the covers of the small bed, she remembered all the little bits and pieces of the day. Especially Allard's kisses. The first one was amazing, but the second one had been spectacular.

Tomorrow night she would be in his bed if they were going to convince everyone their mating was real. Except he wouldn't be sharing the bed in the way her mind was imagining.

CHAPTER TWENTY-THREE

FROM an early age she understood mating ceremonies had nothing in common with human weddings.

No layers of white silk encasing the bride.

No bridesmaids wearing dresses they'd never wear again.

No groom and groomsmen in tuxedos with coordinating bow ties and cummerbunds.

Her plans for the ceremony included nicer clothing, like dresses and suits, some nice flowers, then a catered party afterwards. She also figured her family would be there. His too. Then, when everything had been signed, she planned on continuing to live her life as it was.

But if someone had told Delia that her mating ceremony would be held outside while she wore jeans and a sweater while surrounded by her best friend and everyone else she had known for less than twenty-four hours, she would never have believed it.

Mac read from an old book, reciting the ancient statements from a time when all matings were arranged and approved by Alphas.

Geneva acted as the representative from Delia's pack and Bray stood in for the Broken Peak Pack, since everyone agreed that was Allard's current pack.

And Foster and Maggie loudly whispered questions for anyone to answer. Neither seemed impressed by the ceremony and didn't understand why it even had to happen. The others at least accepted that the ceremony would satisfy the Council's demands and offer the Broken Peak Pack some protection from any outside packs.

Geneva offered Delia a sympathetic smile, but it did nothing to make the morning better. If anything the pitying gesture reminded Delia that not only was the ceremony nothing as expected, it was also completely fake.

Delia glanced over at Allard, who hadn't even smiled once since Vixen ushered everyone outside.

She never should have agreed to the fake ceremony. She could pretend to be Allard's fated mate, but faking the ceremony felt wrong. As though Mac's speaking the sacred words to Allard and Delia somehow invalidated every other ceremony they had been spoken at.

Her feet wanted to run fast and far, but her wolf's close presence to the surface eased the desire to flee.

She wondered if Allard was experiencing the same urge.

Before Delia realized it, the ceremony was over, Geneva and Bray had signed the fake official document.

"Well, that's it. You two are now officially mated." Mac clapped his hands and rubbed his palms together. "And we've got all these witnesses for the Council. How about we celebrate with some moonshine? I have a new flavor for us to try out!"

"We've just had breakfast. I think the moonshine can wait." Eleanor ushered everyone back towards the porch, leaving Bray, Vixen, Allard, and Delia alone in the yard.

"You think they bought it?" Delia asked.

"If they didn't, they're better actors than I gave them credit for." Bray shrugged. "Come on, let's get some food or something. It feels weird just lingering around doing nothing."

"You're Broken Peak now, even if it's just for show." Vixen grabbed hold of Delia's wrist and pulled her back to a slower pace. "No matter what happens, you don't ever forget that."

Vixen didn't wait for Delia to respond. She dropped Delia's arm and trotted up to Bray, wrapping her arm around his waist as she approached him. Allard fell back then, waiting for Delia to catch up before walking through the door.

"You've got a funny look on your face, like you're seeing the world in black and white instead of color," said Allard. "What's up."

"They're pretty special, aren't they?" Delia bobbed her head toward Vixen and Bray.

"Yep. And I'd do anything for them and the pack." Allard responded. "Wait. That came out wrong. I didn't mean…"

Delia shook it off, she hadn't taken his statement to mean anything except what he said. "I get what you meant."

"So, we're mated now, Red."

"Yeah. I suppose we are, mate." She bumped her shoulder against his chest as they pushed through the front door and walked into the main room. "And to think, I hardly know you."

"How much more do you want to know?"

There was no mistaking the hunger in his eyes. Or the intent of Allard's words. It sounded as though he wanted to get to know her in more than the polite chit chatty kind of way.

Instead of being offended, tingles zipped through her body.

Delia coughed and walked further into the room and a few steps away from Allard. "I heard about movie night, but haven't seen any TV screens."

Changes in subjects were good when she needed to stop thinking about images her mind conjured up of Allard and her in various states of undress.

"Yeah, she uses some projector thing and an actual screen."

"So it's a real movie night then?"

"Yeah, it's not like War has a lot of movie theater options."

They circled around talking about nothing, but it was better than thinking about her mate. Especially since she couldn't stop remembering the kisses from yesterday. Or the way his body looked in just a towel. Or the blue of his eyes. Or the sound of his voice.

Allard had still been talking, something about other pack activities, like barbecues and runs, but Delia barely heard any of it. Time to move on to a new subject.

"If Geneva's leaving in a few, I really should say goodbye."

"Yeah, sure." He reached for her hand and led her toward the kitchen where she assumed everyone had gathered.

Did she hear disappointment in his voice? She was sure she had, but didn't know why he was disappointed.

Thinking he might have wanted to spend more time with her alone was a pleasant, but dangerous thought. It led to what else they might do alone when not talking.

And she was definitely going to find out tonight.

Delia gave up.

She couldn't stop thinking about Allard in the ways she shouldn't be. Surviving her stay at Broken Peak was going to be impossible, especially since she had to stay in the same room with him. Her future held lots of showers since she wouldn't even have the privacy of her own room to spend some quiet time with her vibrator.

Assuming Geneva even packed it.

CHAPTER TWENTY-FOUR

THE parking lot at the Dirty Whistle was filled with older cars that looked to be approaching 100,000 miles on the odometer, assuming they hadn't already surpassed it.

Jackson pulled out of the lot and parked on the street, facing the direction they came from. Either he planned for needing to get out of there fast, or just didn't want to circle around until he found a too-tight space to squeeze into.

As soon as the SUV came to a stop, everyone not in the front seat, fell out of the car. They'd been packed in, but it was either sitting three to a row or taking two cars, and after a lot of discussion and a near brawl, Bray stepped in and made an executive decision. One car. Jackson drove. They'd have to figure out the seating arrangements on their own though. Which was how Delia found herself squeezed between Allard and Tevin in the middle seat. The far back seat had held Finley, Maggie, and Danielle, while Jackson and Leighton sat in the front with Eleanor between them.

Delia waited at the curb for everyone to get settled. From what she could see through the window, the bar wasn't so much a bar as a counter with booze filled shelves behind it in a room filled to capacity.

"Is the entire town here?"

Maggie looked up from searching the contents of her purse. She'd borrowed one from Delia, since she didn't have one of her own, and filled it with God only knew what. The raccoon shifter had spent the entire ride wondering out loud if she should have brought the mango flavored lip balm instead of the strawberry.

"Oh, wow." Maggie swallowed hard and took a step back, right into the waiting arms of her mate.

Finley wrapped his arms tight around her middle and held her close. "Come on, Pocket. It will be fun. I promise. Music, drinks, and dancing, right? Something you can cross off your list."

Maggie eyed the bar with as much trepidation as Delia, but finally nodded her head in agreement.

Allard slung his arm around Delia's shoulder and guided her across the street. "Come on, Red, let's show 'em how it's done."

He pulled the door open and held it for her, and everyone else. By the time all nine of them had made it inside, everyone already at the bar had turned and stared at the new arrivals.

Delia plastered one of her polite smiles on her face and headed straight to the bar. She'd been in dives before, but the Dirty Whistle gave the word dive a whole new meaning. The bar top was covered with layers upon layers of grime, so she was careful not to rest her arms on the surface. The wood floor wasn't much better with its ground in dirt. Too bad she couldn't have put on those protective booties before stepping inside.

She ignored the stares from the bar patrons as she waited for the bartender to notice her. After several minutes of ignoring her, she reached into her back pocket and pulled out a fifty.

"Let's see him ignore this." She mumbled under her breath.

The man sitting on a stool next to her glanced down at the bill in her hand then up to her face. "You buying?"

"No, the lady isn't buying." Allard's heavy presence stepped behind her and caged her against the bar.

Even though everyone else in the bar wasn't a shifter, the message was loud and clear. She's mine. Back off.

Allard plucked the fifty from her hand and slid it back into her pocket. She did her best to ignore the feeling of his strong fingers against her ass. Who had strong fingers anyway? She also did her best to not think about the other places those strong fingers might go. Both attempts were unmitigated failures.

The bartender finally made his way down the bar towards them. Sure, now he noticed them. Probably worried about losing out on that fifty.

He stopped in front of Delia and stared at her cleavage. V-neck sweaters were almost always a requirement at bars with male bartenders. "What can I get you?"

"Eighteen bottles of..." Allard growled while surveying the bottles of beer lining the back shelf.

"Miller Lite?" Delia didn't see anything except the usual lagers.

"Miller Lite." Allard agreed.

The bartender's eyes widened. "You sure you don't want a pitcher instead?"

Allard replaced the fifty he'd taken away with a new fifty and a twenty then set them both on the bar. "I'm sure."

Once the bottles had been lined up and opened, Allard handed them back to the others. But he kept one hand pressed against the bar and blocked the man who asked if Delia was buying from getting any closer to her.

When only four bottles remained, Delia picked two up in each hand by the neck and turned around. Allard was staring down at her with a funny grin. Like he couldn't quite believe she was standing in front of him.

"I didn't peg you as a Miller Light girl."

"Chicago's close to Milwaukee," Delia shrugged. "I'm surprised you didn't say Coor's."

He took two of the bottles from her and reached for her hand with his free one. "Come on, Red."

As soon as they stepped away from the bar, she leaned her head towards him. "I kind of feel like we should use some hand sani on these bottles."

"Why do you think I didn't get pitchers."

The others had found an open high-top, one of five in the entire room, stuck in a back corner and were standing around it waiting for them.

"So, this is War?" Danielle looked around the bar.

"You haven't been here before? I thought you'd have visited the town before."

"We used to come to town more often, before Vixen came. Since then, we've stayed close to home." Jackson answered before anyone else could add anything.

"Bray or Vixen will take one or two of us along with them to Costco, but mostly it's been better to steer clear of town."

"I. Love. Costco!" Maggie hopped up and down, barely containing her excitement. "They have everything. And shelves. Lots of shelves."

"Pocket and Vixen aren't allowed to go to Costco together without supervision anymore." Finley pinched the bridge of his nose.

Delia noticed that the males of Broken Peak did that nose pinching thing a lot. And usually when it pertained to something about their mates.

"The last time they went, Vixen had to call home to send another SUV down because they couldn't pack everything in the back." Eleanor grinned.

Delia sipped her beer and listened as the others shared anecdotes of pack exploits. Even though she hadn't been there for any of them, she could imagine them all happening. From Finley stalking Maggie's camper, to Foster running around and picking up whatever moved, including snakes. For the first time since she arrived at Broken Peak, she felt like she was part of the pack.

The others embraced her without question, just because they believed she was Allard's true mate.

For a moment, she wished it was all real. That Allard really was the mate she was fated to be with and the arranged mating didn't matter.

CHAPTER TWENTY-FIVE

ALLARD relaxed next to Delia and slid his arm around her shoulder to protect her from the jostling crowd. He wasn't sure if and when the shifters asking about Broken Peak would make an appearance or if Mac's friend was even around, but so far the night wasn't so bad.

A few more hours, another beer or two, and they could head back home.

Danielle, who must have grown bored with the current conversation, looked between Allard and Delia for a few minutes. She narrowed her eyes and got a look on her face like she was thinking about a problem she couldn't solve right away.

"You two didn't kiss." She tilted her head to the side and grinned, pleased with her observation. "After the ceremony you never kissed. You should kiss now."

The others quickly agreed. Even Eleanor, who'd been doing her best to steer discussion away from the mating ceremony when it was brought up, encouraged a kiss.

His arm tightened around Delia's shoulders and she turned toward him with a hesitant smile and a pink blush to her cheeks.

"They won't stop until we do."

"Oh, I know." Her hesitant smile evolved into an amused grin and her eyes flashed bright gold for a few seconds before returning to their beautiful green.

She tilted her head back, and he bent forward until their lips met. Her soft lips welcomed him with the slight hint of a fruity flavor from the lip balm Maggie had given her as a mating ceremony present.

And just like the previous two kisses, he lost control. His tongue pushed against her lips and her mouth parted for him. Somehow he set his bottle of beer down on the table without knocking it over and wrapped his arms around her, pulling her body close to his until her breasts pressed against his chest.

Delia's fingers tickled the back of his neck as she pulled him closer to her and kissed him right back with even more ferocity.

It was as though they weren't in the middle of a bar, probably named because it had never been cleaned, surrounded by his packmates and human strangers. Everything around them faded away until it was just the two of them.

And then Finley had to come along and ruin it. He slapped his hand against Allard's shoulder and slammed an empty bottle down on the table. "We need more beer!"

Delia pulled away from Allard, but didn't drop her arms from his neck. She blinked up at him with sleepy eyes and Allard wanted to go back for more.

He almost did, but then she lowered her gaze and turned to Finley. "More beers you say?"

Finley nodded with a shit-eating grin spread wide across his face.

"But, of course." Delia returned the grin, just as insincere, and headed back to the bar.

Allard glared at Finley before hurrying after her. No way in hell was he letting her get anywhere close to the crowd at the bar alone. Sure, she could handle herself, she was doing just fine when they first came in, but he didn't want her to have to handle herself.

The bartender had seen her coming and already lined up eighteen more bottles. Before Delia could pay, Allard slid another fifty and a twenty across the bar. Together, they scooped up the bottles and carefully made their way back to the high-top.

Allard noticed no one offered to help carry the bottles, just watched their slow progression. Until Delia stumbled on the crack between planks of wood and nearly fell. Without thinking, Allard reached out and went to grab her before she went over, but forgot about the four bottles precariously balanced in that hand.

Before the bottles left his hand, a man had Delia by the elbow. "Best be careful."

Allard growled low as the stranger got Delia upright without spilling a drop of beer.

The man turned toward Allard and grinned, baring a set of bright white and very straight teeth. "I haven't seen you at the Dirty Whistle before."

The man didn't look like he frequented the Dirty Whistle either. He didn't wear the typical uniform of jeans washed one too many times and threadbare flannel faded to a hint of its original color. Instead the man was wearing suit pants, a collared shirt open at the neck, and leather loafers.

Whoever he was, he sure as hell didn't belong in War.

Allard breathed in through his nose, but didn't catch any scent of fur. What he did sense, or his wolf noticed and shared the observation, was a hint of something unknown. If he didn't know any better, Allard would have called it magic.

"Mac said you would be visiting." He looked between Delia and Allard before finally settling on Delia. The stranger's ice-blue eyes, so pale to be almost silver, flashed in recognition. "I am Alexander, but you may call me Alex."

Allard kept the growl inside, barely.

"Would you like to join us, Alex?" Delia asked. "I feel like we should buy you a drink in thanks for keeping me from going over."

"No thank you, but the offer is appreciated." Alex bent forward at the waist, giving Delia a courtly bow then turned his creepy gaze back on Allard. "I believe I got here just in time. Another group of strangers are a few minutes behind me. I trust you won't cause trouble?"

Delia looked between Allard and Alexander, like they were speaking in an unknown language.

"Nope. We won't cause any trouble at all. We'll just finish our beers and be on our way."

"Very good then." Alexander nodded and slipped away into the crowd.

Delia's forehead wrinkled as she watched him leave. "Who was that?"

"I'm guessing he's the friend Mac and Vixen said would be here."

Her head snapped around to Allard. "Is there anything more you aren't telling me?"

Allard shook his head. "Not here."

It took ten seconds, Allard counted, before Delia nodded once. With her back still facing their friends waiting for their beers, she smiled, but it was one of those polite smiles that never quite reached her eyes.

He hated that smile. He wasn't sure when it happened, but at some point between last night and now, that polite smile of hers had turned into the bane of his existence.

"I take it they don't know about Alex?" She lifted her chin and sort of bobbed her head at his packmates.

Allard discovered something he hated more than Delia's fake smile aimed at him, the name Alex coming from her lips.

"No, and it should probably stay that way for now." Allard wanted to wrap his arm around her shoulder and bring her back to the table. He didn't like talking in the middle of the room where anyone could overhear them no matter how softly they might be speaking. "Come on, let's get back."

"One more thing. The other group coming, they're the ones asking around?"

"Pretty sure that's what he meant." Allard glanced over his shoulder at the door. "And I'd rather be at the table than standing here when they come in."

He hadn't meant to growl at her, but his wolf was anxious now. Between Alexander's appearance, he refused to use the name Alex, even in his thoughts, and knowing the other shifters were on the way, the beast had his hackles up, ready for a fight.

Delia lifted her hands with the bottles still in them. "Okay, okay. I get it."

She turned and headed to the rest of the pack, but he noticed she added an extra sway to her hips with each step.

The little minx.

As soon as they got back to the table, the group peppered them with questions.

"What took so long?"

"Who were you talking to?"

"Did you know that guy?"

"Two more? Are you trying to get me drunk?"

"Don't worry about it." Allard grumbled an answer to all their questions.

Delia ignored them. Instead she took the let's change the subject approach. "Is this the only bar in War?"

"There are twenty at last count."

"And a population of 760, so that's about forty people per bar. There are at least eighty people here, so I'm thinking the other bars might be in worse condition." Danielle calculated the numbers in her head.

"Under 800 people? I didn't realize the town was so small? How's there a Costco here?" Delia asked.

Apparently her 'let's change the subject' tactic worked better than Allard's approach.

"It's not. It's about forty-five minutes away from here, so from where we live, it takes us an hour and a half to get there. It's an all-day event, just with driving alone." Eleanor answered.

The conversation shifted back to Costco stories. Like the time Jackson almost came home with a ship bed for Foster, then segued into other pack stuff that wouldn't attract attention from any humans who happened to overhear.

Allard turned his attention to Delia. The way she looked at whoever was speaking, like they had her complete attention, amazed him. Even Maggie's stories, which tended to wander into the weeds with minor details that didn't matter.

She was sexy as hell too. With her bright red hair brushed back so it fell to her shoulders and the subtle hint of makeup, she stood out from the other females, but not in a flashy way.

A bell over the door chimed as it opened and immediately drew Allard's attention away from Delia. All conversation in the bar halted and everyone's attention was on the door. Just like when Allard and the others had walked in.

Three males stepped into the bar, letting the door slam closed behind them. They surveyed the room, their heads swiveling back and forth as they scented the air.

Allard didn't recognize them.

They didn't come from his father's pack, so where did they come from?

One after another, Jackson, Finley, Leighton, and Tevin, turned their heads until they had an unrestricted view of the door and the males standing there.

"Five to three," Leighton mused.

"Be stupid to try anything," Jackson agreed.

Eleanor and Danielle didn't have the gift of a sensitive nose and appeared confused by the unfolding events. But Maggie did, and the sight and smell of the three large males turned on all her fidgeting. She bounced from foot to foot while slipping around the table until she stood closer to the human women. Delia did the same, but without any of the nerves. No, she was steady as she stepped nearer to Danielle while never letting her gaze drop from the new arrivals.

Leighton stopped staring long enough to glance between Delia and Allard. "You two don't seem surprised."

"We had advanced warning."

"And didn't say anything?" Jackson growled out between gritted teeth.

"We weren't positive. Just hints that someone was in town and asking questions they didn't need to be." Delia supplied.

"I did think it was kinda strange for Vixen and Bray to suggest we head to town tonight." Finley said. "But hey, things at home have gotten kind of boring in the past two weeks."

"Excuse me." A deep whiskey worn voice came from behind the wall created by the three males. "I said, excuse me."

Two hands appeared between the male in the middle and the one to his right and pushed them apart. Once there was enough space between them, a tall blond woman pushed her way through.

"Didn't your mamas teach you boys any manners?" She harrumphed her way past them and to the bar. "Sheesh, you'd think you'd been born in a barn."

"Am I needed here?" Tevin asked with a grin. "Or do you all think you can handle this. Because there's a woman over there who has my name written all over her."

Allard waved him away. "Yeah, go for it."

"Don't wait for me, I'll make my own way home." Tevin grabbed the two bottles of beer in front of him and headed to the woman who had pushed her way into the bar and was now waving dramatically in an attempt to get the attention of the bartender.

"Well, that's…" Eleanor watched Tevin's exodus with bemusement.

"Odd."

"Strange."

"Unexpected."

"Not something I want to think about."

The others at the table offered their suggestions while still watching the three males. None of them would act unless the newcomers turned aggressive. Vixen and Bray had trained them too well. When humans could witness everything with cell phones, reacting would always be preferential to making the first move.

Allard reached across the table and slid Delia's purse toward Danielle. "There's a radio in there."

"Got it." With a quick apologetic glance to Delia, Danielle dug through the contents until she found the radio, no bigger than an old-fashioned flip phone. Once in hand, she pressed some buttons then set it down in the middle of the table. "Keep the volume down, but they'll hear everything."

Jackson raised a questioning eyebrow at Allard.

"Bray insisted."

Delia looked away from the three males long enough to give Allard a glare. "When did you put that in my purse?"

"Worry about it later."

"He didn't." Maggie blushed. "He asked me to. Said it was a tracker to keep you safe. And since I like you and want you safe too, I did it. It was on the ride here, you didn't even notice."

"Pocket," Finley grumbled.

"What? Oh, yeah, possible bar brawl." She grinned at Delia. "This is on my list of things to do too, so I can cross it off. Hey, we haven't danced yet."

"Focus, Pocket." Finley reached out and gave the back of Maggie's neck a gentle squeeze.

While the three shifters at the door stared at the shifters of Broken Peak, the rest of the bar returned to whatever conversations they'd broken away from. As soon as the noise reached its normal volume, the three males stepped further into the bar.

Allard and the others shifted their weight, preparing for whatever was about to come their way.

But before the strangers could get any closer, Alexander stepped in front of them. With his arms crossed over his chest, he stared down the males until they took a step back. And then another step back. Whatever he said to them, Allard couldn't hear. The noise from the crowd was just too loud. Except, he also had a feeling that Alexander didn't want anyone else to hear what he said.

"You!" The tall blond Tevin was actively chatting up at the bar, shouted and pointed at Alexander. "This is all your fault!"

Alexander turned away from the males and flashed a wide smile at the woman. "I know."

He didn't yell, but Allard could hear his words clearly. Which confirmed his suspicions that Alexander was using some kind of power to focus his words. He'd have to ask Vixen or Mac about it later.

Alexander turned back to the three males. Allard didn't see what happened next, but the three males turned and hurried out of the bar like it was on fire.

"Did you get a look at them?" Allard glanced down at Delia who was staring at the closed door.

"Yeah, but didn't recognize them. You?"

"Never seen them before."

The others around the table turned back to Allard and Delia. After several long seconds of everyone staring at them, Jackson finally broke the silence.

"You got something you want to share with us?"

"Later," Allard shook his head slowly from side to side. "Should we finish our beers?"

Leighton glanced back at the front door of the bar. "Nope, let's head home."

They left their bottles of beer, empty and half-filled, on the table and headed out as a group. The males surrounded the females in a protective wedge, just in case.

Before they walked out the door, Allard whistled loud to grab Tevin's attention. "You coming?"

"Nope, I'll see you later." He spared Allard a brief glance before refocusing his attention on the woman next to him.

CHAPTER TWENTY-SIX

THE following morning Allard woke when he felt something heavier than a blanket covering his back. His barely awake mind registered the warm body and the arm covering his face, but it took him a few more minutes to remember who was currently clinging to him like a koala.

That someone being Delia, and she was still asleep from the sound of the even cadence of her breathing.

The clock by his bed said 7:30 AM, which wasn't all that early for him, but he hadn't had much sleep the night before and debated staying in bed for another thirty minutes. After they got back, Vixen and Bray had questioned everyone about what happened at the Dirty Whistle. And then they spent another hour questioning just Allard and Delia until Vixen was satisfied neither of them recognized the males. She'd even gone as far to bring out a binder filled with images of shifters and their associated pack.

By the time they made it back to his room, they both fell asleep as soon as their heads hit the pillow. Which was probably a good thing considering how tightly she was pressed against his body when he woke up.

As much as he wanted to go back asleep, he knew it wouldn't happen. He carefully slid out from under Delia and replaced his body with a pillow. Amazingly, she slept through his maneuvering.

Silent steps carried him out of the room and into the hallway. He even closed the door slowly in case a hinge decided to protest. As soon as the door latched closed, he stretched and yawned loudly then headed for the kitchen. From the smell of it, someone had cooked up some bacon and, if he was lucky, there would be a few pieces left.

Sure enough, a small buffet of breakfast foods had been set up on the island. During one of the trips to Costco, Vixen stumbled across some warming pans. They had all laughed at the time she purchased them, but a morning hadn't gone by since then that they didn't get used.

Allard stacked a plate full of eggs, bacon, toast, and some cottage fries, then thought better and stacked a second plate full of the same things. He also added some fresh fruit to the second plate. Delia might not be awake just yet, but he bet if he brought her food, she'd wake up. And then if she wanted, she could go back to sleep. But his wolf was annoyed that Allard considered eating anything before her.

He found a tray, stacked the plates on them then added large mugs of coffee and some creamer and sugar. He didn't know how Delia liked her coffee. Or even if she liked coffee. That was how the glasses of orange and apple juice found their way on the tray too. Before he emptied the pantry, he headed back down the hallway to his room.

When he got there, the bed was empty.

Shit. Had Delia wandered off somewhere?

With the tray still in hand, he wandered back down the way he came. As soon as he passed the bathroom door, the sound of water moving through the pipe hit his ears.

Shower.

Delia was in the shower.

Naked.

Allard groaned. It was bad enough waking up to her clinging to him, now he had to deal with the thoughts of her naked in the shower?

He turned back and returned to his room. If he had to imagine her naked and wet, at least he could do it in the privacy of his bedroom. He sat down on the bed, put the tray full of food next to him, and closed his eyes.

The pack needed a second bathroom. At least. There was no way Allard was going to survive the intoxicating thoughts of Delia without having access to a shower.

Sure, he could take things in hand, so to speak, right in his bedroom, but there was always the chance that Delia would finish her shower before he did. What would happen if she walked in on him? In his fantasies, she'd help him with his growing problem, and it was definitely growing. But in reality, he assumed she'd run off and the next few weeks would be even more uncomfortable than they already were likely to be.

Shit.

He needed to change.

The loose pajama pants he'd pulled on the night before had turned into a tent. In a rush, he kicked off the flannel pants and yanked up the pair of jeans he'd worn the night before. He was just finishing zipping up the fly when Delia returned.

"Oh, I didn't know where you went off to." She clutched the towel wrapped around her body closer to her chest, which just squished her breasts together so they pushed up over the edge.

Allard closed his eyes and looked away from her. "I, uh, got breakfast."

I got breakfast. Real smooth.

She stepped inside the room and closed the door, but didn't move any more than that. Yeah, not that he blamed her. After all, he'd done the getting dressed in under ten seconds a few minutes earlier.

He turned his back to her and faced the far corner. "I brought breakfast for you too. In case you know, you were hungry."

"Thanks."

He heard zippers opening and closing and fabric rustling. Her family had shipped her entire closet from the amount of cases that Tevin and Leighton had dragged up after the General dropped Geneva off at the airport. They'd need to build an entire new wing to accommodate her wardrobe.

"You can turn around now."

She was standing in front of the mirror brushing her wet hair and dressed in a pair of those super tight jeans that looked painted on and a huge sweater that swallowed all her curves. He loved the jeans, but wasn't thrilled with the sweater. At least the ones she had worn before showcased her breasts.

Even if he hadn't actually seen them in their full and naked glory, he just knew they were magnificent and didn't deserve to be hidden beneath layers of fabric.

"Breakfast?" He blurted the word out while still staring at where he imagined her breasts were hiding under the thick yarn of the sweater.

"Sure." She set the brush down and sat down on the bed, crossed-legged style. "You are eating with me, I hope?"

He nodded and followed suit so they faced one another on the bed with the tray of food between them.

They ate in a somewhat comfortable silence, which surprised Allard. He'd expected there to be more tension, but Delia was relaxed.

"What are your plans for today?" She asked between bites of eggs.

"I have early evening patrol, but other than that, nothing." God, is this what being mated was like? Talking about their plans for the day? If they lived in a city, he imagined there'd be a lot more to do. "You?"

"I'm supposed to talk with Eleanor and Mac about something, then Vixen wanted to do those drills you talked about. But other than that, I guess nothing." She grinned at him and waggled her eyebrows. "Why, you wanna do something? Short sheet all the beds? Put saran wrap on the toilets, maybe?"

Allard shook his head with a chuckle. It shouldn't be this easy to talk with her. "As much fun as it might be, the retaliation would surely be swift and twice as bad."

"Oh, a prank war. I haven't been part of one of those since I went away to summer camp one year." Delia looked positively mischievous sitting there considering the kinds of pranks she could play.

He needed to distract her. And quick.

"We'll have to ask Vixen when the Council is supposed to arrive."

"Is there any room for them to stay here?"

"No. But they won't let them stay here. Not with Vixen being what she is."

Delia looked over at the door, reassuring herself it was still closed. "What is she anyway?"

"I'll let her tell you. If you ask nicely, she'll probably let you know when you do your drills with her. She might even show you."

"I don't get what the big secret is."

"Sorry. I'd tell you, really I would, but she's pretty much made us all take vows of secrecy. Well, more Bray than her."

Her lips tightened into a thin line, but she nodded, accepting his explanation, even if it didn't make her happy.

"Hey, anytime you're out in the woods, make sure you have one of Danielle's trackers with you. And it'd be even better if you weren't alone. In fact, don't go out in the woods at all without someone with you."

She wet her lips and rolled them between her teeth. "What do you mean? I thought Broken Peak was supposed to be safe."

"It is. For the most part. But I don't want you taking any risks. None. And with us not knowing whose pack those three wolves from last night belong to, it's much better to be safe than sorry."

Delia tilted her head to the side and considered his words. After several seconds, she wrinkled her nose at him. "Okay."

Just okay? He expected more push back from her, something along the lines of why or I don't have to listen to you since we aren't really mated. He almost questioned what she meant by the word okay, but Delia had returned to eating and watching anything go near her lips was distracting.

"What should I do with my clothes?" She asked between bites. "I don't mind living out of a suitcase, but if the Council wants a tour of the Lodge seeing my suitcases might not settle with them."

"I have room in the closet, but I don't think there's enough closet space in the entire place for all your clothes." He leaned back on his hands. "I think we might have a spare office. If we get some of those wheelie clothes rack things, we could create a closet for you. But it will be clear across the way by the laundry room."

"You have a laundry room here?"

He didn't understand why she was surprised. Of course they had a laundry room. They had to clean their clothes somehow. "Yes. It's a new addition since we hated lugging our things to the river to beat with rocks." He added dryly.

Delia rolled her eyes at him. "From the pile of clothes you have in the corner, I figured you just bought new things when you finally ran out of clean clothes."

Damn, not only was she sexy, but she had a sarcastic streak a mile long. People claimed smart was sexy, and it totally was, but wit was even sexier in Allard's book.

"Eleanor usually collects laundry once a week and does a bunch of loads at once. She won't fold the clothes though."

"I can fold, and even wash, but I draw the line at ironing your socks and underwear."

His eyes lit up in excitement. Washing clothes was his most hated chore, which was why the pile in the corner kept growing. "Okay, no ironing underwear or socks."

"And what do I get in return?"

"What?"

"What do I get? Foot rubs? Back massages? Will you hand feed me bonbons?"

"I'll kill the spiders for you."

"I'd prefer the bonbons." She said it all with a straight face, but couldn't hide the tiny crinkles in the corner of her eyes as she struggled not to laugh.

"Okay, bonbons and spiders it is then."

"Um, I will need a drawer. Or two."

Drawer? What did she need a drawer for? And what did drawers have to do with spiders and bonbons?

He must have had a silly look on his face because she quickly added, "I have to have a place to put the socks and underwear, which I don't iron, and I don't think hanging them up in the closet will make you thrilled. Although, I will have to hang them somewhere after I wash them."

"Hang your socks after you wash them?"

"No. My lingerie, silly."

"Oh." Yeah it was a stupid thing to say, but his mind was busy going to places it had no business being. Not if he didn't want to run to the shower to take care of the growing concern between his legs.

Before he said anything more stupid than oh, like hey, can you model that lingerie for me some time, he hopped off the bed and grabbed the tray. "I'll go take these to the kitchen and find a room for you to store your clothes."

CHAPTER TWENTY-SEVEN

AS SOON as Allard left, and Delia could no longer get a clear view of his ass as he disappeared down the hallway, she eyed the pile of suitcases. She didn't need to unpack all of them, but emptying a few would help with the facade they were building as mates.

Twenty minutes later and Allard still hadn't returned. Not that she expected him to, but it would've been nice to have company while she organized her clothes into neat stacks on his bed.

Forty minutes later and Maggie was standing outside the door. She was leaning forward, as though she might tip over at any minute, but wouldn't allow her feet to cross the threshold.

Delia grinned. She enjoyed the female's company and if anyone could make unpacking less boring, it was definitely Maggie.

"You want to come in?"

Maggie nodded, skipped over to the bed, and flopped down on the mattress. "Whatcha doing?"

"Unpacking." Delia glanced down at the still mostly-filled suitcases. "Or at least trying to. There's not much room here."

"You can borrow our closet. I don't have much, and Finley only has a few pairs of jeans and shirts he just rotates through."

"Thanks." The stark confession of Maggie not having much sent a pang through Delia's middle. A bright idea formed in her brain. "Do you like music?"

"Sure, I guess."

"I'm sure Geneva must have packed it for me. She included everything else." Kneeling in front of one of the larger suitcases that had the dimensions of a steamer trunk, Delia dug through its contents. Sure enough, near the bottom, she found what she was looking for wrapped inside a towel.

A towel? Why had Geneva bothered to pack towels? Never mind, wasn't important.

"Aha!" Delia emerged from the trunk with her prize in hand. A portable bluetooth speaker. Her phone might not dial out because of the blocking thing they did, but it would still be able to play music. She handed the gizmo over to Maggie. "Can you find an outlet to plug it into?"

Maggie grabbed the silver speaker like it was a treasure and stroked it while looking for a nearby outlet.

"Okay, now what?"

"Um, there's a little cord that you can plug my phone into since it will need to charge up, then hit the button with the music note and pick a playlist that looks interesting to you."

"Oh, these are like the phones Danielle gave us. I have music on mine too. Did she give you this phone?"

Delia half-listened to Maggie while surveying the rest of the contents of the mammoth suitcase. Why had Geneva packed cocktail dresses and was that a beaded tank? "Um, no. But she'll probably give me one today."

At least Delia hoped Danielle would. She wanted to call home at least and let her parents know she was safe. Although, she was certain they already knew she was safe since Bray or Vixen had probably already called them.

"Oh my God! I need this playlist on my phone!" Maggie squealed and then Britney Spears's Sometimes came out of the speaker.

Maggie had found the 90s playlist. At some point, when they were younger, Geneva and Delia decided the 90s had the best music and insisted it was all they wanted to listen to. Thankfully, that phase only lasted for three months before they moved on, but Delia kept the playlist around because it had an odd combination of punk rock and pop songs.

Delia did her best Britney dance while moving around the suitcases and soon enough, Maggie was copying her. Eventually those steps that Delia had memorized from the video came back and unpacking was forgotten.

The song faded away, and both females collapsed on the bed in a fit of giggles. The neat stacks of clothing turned into disorganized piles, but Delia didn't mind. Dancing around like she did when she was thirteen was a better way to spend the morning than dealing with an out-of-control wardrobe.

Immediately after Britney's sweet voice trailed off, heavy breathing replaced it.

"What's this?"

It took a few seconds before Delia recognized the artist. "Offspring."

"Ew, you can't dance to this."

"Sure you can." Delia jumped to her feet and thrashed her head back and forth to the beat of the song.

"That's not dancing." Maggie reached for the phone and tapped the screen.

Ace of Base came on and they were both back to dancing.

"This music is so much better than the songs Danielle put on my phone." Maggie hopped around the room with a funny wiggle of her hips.

The dance looked like so much fun, Delia was soon copying her.

And that was how Allard found her. Hopping around the room with her arms waving overhead and bent slightly at the waist so her butt stuck out while she wiggled it. Sure, she could have stopped the silly dance, but then she couldn't enjoy watching Allard's amused grin.

"Wanna join us?"

"Um, no thanks. I'm not really into dancing."

"Aww, too bad. This is going to be the next big thing on Tik Tok."

"What's Tik Tok?" Maggie stopped dancing.

"Um, it's an app, a way to share videos with others."

"Can we Tik Tok?"

Allard gave Delia a tight shake of his head. Yeah, Maggie on Tik Tok might be a viral hit, but it would also probably backfire magnificently.

"It's too public. Most packs really restrict the use for their young." Delia had more tact than to say, 'no, you'd out us all in thirty seconds.'

"Oh." Maggie thought about Delia's words for a few seconds, then resumed dancing. If it could actually be called dancing.

Allard stepped into the room and looked around the piles of clothes. "I found a room for you. And even some racks, well shelves actually, but you can hang things up on them."

Delia pressed her hands to her waist with her elbows sticking out. "All right. The things on the bed should stay, so can that smaller bag over there, but the rest can go."

"You've been hard at work since I left."

"Not really, it was more needing something to do and not knowing what else to do." No point in coming up with a polite excuse when the truth would do just fine. Besides, it wasn't like anything else about her tenure at Broken Peak was based on truth, no need to add white lies to the long list of not-white lies.

"Come on, Maggie, wanna help move clothes?"

The dancing stopped and Maggie looked around the room. "Some of her clothes can stay with me. I'll take good care of them."

Allard shook his head with a smirk, "if we run out of space in the room I claimed as her closet, sure."

"Okay, in that case, fun things come out of that big one, so let's save that for last. And let me get Finley, he's stronger than me."

Both Allard and Delia watched Maggie leave the room in a whirlwind, the same way she had entered.

"You could have a reality show with her as the star."

"Oh, yeah, I can see it now, The Real Pack: Broken Peak."

"Whatever happened to The Real World?" Delia picked up one of the suitcases, not having anything better to do with her hands unless she considered running them across Allard's bare chest a good idea. He still hadn't put on a shirt since he left with their breakfast dishes.

As if he could read her mind, Allard opened a drawer and pulled out a t-shirt. "It sort of just faded away I think when reality stopped being entertaining and they couldn't find another gimmick to make it interesting."

He pulled his shirt down over his head and Delia stared at the clearly defined muscles on his chest and stomach as they slowly disappeared behind his shirt. She shook free the image of running her tongue along those crevices between his muscles.

"Want to lead the way? I don't know where I'm going."

"By all means, Red." Allard hoisted a large duffel over his shoulder.

Instead of waiting for her to leave the room, he slipped past her, brushing his chest against hers. If she didn't know any better, Delia could have sworn he intended to press against her.

"I think at some point, Eleanor wants to use this room as an archive so she doesn't have to run to Mac's every time she needs to find something, but it will look permanent enough to any Council members who come to investigate."

A bucket of ice water dumped on her head would have had the same effect as his words. Their mating ceremony had been a fake, they weren't the fated mates they pretended to be, and Delia would leave Broken Peak once it was safe.

Her feet continued to move, almost as though they had a will of their own, for which she was grateful. If they hadn't kept moving, she would have froze in place and come across as an idiot. The last thing she wanted, or needed, was for Allard to see how his words affected her.

Allard led her to a small room with wire shelves lining the wall. Eleanor had probably installed the shelves as a place to hold books, but they could hold hangers just as well.

Besides. It was all temporary.

Right?

Delia fell down on the bed and curled into the fetal position, hugging her knees to her chest. Except even that slight movement sent ripples of achiness through her muscles. Muscles she didn't even know she had.

A one hour workout with Vixen might have broken her. And the Alpha expected Delia to do it all over again tomorrow.

Her wolf stretched inside of her and urged her to shift. Except Delia didn't think she had the strength left to blink her eyes much less stand up and go outside. Delia thought she was in shape, but nothing in her life had prepared her for the torture Vixen put her through and planned to continue putting her through.

The worst part about it was Maggie. The ever-cheerful raccoon shifter did all the same exercises, except twice as many in the same amount of time, and hadn't even broken a sweat.

Shower.

Yes. She needed a shower.

But that required moving.

A part of her, albeit a very small part, felt guilty about still being dressed in her sweaty clothes and lying down on Allard's side of the bed. Hey, one night in the same bed together and she thought of him as having a side.

Yep. Definitely broken. Her mind wandered off on random tangents when she needed it most if she ever hoped of moving again.

Workout clothes. She'd need more workout clothes too.

Tomorrow, Vixen had planned for two sessions and with how much she had sweat during this afternoon's workout, she'd need to change between sessions.

Whad'ya know. There her mind went, wandering off in a random direction.

She couldn't stay in bed much longer or she'd risked never getting out of bed again.

Except that idea had definite merit.

Food wouldn't be a problem. Delia could barter her clothes to have Maggie deliver it. The only issue was the bathroom.

That's right. She needed a shower.

"Brain, I need you to focus," she muttered.

Her wolf laughed. Well not so much as laughed as ran in circles with her tail wagging and her tongue lolling out the side of her mouth.

Legs first, then she could figure out if they still worked enough to carry her out of the room and to the bathroom.

They refused to budge. She tried again to stretch them out, but they weren't moving in the slightest.

Oh, that's right, her arms were still holding on to them.

So, arms first. That task she managed, but she was pretty sure it took a few minutes just to move them a few inches.

Okay, now the legs.

Look at that, they could unbend when a pair of arms weren't holding them in place.

Except now, she was just stretched out on the bed lying on her side.

The effort it took to roll to her side, she didn't trust rolling on to her stomach, was monumental. A few minutes rest wouldn't be the end of the world. Right?

Her wolf nudged her. There had been times when she allowed her wolf deeper into her consciousness, like when she was in high school during gym class and had to run a mile. Using her wolf to get her up and moving so she could take a shower didn't carry quite the same hint of cheating to Delia as when she was in gym class.

It didn't take any effort at all, which was a good thing considering how near to exhaustion she was. The wolf slid into her consciousness, and there was a moment of vertigo as she acclimated to the wolf's immediate presence. As quickly as the wave of dizziness arrived, it left and Delia found herself standing on her feet by the bed.

A few minutes later and almost warm water pounded down on her skin. She didn't wait for the temperature to warm before stripping out of the sweaty clothes and stepping under the water. By the time the water warmed enough to ease some of the soreness from her muscles, Delia had cleaned the dried sweat from her body. Her hair remained unwashed, but only because she wasn't sure she could lift her arms high enough over her head without her shoulders protesting.

She didn't know how long she stood under the pounding water, but it finally turned cool and Delia wanted out before it went from cool to cold.

Turning the water off was a struggle. Grabbing her towel hanging from the hook almost didn't happen. The only reason she summoned the will to lift her arm enough to pull it from the hook, was she didn't fancy trotting down the hallway bare-assed naked. She also didn't think Allard was a good enough actor to go on a full-blown possessive tear of a fated mate.

With the towel tucked firmly around her, she headed back to their shared bedroom. Part of her wished Allard would be there. She wanted to upgrade from foot rub to a back massage. Her wolf fully agreed with this part. The other part wanted the room to herself so she could crawl under the covers and go to sleep and never wake up again.

The bedroom was as empty as when she had left it, so she closed the door, dropped the towel and slid between the cool sheets. Only this time, on her side of the bed. A light was still on, but she couldn't bother to do anything about it.

A nice long nap and everything would be less bad. It wouldn't be better. But then after Allard's reminder this morning that everything about Broken Peak, including him, was temporary, she didn't think it was possible for better.

Better was a dream on a wing and a prayer.

Less bad was an achievable goal.

So was sleep. And she wouldn't even have to work at it. Her wolf slipped back into the recesses of her consciousness with a satisfied growl and Delia's eyes closed as sleep overcame her.

CHAPTER TWENTY-EIGHT

ALLARD stood next to the bed and stared down at Delia's sleeping form. An adorable little snore came from her with each soft breath and he was tempted to brush his knuckle against her cheek.

When he found her in bed asleep, he knew he should turn right back around and leave her alone. His feet didn't agree and carried him into the room.

Thankfully he closed the door, or his packmates might have caught him staring at her naked back. But who could blame him? The pale skin, dotted with freckles, practically glowed in the soft light coming from the lamp on the dresser.

He really should leave. Turn off the light and head straight to the shower to take care of the growing problem between his legs.

A naked back really shouldn't get him hard. Right? But it wasn't just her naked back. It was also, that the thin white sheet did nothing to hide the fact that she wasn't wearing anything at all. Not even those sexy lace panties he watched her fold and place in a drawer.

Although, truth be told, he wasn't sure which he preferred. No panties, or the panties currently residing in the drawer that used to hold his socks.

"Allard? That you?" She garbled her words, so it sounded more like 'lirdateww' and it took a few moments before his brain processed the sound.

"Yeah." He should have stepped away from his bed. He knew it, but his feet once more had a mind of their own and refused to budge. "Workout with Vixen?"

"How'd you know?" Except it came out as hochano.

The garbling of her words might have had something to do with the way she smooshed her face against the pillow.

"Been there before. We all have."

"Mag-"

He stopped her before she finished the word. "Maggie is a freak of nature and can run laps around all of us unless we're shifted. Her raccoon can't keep up with our wolves, but we can't keep up with her, so it's probably all fair in the end."

"Too happy." She lifted her head enough so her mouth wasn't pressed into the pillow.

"If I know Vixen, your arms are probably feeling like they want to fall off."

"And my legs."

"How about a shoulder rub?"

She opened one eye and lifted her head up enough so she could see him. "At the summer camp I went to, we weren't allowed to give each other back massages because massages always turned sexual."

"Red, it's a shoulder rub. Not a back massage."

"There a difference?"

"Fine, if you don't want one, I'll take my hands somewhere else then."

Where he really wanted to take them was under the sheet so he could feel her ass without that layer of denim blocking his way. The night before in the bar, when he slid her money back into her pocket, it almost killed him. And ever since, he'd been trying to come up with more reasons to touch that gorgeous ass.

But he didn't say that.

"Where do you want me?"

On your knees with me behind you was what he thought, but said, "there's fine, but can you move over so I can sit on the bed?"

Hopefully she was too tired to catch the lie.

She slid over towards the middle of the bed and Allard settled next to her hips.

Just her shoulders. He repeated those words over and over until he was certain his hands wouldn't take over and go lower. Lower in every other situation would be good, but when it came to Delia, it would be bad. She might not have actually been his fated mate, but he found himself enjoying her company. Delia was smart too, she read the room at the bar last night and adapted fast. Faster than even Jackson and Leighton. Not to mention the female was sexy as fuck.

And all of those qualities came together to create a huge problem for Allard. He'd agreed to the fake mating because it needed to be done, but now he regretted the fake part. Perhaps if he took more time to get to know her, he'd have agreed to the mating. Then he wouldn't have to spend his time in the shower taking care of a hard-on that never seemed to go away when Delia was around.

He laid his hands down on her shoulders and it was like a static shock charged through him. Her skin was like silk beneath his hands and her bones were like the delicate fine china his mother used to pull out for formal events.

God, he was going to break her.

"You're not rubbing. Rub. I won't break. I promise."

Could she read his mind? Shit. He'd have to keep all his thoughts about her nice and clean now.

As soon as he considered the mind reading thing, he tossed it aside. Delia might be an Alpha, like him, but she didn't have any special powers.

Allard kneaded the tight muscles, using his thumbs to rub out the particularly stubborn knots. He focused on those instead of the way she felt compared to everyone else he'd ever touched in his life. And the tactic worked for a while, but then she started groaning. And it wasn't a polite noise either.

"More."

More? He wasn't sure how much more he could handle.

"Harder."

Yeah, that's what he needed to be thinking about while he rubbed her shoulders. Harder. Like the current state of his cock. Or like how he wanted to be pounding into her.

He obliged her request, assuming she meant the pressure of his hands. As soon as he did, her moans turned into groans and he couldn't keep the iron grip of his self-control in check any longer.

Allard jerked his hands off her back and jumped off the bed. "I can't."

"Can't what?" She lifted her body slightly and while her arm made a valiant attempt at covering her breast, it didn't succeed. In the slightest.

He tore his gaze away from the hint of a nipple peeking out at him, an incredibly hard nipple if his brief glance had been accurate and paced the width of the room.

"I can't do this, Delia." The more he touched her, the more he wanted to fuck her. And he couldn't come up with a good enough reason for it not to happen.

Allard stopped his pacing as far away from her as possible and turned to face her. And that was a mistake of the nth degree. Delia was sitting up in bed with the sheet pulled to her chest, but with her lips slightly parted and her green eyes flickering with gold, it was all he could do to keep his wolf from urging him to take her.

One step closer, then a second and a third, and he found himself standing beside the bed again, staring down at her. But she wasn't asleep and if her heated gaze warming his body was any indication, she wanted what he wanted.

"Is this happening?" Allard asked.

Delia nodded, "Yes."

"You want this?"

Another nod, "very much so, yes."

He bent down until his face was so close to hers that he could feel her sweet breath dance across the skin of his cheeks.

"Is this us?" Allard asked.

"Or our wolves?"

Allard nodded.

"Does it matter?"

Did it? Yeah, he'd pushed his wolf away since coming to Broken Peak, but he never ignored the beast's silent nudges urging him toward something. He still trusted his wolf. Even with Delia. Especially with her. "No."

Once he said the word, the carefully erected walls came tumbling down faster than they had at Jericho.

Her arms snaked around his neck and lifted closer. Oh so close.

Their lips brushed, and a spark jumped between them.

She opened her mouth, welcoming him and he dove in, all thoughts and cares tossed aside. Her taste filled his mouth with a sweetness he couldn't ever remember experiencing before and her scent filled his nose, overpowering him with a heady combination of arousal and need.

He lowered his body over her. His hands sank into the mattress, caging her with his arms. Delia's arms wrapped tighter around his neck, pulling his body closer to hers until all that stood between them was a sheet and his shirt.

She realized the problem as soon as he did and her fingers trailed down his sides to the bottom of the shirt. Without breaking from their kiss, she tugged his shirt until it came to a stop at his arms and neck.

Too much fabric. Not enough skin. He pulled away slowly and yanked the t-shirt off before returning to their kissing, but this time his hands found her tits. The perfect breasts he'd imagined didn't compare to reality and he couldn't wait to feel them beneath his fingers.

She pushed up against his touch and whad'ya know, her hands found their way to his jeans.

Where had all these clothes come from? And why wasn't he as naked as she was?

He groaned as her fingers discovered the button and zipper. Want for her tore through his body, driving him to take her hard and fast.

Except Delia didn't deserve that. Her body deserved to be worshiped and appreciated and Allard planned on doing just that.

"Allard," she moaned into his mouth and he nearly came from the sound alone.

"I got you." His tongue dragged down along her neck, over her collarbone, and between her breasts before finding a nipple. Pulling her taut nipple between his lips, he sucked hard enough to bring about another moan from her.

His cock jerked at the sound.

God, he loved the noises she made. He could spend hours listening to those noises.

His thumb circled her other nipple, gently flicking it while his teeth pressed into the tender flesh of the nipple his mouth was focused on.

As far as he was concerned, Allard would be content spending the rest of his life just paying attention to her tits.

He'd never been into breasts. Sure, he enjoyed them when he came across a nice set, but he'd never been attracted to a female just because of her tits. And not that he was only attracted to Delia because of her tits. Even if they were fucking amazing breasts. Everything else about her turned him on too. Her confidence, her wit, her hair, her skin, her eyes, her mouth, her ass, and, of course, those tits.

"Allard…" The moan turned into a whine and her body writhed beneath his with an urgent need.

The way she pressed up against his hard cock, still confined by his jeans, nearly sent him over the edge. Fuck, he never would've believed dry-humping could be this hot.

"Now, Allard." The small growl urged him on.

He pulled free from her nipple with a pop and knelt over her with his thighs straddling her hips.

Their hands and fingers tangled with one another in an attempt to get his pants off. Finally, after several seconds of chaotic struggling, his jeans were at his ankles and he kicked them to the ground. The tight boxer briefs came next. She yanked them down, her lips dangerously close to the head of his cock as it popped free.

Delia looked up at him, her eyes dancing with mischief and hunger. The tip of her pink tongue snaked out from between her lips, swollen from their kissing, and licked off the drop of clear pre-cum.

If she wasn't careful, he'd be feeding her his cock and coming down her throat before he had a chance to feel the embrace of her pussy.

Allard growled. Delia looked up at him and licked her top lip. He groaned. She laid back on the bed with her legs parted and his gaze, still focused on where her head once was, now saw her pussy. Her very pretty pussy.

The tiny thread holding his control in check snapped.

He pounced down on her, pressing her body down against the bed.

Delia yelped, but didn't protest.

"Fuck, Delia, your tits are perfect."

His mouth covered a nipple, and she arched, offering him more. He moved to the other nipple, giving it the same attention before finally pulling back so he could once again gaze down at her.

Maybe he could convince her to remain naked in his bed forever?

Fuck, how had that thought crept into his head? He shook it free and focused on what was in front of him. Or more exactly, who was in front of him.

"I need to feel you around my cock."

But before he did that, he wanted to taste her. Planting his lips between her breasts, he moved down her stomach. After a brief detour to circle the tip of his tongue around her belly button, he moved lower. To her pussy. Her delightfully nearly bare pussy. The only hair was a small patch of red just above her clit.

Fuck, her hair was the same color everywhere. Not that he doubted she was a natural redhead for a minute, but to see that bright red, just above her clit, it was like a huge neon sign telling him exactly where to go.

His tongue avoided her clit and instead lapped at the seam of her outer lips. She was wet. When his tongue broke through her lips and speared her entrance, her sweet taste flooded his senses.

Like honey and cream and so much more.

"Fuck!" Delia groaned out the word through gritted teeth.

Allard peered up over the length of her body to find her head pressed back against the pillow, her back arched, and her fingers plucking at her nipples.

Hottest. Fucking. Sight. Ever.

He dove back in, but this time, while his mouth was busy with her pussy, he let his nose bump against her clit. He stiffened his tongue and fucked her with it, alternating the intensity of the strokes between hard and soft. His mouth teased her, keeping her on the edge of an orgasm.

Her legs wrapped around his neck, her thighs locking him in place. But she didn't have to worry, he wasn't planning on going anywhere any time soon.

Each breath brought more of her scent into him, and his cock jerked, impatient for a taste of what his mouth was enjoying.

Redoubling his efforts, Allard reached up and gently pried her legs apart, opening her up even more for his tongue. It was like he flipped a switch inside her. With just his tongue, he pushed her over the edge. Her pussy tightened around him and the hold he had on her legs was lost as she snapped her thighs against his head.

When her orgasm finally slowed and her body relaxed enough to release its tight grip on his head, she fell back on the bed. He knelt up and his cock bobbed against his stomach.

Delia watched his cock with heated eyes. She licked her lips and his cock jerked towards her. Her mouth could wait. He wanted inside her and if he didn't, he'd shoot his load down her throat, which was definitely tempting, but not nearly as tempting as her pussy.

Allard slipped his arms under her thighs and lifted her legs and hips, guiding them towards the head of his cock. When it pressed against her wet entrance, he bit back the urge to plunge inside her and take her hard.

"Allard." She wailed out his name with a lift of her hips.

His cock slid into her, much further than he planned. Her pussy was tight, but easily welcomed the girth of his cock.

Allard wasn't a small male, by any means, and he was large all over. Most of the females he'd been with in the past took time to accommodate, but Delia fit him like a glove. Like he belonged inside her pussy and only her pussy.

"Fuuuckkk." Allard ground his molars together to keep himself from coming. For as often as he took care of business in the shower, he should have more control than he did, but Delia's body was a paradise he'd never experienced before.

"I agree." Delia shifted her hips from side to side.

Allard pulled back instead of giving her more. He slipped back in slowly and then slid out just as slow. With each gentle push in, he slipped deeper into her until his cock was entirely inside of her.

Her wiggling stopped, and she stared up at him with parted lips and hungry eyes. Eyes that had turned from green to bright gold.

It was as though she flipped a switch inside him.

He pulled out completely, letting the tip of his cock tease her entrance before plunging back into her hard.

Delia's body moved with each thrust and her bouncing tits caught his attention. He stared down at her, watching her as he fucked her hard and fast.

But he needed more. Lifting her up by her legs, her body shifted and her pussy welcomed him in even deeper. If that was even possible.

"Fuck, you feel perfect." Delia's body lifted to meet each of his thrusts.

Allard agreed, but couldn't get the words out. His brain stopped working as soon as his cock felt her tight embrace.

Their hips slapped against each other with every pounding thrust. She reached up and wrapped her arms around his shoulders, pulling him down over her body until he had to slip his arms out from under her legs.

His mouth found hers. Or her mouth found his. It didn't matter. Her lips parted and their tongues met, dueling with one another.

Delia broke from the kiss long enough to whimper out a "please".

Pride swept through his body at the sound of her pleasure. Pleasure he gave her.

"So close, Allard."

The second plea drove him on. He thrust into her harder and faster, pushing her body up the bed until he feared her head would hit the wall. Finally, he knelt up, grabbed her hips, and pulled her down just as he plunged into with a final hard thrust.

She cried out.

He growled.

Her pussy clamped down tight around his cock, squeezing him harder than his own fist.

She came hard, and Allard's cock responded. The orgasm he'd been holding back exploded.

The world shook. Maybe it was the bed.

He saw stars. Or his eyes were just closed, and he saw those sparkling lights on the inside of his lids.

"Fuck!" Allard growled out and ground his hips against her, like he could get even deeper inside of her.

She didn't push him away, but pulled him closer and her pussy rippled around him, pushing out the length of his orgasm.

Before he collapsed on top of her, Allard rolled to his side then on to his back, bringing Delia with him so she sprawled neatly across his chest with his cock still firmly embedded inside her.

She nuzzled her mouth against the side of the neck. "Am I alive?"

"If you aren't it means, I'm dead too." Allard dragged his fingertips along the length of her arm from her elbow to her shoulder. "So, I'm going with yes, you are."

"I wasn't sure if you killed me." Her teeth nipped at the sensitive skin between his neck and shoulder.

A place where he wouldn't mind her bite.

His eyes widened in shock. What? No! No bite. No mark. Biting and marking led to bonding and the last thing the pack needed was Allard bonding to Delia, especially if she was leaving.

Delia's heavy breathing and warm breath against his skin announced that she'd fallen asleep. Allard turned his head and kissed her forehead then adjusted her body until she fit tight against him. Just as she should be.

He planned on joining her for a quick nap, except before sleep came, Allard wondered where Delia would go after she left Broken Peak and who she would see.

His hackles raised at the idea of her with another male.

His wolf growled. Or maybe it was him.

Fuck.

CHAPTER TWENTY-NINE

A LOUD knocking at the door roused Allard. He opened one eye, then the other and peered at the barrier. Another set of loud knocks woke Delia, who stared at the door with wide eyes.

"Shit. Did they hear us?" She whispered.

Allard didn't mind if they did, but from the way Delia hopped out of bed, with a pillow covering her body, while she jumped around collecting her clothes, she wasn't pleased with the prospect.

"What?" Allard bellowed, and the knocking ceased.

"Visitors." Tevin's voice came through the closed door. "Vixen and Bray said to come and get you."

Visitors?

Fuck. So soon?

Allard had been expecting a few days of practicing the mating thing before anyone came to verify that Delia and Allard had indeed fulfilled their arranged mating. He rolled out of bed, not bothering with covering anything, and pulled on his jeans. "We'll be right there."

He grabbed a clean shirt and put it on then turned to watch Delia struggle to pull up a pair of yoga pants. God, he wished he'd seen her in them before she pulled them off.

"Red, put on jeans and a sweater, might be easier."

She growled at him mid-hop, but didn't argue. Instead, she headed to the closet, keeping the pillow on her front at all times and found some clean clothes to put on.

How she managed to dress without flashing any of her bits was impressive, and Allard had been watching closely, hoping for another glimpse.

Once dressed she turned to him. "How do I look?"

"Fine, Red." He opened the bedroom door and waited for her to step out before wrapping his arm around her waist. "Let's do this."

They headed toward the front room of the Lodge and halfway there, Delia wrapped her arm around his waist as well. He rather enjoyed the way she fit against him, but stayed quiet. Although his wolf gave a happy howl inside his head.

As soon as they stepped into the front room, Eleanor greeted them. "They're outside. Three of them."

"Three?" Allard asked.

"The same three from last night at the bar?"

Eleanor shook his head. "No, two males and a female, all older. And right now they're more fascinated by Vixen than anything else. Which could work in our favor or backfire spectacularly."

Allard peered around Eleanor's shoulder and looked out the front window. Sure enough, three wolves stood a safe distance away from

Vixen, who was standing right in front of the window on the porch. Like she was on a TV screen for anyone inside the Lodge.

"I'll put money down on a spectacular backfire."

"Yeah, but even when one of Vixen's plans backfire, it still manages to work itself out in the end." Eleanor added.

Delia narrowed her eyes as she stared out the window. In the short time since they'd left his room, she'd transformed herself. Gone was the witty, if somewhat snarky female and in her place stood an Alpha, proud and regal and preparing for battle.

If he hadn't been standing right next to her and witnessed it with his own eyes, he'd never have believed the same female who'd just been in his bed was standing next to him.

Magnificent didn't even begin to describe her.

With a deep breath, her shoulders went back and her spine straightened. She lifted her chin and jutted it out in that way that said she was better than everyone and everything around her. "Shall we?"

Damn. His fake fated mate was even sexier when she went all Alpha.

Allard nodded and readjusted his cock before heading outside. The Council members didn't need to know he had a semi. He led them to the door, still arm in arm, and held it open for her.

Bray hovered at the top of the steps, but didn't interrupt the current staring match between Vixen and the Councilors. He turned when the door opened and gave Allard a slight chin lift.

Delia stepped out of the Lodge and instead of heading down the steps or waiting for Allard, she crossed the porch and stood next to Vixen. Shoulder to shoulder.

Allard's jaw almost dropped at the sight of the females side by side. So different, except so similar. Vixen could eviscerate anyone with her dagger or talon, and Delia looked just as capable of doing the same. But instead of a weapon, she'd use her tongue.

"Shiiiiiit." Bray exhaled softly.

Shit was right. Broken Peak didn't have one Alpha female. It had two.

"Councilors." Delia peered down at the three wolf shifters from the porch. "I didn't realize it was within the bounds of the Council to make unannounced visits."

The female glanced at the younger of the two males from the corner of her eyes. Despite the subtlety of the gesture, Allard had no doubts Delia caught it. The female Councilor laid the blame for the surprise visit on that unfortunate male.

"Broken Peak Pack was willing to accommodate your visit and made no attempts to stall or thwart you. I am confused as to why you felt it appropriate to arrive earlier than planned." Delia let the unasked question hang in the air.

Vixen, who had been eerily still since Allard and Delia stepped outside, raised her arms and crossed them over her chest.

The oldest of the Councilors, hell, he was probably older than even Mac, lips cracked apart in a wide grin. He smacked the younger male on the shoulder with the back of his hand and stepped forward.

"Forgive our impertinence, but you must admit, the circumstances of this…" He waved his hand in the air in small circles, as though searching for the right word.

"Mating. Our mating." Delia declared.

"Ahh, yes. Well, the circumstances are odd, and we wished to put an end to any of the rumors. We would have called to announce our earlier arrival, but it's not always easy to reach your pack."

Delia tilted her head to the left. Just enough to lift her chin even further up in the air. Her unfaltering gaze landed on the younger male. The simple gesture demanded the male's attention.

Hell, it demanded Allard's undivided attention, and it wasn't even aimed at him.

"Spencer Pearce, I didn't realize you were on the Council now."

"He's not." The female answered. "The packs demanded that someone not from the Council, join us as an independent observer."

Interesting. Allard wanted to run back inside and grab some popcorn because he knew Delia was about to deliver that evisceration her body language had promised earlier.

Delia's head tilted in the other direction and even though he couldn't see it, Allard knew she was smiling. Not one of her fake plastered on smiles either, but a hungry smile.

Delia was about to feast and her meal would be Spencer Pearce, whoever he was. Allard recognized the name, but couldn't place it with any pack. Not that it was surprising, since he'd been away from the shifter world for so long.

"Whatever made you think it would be okay to walk into a pack's territory without their explicit permission?" Delia's husky timbre held the hint of a growl. "Any other pack would have called your act, a declaration of war. Is that what this is, Spencer? Are you declaring War on behalf of the Northwest Pack?"

"Delia, you have to admit, everything happ-"

"I have to admit nothing, Spencer Pearce. Can you blame me for coming here after the way your pack's enforcers behaved?"

Allard's ears perked. So did his wolf's.

Did Delia just name the pack who tried to grab her off the street?

Oh, hell, no!

He strode across the porch and down the steps until he stood in front of this Spencer Pearce. His hands grasped the collar of Spencer's shirt and he yanked the male toward him until they were nose to nose. Spencer's toes barely touched the ground as he hung from Allard's grip.

"Did you send others here? Before you arrived?" Allard snapped.

Spencer's eyes widened for a moment before the male regained his self-composure. He clenched his fingers around Allard's grip to keep his shirt from choking him out.

Was that surprise about the other males?

Or surprise at Allard's response to learning that Spencer's pack was responsible for attempting to grab Delia?

It didn't matter. Not if Allard's wolf got his way. And he had half a mind to let the beast free just to rip the male's throat out. He deserved nothing less.

"Allard," Delia's soft voice carried across the yard and reached his ears. "Release him, please."

Her words had the same effect as if she had physicaly yanked him back to the porch. Allard's hands opened and Spencer fell to the ground in an undignified lump, hopefully ruining his nicely pressed slacks with grass stains.

"He isn't worth it. And even if his death is justified, and it is by all shifter customs and laws, it would be a tedious mess to clean up." She'd move to the top of the steps and neither Allard nor his wolf was happy about that.

Delia was vulnerable to any stupid ideas Spencer might have. And considering his pack thought it would be a good idea to send him to Broken Peak, Allard figured Spencer only had stupid ideas. Allard turned, careful to step on Spencer's hand as he did so, and covered the distance to the porch in half the usual number of steps.

He wanted to grab Delia, wrap his arms around her, and hold her close to his body. Somehow, he understood Delia wouldn't appreciate the gesture. Except as soon as he reached the top of the steps, Delia stepped into his side and wrapped her arm around Allard's waist. His arm dropped around the back of her shoulder and he pulled her close.

His wolf rumbled out a satisfied growl. He needed Delia's touch more than anything else, and she gave it to him without a struggle.

"Satisfied?" Bray asked from behind Delia and Allard.

The older male, he'd never introduced himself, raised an eyebrow and glanced down at Spencer, still on his knees. "Bray, you know me, an altercation was never our intent."

"No, Mac knows you. As for what your intentions were or are, it doesn't matter now, does it?" Bray stretched his arm out and Vixen slid into place next to him.

Apparently Bray's wolf was as unsettled as Allard's.

The Councilors stood behind Spencer, looking up at the four shifters on the porch, but said nothing.

Spencer, though, proved that not only was he full of stupid ideas, but that he probably also qualified as stupid. "I want to see the documentation from the ceremony."

"Out of respect to traditions and customs, the Councilors may view the documents, but no one else. We'll arrange to bring the documentation to them. Outside of our territory. But not today and not here." Delia stared down at the male as though he was a bug to be stepped on under the toe of those sexy boots she wore to the bar. "Leave, before I let my mate rip out your throat like he wants to."

"You aren't the Alpha here, Delia."

"No, but I am, and I want you to leave." Vixen commanded.

And it wasn't an order given to a pack member either. Her words carried the full weight and power of an Alpha and only the strongest among shifters could ignore the compulsion to obey. They'd learned Vixen's power with the Alpha command was stronger than most, and Mac had been working with her to keep from letting it out accidentally. But this wasn't accidental. This was intentional.

Vixen wanted the Council and the Northwest Pack to know just how strong the Broken Peak's Alpha female was.

Allard wasn't convinced it was the best decision, but it was better than Vixen letting her griffin out. That would have been an unmitigated disaster of a backfire that didn't come out okay in the end.

Members of the Council didn't have to be Alphas, but they had to be strong and dominant. They also usually had additional gifts. Not magic or crap like that, but something that gave them an edge over others. They also held their position for life. Which meant a vacancy on the Council only came when one died. Or was killed. That a successful challenge hadn't occurred in hundreds of years, told just how powerful the current Council was.

Except Vixen's command pushed all three halfway across the yard. And since Allard was standing in front of her, his body took a hit as well. Delia's arm tightened around his waist, as though she was using him as an anchor. That they were able to withstand the compulsion to obey Vixen, was both a surprise and a small miracle. She must have made progress on her targeting practice with Mac.

Of the three visitors in the yard, only the older male appeared unsurprised by the developments. If anything he looked, almost relieved, like someone came and took away a heavy box he'd been carrying a long distance.

"Go home, Spencer. Tell your brother the mating took place and his sons will just have to find other daughters to mate to help fill up his coffers."

Delia leaned into Allard, and he took the cue from her body. They turned and walked back into the house.

His wolf wasn't at all happy about the prospect of turning his back on three unknown shifters, but he put aside his discontent and pranced around in pride at his mate's performance.

Fake mate. Allard reminded his wolf. She's our fake mate.

Vixen and Bray followed behind them and someone closed the door harder than necessary. Not quite a slam, but damn close to anyone near enough to hear.

The two Alphas of Broken Peak shared a look with each other before Vixen turned the full force of her stare on Delia. Allard pulled Delia tighter against him.

Instead of cowing to the glare, like Allard expected her to, Delia's chin jutted out in that way that said she'd do exactly as she pleased.

"That was enlightening." Delia spoke first.

"It was. And tomorrow you'll speak with Mac. There's a reason you're here, Delia, and it's not because of an arranged mating or Allard."

"Fake mating." Both Allard and Delia spoke at the same time. But Allard couldn't say if it was because they were reminding Vixen or themselves.

"Yes, yes, whatever." Vixen brushed aside their minor protest with a wave of her hand.

"Don't you think it's too soon for the mumbo jumbo crap?" Allard asked.

"What mumbo jumbo crap?" Delia looked between Allard and Vixen, expecting an answer to her question.

Allard opened his mouth to speak, but Vixen cut him off. "Tomorrow. It can wait until tomorrow. As for what just happened, Bray and I need to talk and figure out a plan. You bought us some time though, Delia. Nice job."

Nice job? Vixen never used the words nice and job together when praising any of the pack. The best Allard had ever gotten from her was an okay and Maggie, Vixen's favorite, got the occasional that was fine.

"We'll figure things out and fill you in with our plan in the morning, but it's been a long day for everyone." Bray dismissed them, and, as if on cue, Delia yawned.

"Come on, Red, let's get you to bed." Allard pulled Delia along with him out of the room.

She opened her mouth to protest, but Allard gave her a tight shake of his head and mouthed the word later. A small nod signaled her reception of the message, and she went along with him without argument.

CHAPTER THIRTY

DELIA rolled over in bed and right into a warm hard body. She nuzzled her face against the bare chest and breathed in his scent. If the presence of a half-naked male wasn't enough to wake up, Allard's distinct scent was.

His arms wrapped around her and he rolled with her onto his back so she covered his chest.

So much better than an alarm clock.

Oh.

Not half-naked. All-the-way naked. And all-the-way hard too.

Well, how was that for a good morning?

Delia slid her body against his, shifting her hips against his so his hard cock rubbed against her.

She wanted, no needed, to feel his warm skin against hers. Except something was in the way.

The sheet? No. At some point the sheet had been kicked to the foot of the bed.

Her shirt! The night before she pulled on one of Allard's larger-than-life t-shirts instead of digging around for her own pajamas, and now it was the only thing between her and a naked Allard.

Pressing her hands down on his chest, she pushed herself up until she could easily pull off the offending shirt. As soon as their skin came in contact with one another, her breath caught.

Bending down, she planted a soft kiss at the spot between his shoulder and neck and Allard's breath caught. Encouraged by his reaction, she kissed her way across his collarbone, pausing for the occasional nipping.

Allard growled low and stroked his hands over the length of her back.

Delia moved her lips over his chest, sliding her body across his hard muscles as she continued down to the hard planes of his stomach. She traced the creases defining his muscles with the tip of her tongue and a shudder rolled through his body.

When her mouth finally reached the sharp lines that pointed down, his cock bobbed up in anticipation and her mouth watered.

"Delia," Allard groaned when she didn't move quickly enough.

She wanted the taste of him on her tongue as much as he wanted her to continue, but she took her time. Her lips slid across the silky skin of his cock down to the base then up to the head.

Damn, he was big. Not that she expected him to be small, and she'd definitely felt how big he was when he was inside her the day before. But now that she was facing the full size of his cock, she wondered how he was going to fit in her mouth. She'd be lucky if she got a third of the way down his cock before he hit the back of her throat.

A clear drop of pre-cum pooled at the tip of his cock and she lapped at it. She'd had a brief taste the day before, but his sweetness still surprised her. She'd expected salty or even slightly bitter, but Allard tasted wild and fresh. And male.

Her tongue circled the head a few times before returning to flick the tip. Continuing to tease him with what would come later. If he could last that long.

After circling the crown of his cock again with light kisses, she looked up at him as she ran the flat of her tongue along the full length of his cock.

Allard's head was thrown back and the muscles in his neck corded with tension. Even the muscles in his stomach seemed harder than before. As though he struggled against holding his entire body still.

Delia grinned to herself, enjoying the sight of his reaction. She wrapped her mouth around the head of his cock and sucked hard on just the crown.

His fingers combed through her hair and he pulled her away from him. Hungry gold eyes gazed up at her. Allard was a dominant wolf and while he might have let her have her fun for a while, he was done playing. And apparently, so was she.

With a gentle, but firm tug, he guided her up until their noses touched. That was when the gentleness stopped.

Allard rolled her onto her back and slid between her legs. He didn't wait to see if she was ready, he just lined up his cock to her entrance and thrust into her hard and deep. He pulled out completely and slammed into her again.

His cock stabbed into her with each piercing lunge. All of his control was gone, and Delia loved it. She loved the way he filled her and the tight burn that lingered just beneath the growing pleasure from the hard fucking.

And that's exactly what they were doing. Nothing about Allard's driving into her with his hard thrusts resembled their time together the day before.

But Allard needed this. His wolf needed this. And if Delia was honest with herself, she needed this.

Without a word, he pulled out of her, grabbed her by her hips and flipped her over. She didn't even have time to put her arms under her before he lifted her ass up in the air and slammed back inside of her.

Whatever she felt before didn't come close to what he was doing now. His cock conquered and plundered her surrendering body.

Allard's hand circled the back of her neck, pushing her chest and shoulders down and Delia turned her head to the side before the pillow smothered her. She lifted her hips up further by tucking her knees beneath her. His knees pushed between her legs, spreading her further apart and allowing his cock to drive into her even deeper.

Her body responded with each touch, thrust, and exhibition of control with tingles of pleasure.

Allard bent over her, his hands pressing down on hers, keeping her in place. His breath tickled the side of her neck and his groans pulled more pleasure from her.

"Mine."

Her body tightened around his cock and Allard moaned.

"You're so wet, Red. Is this for me?"

She nodded and moaned, not able to form words. What the hell was he doing to her?

"That's right." Allard's soft chuckle sent a shiver down her spine. He pulled out and slammed back into her with each word he spoke.

Her climax approached, the intensity of the pleasure from Allard taking her as hard he was, overwhelmed her until she teetered on the edge. And he knew it too. He redoubled his efforts, claiming her body with each thrust.

Everything tightened inside of her and she exploded, bringing Allard with her over the edge. His teeth clamped down on the flesh between her neck and shoulder and another orgasm ripped through her body as his release flooded into her.

Delia threw her head back and screamed out his name, but Allard silenced her with a kiss.

A final thrust, a reminder, then they collapsed together on the bed.

No one spoke for several minutes and the only sound in the room came from their heavy breathing. Until Allard rolled to his side, brought her with him, and saw the mark on her neck.

"Oh fuck, Delia..."

She heard the regret in his voice and knew the next word out of his mouth would be sorry.

"No." She preempted his apology. When he tried to release her, Delia held his arms in place and pressed her back against his chest. He didn't need to feel guilty for a natural act.

"Delia," he whispered in her ear.

"No sorries. Okay? We'll figure it out, but no sorries."

As long as she never marked him back, it should be all right. Delia had heard about this happening before with extremely dominant males. Instinct took over and their need to claim overrode all reason. None of those stories ever ended with the pair bonding, unless the female made a claiming mark of their own.

It would all be okay.

She hoped.

"Uncle Allard?" The high-pitched voice of a child called through the door.

Allard rolled out of bed and pulled on a pair of loose pajama pants before opening the door. Delia hid under the covers, not knowing where the tee-shirt she'd been wearing earlier landed.

"Whad'ya need, pup?"

"Breakfast." Foster, the youngest member of the pack, nodded vigorously while trying to look around Allard's body without success.

"And your mom or dad can't help with that?" Allard stepped out of the room and closed the door behind them.

They must have headed to the kitchen because Delia didn't hear anything else from them.

She looked over at the clock. 6:29 am. Ugh, way too early by her normal standards, but she had a feeling Broken Peak rose at the crack of dawn on most mornings. She considered rolling over and trying to go back to sleep for another thirty minutes, but her mind was too focused on Allard and the mark he left.

She might as well get up and jump in the shower to start her day. Besides, she never did learn what the mumbo jumbo crap was that Allard mentioned. There was a chance she'd have enough time to corner him, while completely avoiding any conversation about the mark on her neck, and get an answer before Vixen found her.

Once she decided on her plan of action, Delia jumped out of bed, and headed to the closet to find her bathrobe. Bathrobes were easier to run across the hall to the bathroom than in a towel. Plus, she wouldn't have to worry about leaving anything behind.

The only problem with her plan was the time it took to shower. Too much time for her mind to wander and circle around, a rather disconcerting fact.

Delia wasn't upset that Allard marked her. She should have been fighting mad, but a part of her, a much bigger part of her than she wanted to admit, liked that he marked her.

And her wolf hadn't stopped prancing around proud as could be. She also hadn't stopped pestering Delia to let her out so she could run. Preferably, with Allard's wolf. Except that was the last thing they needed. If Delia's wolf claimed Allard's, it would be the same as if Delia marked him herself.

And then where would they be? Bonded under a fake mating to satisfy an arranged mating?

Gah, she needed to stop thinking and focus instead on her plan for the morning. Learn what the mumbo jumbo crap was, talk with Mac, then talk with Vixen and Bray about Spencer Pearce's appearance and what it meant. Her mind got back on track right about the time she rinsed the last of the conditioner from her hair.

Perfect timing. Now all she had to do was figure out if she needed to wear workout clothes or jeans. Jeans, definitely jeans. Workout clothes would only remind Vixen that she wanted Delia to have multiple sessions today.

The morning passed quickly enough.

Once showered and dressed, she headed to the kitchen, but before she could sit down for a quiet conversation with Allard, the rest of the pack filed in. All eyes were on the mark on her neck, but no one said anything. Probably because of Vixen's glare.

As soon as breakfast was over, Bray sent the males off to do whatever it was they did, Eleanor sat Foster down for some school work, Danielle and Maggie wandered off with their heads together, and that left Delia alone, with Vixen and Bray.

Before Vixen even broached the subject of finding Mac, she peppered Delia with question after question about Spencer Pearce. Delia did her best to answer them, but some pieces of the puzzle still seemed to be missing.

Bray kept circling back to the three males at the bar. Everyone was sure that Spencer hadn't known anything about them from his reaction, but that left yet another pack that was circling around Delia and Broken Peak and even more questions.

Finally, an hour later, Delia learned what Allard meant by mumbo jumbo crap.

Mac handed her an old leather-bound journal with specific pages marked and made her read each of those pages.

And the pieces fell into place.

She'd always thought that family legend about the Destined Heir and the Daughter of the Moon was the pinnacle of the Lyall hubris, but she was wrong.

Delia would be more powerful than her brother. Than all the other Alphas even.

She finally put the journal down. She stared at Mac and hoped she hadn't interpreted the journal entry the wrong way. Except she didn't think she had.

"You get it, don'cha?" He carefully lifted the journal from her lap and set it down on the small table in front of his couch. "The others don't. They think it's all about Vixen cause of what she is."

"Is she really a griffin?" Delia glossed over the bit about the Hero supposedly being a griffin and the Rebel having a bit of dragon in her.

"Yep. And she's a weapon fer sure, but she ain't no leader. Not really. She can command and order and sometimes even lead, but she ain't a leader." Mac nodded and stroked his beard. "You are though, Delia Lyall. You're the natural born leader. Joseph saw it too."

"Who's Joseph?"

"The Councilor who came knocking last night. He's a good male, just very tired. And now he's very relieved."

"Why is he relieved?"

"Because, Delia, you're the Crown. You faced down two Councilors, yanked Allard back from the brink of killing another male, and humiliated the brother of an Alpha of a decent sized pack." Mac leaned back against the couch cushion with a satisfied sigh. "Broken Peak might be waiting on one more, but with you here, the Council can retire."

"Yeah, somehow I don't see any of the packs going along with that idea."

"They don't have a choice."

"And the other Councilors? What about them?"

"They'll do what Joseph tells them to do."

Delia considered all she learned from the journals and then read between Mac's lines. The final piece fell into place. "Pearce doesn't want me for his son, does he?"

"Probably not. I'm assuming his family has some history that's been passed down, like all of us."

"But he's mated." Delia chewed on the tip of her thumb. Maybe the fake mating wouldn't solve all their problems.

"For how long? Accidents happen all the time. Just ask Vixen. Before she came here, she was responsible for a lot of accidents."

The mention of the Alpha female's name, jarred some sense back into Delia's thought process. "She's the Alpha of Broken Peak, she should be the Crown."

"Like I said, she ain't no leader. She's the weapon you aim at whatever or whoever you wanna destroy, but she won't be able to compel the others to go along. You and your brother are gonna take care of that." Mac patted her knee in a grandfatherly way. "Besides, you think any shifter is gonna listen to a griffin? A lion? Sure. Bears? Yep. Wolves? Of course, y'all have been the de facto leaders fer some time now. She needs you more than you need her. Which has got to stick her craw something fierce."

"But why is all this happening now?" Delia didn't necessarily believe in the mumbo jumbo crap as Allard called it, but she wasn't willing to toss it all away as a myth or fairy tale either.

"There's a war coming with the humans. Whether it's in months or years, I don't know, but it's coming. If the journals are right, no one was unified during the last war with humans. The shifters could have been, under the Griffins and Dragons, but pettiness and pride got in the way of good sense. The only way we're gonna survive what's coming is if we all stand together. Your brother brings the wolves and you bring the shifters. And the others will follow."

"Others?"

"There are lots of others out there. You read that bit about the Mage and Sage? Danielle and Eleanor both came from that line. Magic exists. Just cause you don't see it doesn't mean it's not there."

"Mindwipers."

"A sort of species of vampires. And, yes, before you ask, there are vampires and witches and wizards. Not quite as numerous, but they're out there."

Delia closed her eyes and took in a deep breath, filling her lungs with much needed oxygen. "That's a lot to swallow."

"Yeah, but you've been ready for this haven't you? Your mother's been sharing stories with you since you were a pup. You're more open to believing than the others. They all came around, eventually, but deep down inside, you know this is right. You know you're where you're supposed to be, and you'd be here even if Allard wasn't."

There it was. She'd been waiting to see how Allard fit into Mac's tale, and it turned out, he didn't.

"That's why you agreed to having the fake ceremony?" The thought didn't make Delia happy. It turned Allard into a pawn, something he didn't deserve.

"Nope, I did that because Vixen asked. Anyone else, and I woulda said no. But that one's always ten steps ahead of everyone else. Even you." Mac stood up and helped Delia to her feet. He led her to the door and practically pushed her outside. Before she walked away, he gave her a slow wink. "She could have handled the Councilors last night, but she let you. Think about that while you head back to the Lodge."

CHAPTER THIRTY-ONE

ALLARD walked into the Lodge and found Delia fast asleep on one of the oversized chairs. Maggie was with her, contorted into a weird shaped ball, but just as asleep as Delia.

Vixen must have worn them out.

As he contemplated how to move one without waking the other, Finley came up behind him and whispered, "they've been out for the past hour."

"That can't be comfortable. We should probably move them."

"What do you think I've been doing since I found them? Every time I try to pick Pocket up, she twists around and just ends up looking more uncomfortable than before."

Allard rolled his eyes at Finley's efforts. It wasn't like Maggie was all that big. He crouched down next to the arm of the chair and ran his fingertips across Delia's shoulder. She moved, but settled right back into place. And Maggie, who he hadn't even gone near, twisted herself around until her knees were practically up to her ears.

"My mate is not normal." Finley stared down at Maggie and shook his head, as though he couldn't believe what he was seeing.

Allard leaned close and whispered softly in her ear, "Red, you need to wake up. You don't want to sleep here all night, do you?"

"Hm?" She woke up enough to rub the back of her hand across her nose.

He gave up trying to wake her gently and resorted to scooping her up. He thought for sure she'd at least open her eyes, but instead, she snuggled in closer to him. She nuzzled her cheek against his chest and her hair fell away and the mark on her neck was even more obvious than it had been at breakfast.

Fuck.

How had he lost control like that? Even when he was young, he kept a tight rein on his wolf. Biting her was inexcusable.

Not that he regretted marking her though. He definitely didn't regret it after Spencer Pearce showed up. Allard had half a mind to take her back into town to The Dirty Whistle and make sure those three males showed up and saw his mark as well.

"Come on, Red, let's get you into the shower then bed."

Delia mumbled something under her breath, but Allard couldn't make out the words.

"My mate is not normal." Finley repeated his previous statement and Allard glanced over at him.

Maggie was now sprawled across the chair, her body spreading to take up every square inch of the piece of furniture.

"Good luck." Allard chuckled and carried Delia down the hallway toward their room.

Their room?

Since when had his room become their room?

Since he marked her.

Fuck.

When he and Eleanor had spoken about Vixen's plans backfiring, he didn't think they were talking about his marking Delia.

She finally woke up when he walked into the bathroom. He set her down on the toilet and she rubbed her eyes while he turned on the shower and adjusted the temperature.

"Big day?"

Delia nodded. "Vixen ran us until I finally collapsed. Maggie was still bouncing around though. She's like the Energizer Bunny, isn't she?"

"Wait 'til you meet her raccoon. For being as small as she is, she packs a huge punch."

Once the water was warm enough, Allard nodded to the shower. "Hop in, you'll feel better after the hot water hits your shoulders. I'll grab you a towel."

"Bathrobe."

"What?"

"My bathrobe please. It's in the closet."

"Sure. Okay."

Allard raced out of there before Delia happened to glance in the mirror and saw the reminder of his lack of control. They still hadn't talked about it since Foster conveniently interrupted them this morning. Frankly, Allard was kind of happy with her ignoring it.

As he stared at Delia's clothes filling his closet, he found himself smiling.

Yeah, they might be fake mates, but if their mating hadn't been arranged, and he'd met Delia at some event, he'd have wanted to spend time with her. Shit, he could even imagine being mated to her for real.

She fit into the pack, got along with everyone, even Maggie, who tended to push more than a few of them past their patience's breaking point.

Sure, she might have been the crown princess of the Chicago Pack, but you'd never know it. She hadn't complained about anything, not even Vixen's workouts. Shit, he'd dragged her to what might have been the worst dive bar he'd ever stepped foot in and she hadn't even flinched. Not to mention what she was like in bed.

He grabbed her robe from the hanger along with the massive towel hanging from one of the hooks. The more skin she covered between bathroom and bedroom, the better.

That was another thing. Delia hadn't whined to anyone about having to share a bathroom. Hell, even some of the guys complained about it, but not Delia.

Fuck.

Why did their mating have to be arranged?

Allard hadn't been lying when he told her he would mate her if it didn't have anything to do with the arrangement. He just hadn't planned on enjoying her company as much as he did though, or on wanting her to stick around Broken Peak.

Or wishing that Mac lied and the fake mating ceremony wasn't all that fake after all.

Shit.

How much time had he spent staring at her clothes in the closet? Delia had probably finished her shower already. He raced out of the room with her robe and towel in hand.

"Red, it's Allard. I'm coming in." He yelled through the door, but if she was still in the shower, she might not hear him. Cracking the door, he stuck his head in. "Red?"

"Yeah?"

"It's me."

"Okay?"

"I'm coming in." He didn't wait for a response, just pushed through the door.

A bare arm pushed through the curtain and Allard almost dropped the towel and robe to join her under the water. He handed over the towel first and soon after, she turned the water off. Delia's arm came out from behind the curtain again and he gave her the robe.

When she finally emerged from the shower, all fresh and clean with pink cheeks from the heat of the water, she had the robe tied securely in place and the towel wrapped around her head and holding her wet hair in place.

"Better?" Allard asked, unable to pull his gaze away from her.

She nodded, but her eyes were still heavy with sleep.

"Come on, let's get you to bed before you crash." He held his hand out to her, and she took it.

"Vixen is evil."

"Yeah, you and Maggie looked worn out. But why didn't you lie down on the couch?"

"Chair was closer."

She stumbled along behind him and Allard took pity on her. Even though it wasn't far to his bedroom, poor Delia looked ready to fall over. He pulled her closer and swung her up into his arms.

"Mmm, nice." Delia rubbed her nose against his chest and Allard chuckled.

"The free ride?"

"Your smell."

Whoa. Delia got honest when sleepy. Allard would have to keep that in mind.

"Glad you like it, Red." He stepped into the bedroom and kicked the door closed behind him, then carefully locked it.

"Do you like my smell?"

Allard growled low. Damn, how did he answer that question? Fuck yes, he liked her scent. He loved her scent.

She didn't even have to be in the same room with him for her scent to get him hard. He'd run by Mac's to pick up some books for Eleanor and Delia's scent lingered from her visit earlier in the day. Hello awkward hard-on.

Standing over the bed, he gently lowered her to the mattress. The robe fell open, revealing her long legs and their smooth skin. His fingers itched to touch her.

"Do you?" She asked.

"Do I what, Red?"

"Like how I smell?" She turned on her side and tucked her legs up closer to her chest.

"Yeah, Red, I do."

"Come here." Delia patted the space on the bed next to her. "Don't go."

"Wasn't planning on it, Red." He swung around the foot of the bed to the other side, the side she usually slept in, and tossed the blanket over on top of Delia before sitting down on the bed so his legs stretched out in front of him and his back against the wall.

Which turned out to be a rather uncomfortable position. He pulled the pillow out from under his ass and slipped it between his back and the wall.

Better, but now what? No way he'd last long lying in bed with her and twiddling his thumbs. And he wasn't tired enough to sleep. If he waited until she fell fully asleep, he could sneak out and grab a book or something and be back before she woke.

Delia flopped over onto her stomach, throwing an arm and leg over Allard. Okay then. Sneaking out just went out the window.

"Stay."

"I am, Red." He dropped his arm down on her back and drew random shapes over her back. "I am."

"What if the mumbo jumbo isn't bullshit?" She sounded more awake than before, but sleep lingered in the rasp of her voice.

"Talked to Mac?"

"Yeah."

"And what if it isn't bullshit, Red?"

"I asked you."

Allard gave her a soft laugh. "We've been here for years before Vixen came and Mac never shared anything about this Sentinel bullshit with us."

"That's what we are? Sentinels?"

"We? Are you buying into it?"

"I don't know. But some shifters do."

"Why are you sure about that?"

"They want me, Allard, they don't want the daughter of an Alpha. They believe in the mumbo jumbo, or their version of it, and they want me because of it."

Allard growled. Over his dead body would they ever get her.

"Thank you." Her small hand, the one attached to the arm covering his stomach, patted his body. "Now I know why Vixen has been running me ragged. So I can handle myself."

Had he said that out loud?

Shit.

Fake mate! She was his fake mate! Not his mate and certainly not the fated mates they pretended they were.

She lifted her chest and tilted her head back so she could see his face and his heart thudded hard against the inside of his chest. With her red hair and the way the light from the dresser shone at the back of her head she looked like she had a halo, or a crown. Yeah, definitely more crown than halo, considering what she was capable of in the bedroom.

"What's on your mind, Red?"

"What happens if I stay here? I mean between us?"

Fuck. What did happen if she stuck around? No way he'd be able to handle seeing her with another male. But it wasn't like he could just tell her that. Hey, Red, I know this is fake and all, but I will kill any male who looks twice at you, so if you stay, it will be with me, in my room, in my bed, and as my fake mate.

He supposed he could say those words, but Delia was fierce. He'd seen her rip apart Spencer Pearce with just the tip of her tongue and really didn't want to experience that himself. She would rip him a new asshole if he even hinted that there might be conditions to her staying around longer than planned.

"We'll figure it out, Red."

The hand on her back slipped down over her hip to her leg, the one over his own legs and encountered bare skin.

His cock jerked at the reminder she was bare under that robe of hers. Completely bare.

Her gaze hadn't left his, and she hadn't pulled away.

His fingertips danced around to the inside of her thigh and skirted their way up until he touched the bare lips of her pussy. Delia's eyes flashed a brilliant gold before returning to their bright green. The thought that her wolf was so close turned him on even more.

His fingers brushed against the wet seam and Delia let out a soft moan.

"You're gonna make that noise for me again, Red." Allard rolled her over to her back and slid down her body until he was planted between her legs with his broad shoulders pushing her thighs apart.

He lowered his head and ran his nose up and down her lips, plump with arousal. With each breath, he took in more of her scent, a heady combination of wildflowers and arousal.

God yes, she wanted him as much as he wanted her.

His tongue found her clit, and he licked, circled and teased her.

The moans coming from her grew in volume until they became whimpers. It wouldn't take long to bring her over the edge, and he had no intention of making her wait. One finger slid inside her, and when her warm heat constricted around him, he added two more. Turning his hand so his palm faced up, he curled his fingers and pressed against her G-spot. Each swipe of his fingers matched the movements of his tongue.

Delia exploded. Her body vibrated with tension as her orgasm rolled through her body.

Allard didn't stop. He pulled her through the first wave and brought her right to the edge of a second. Just as she came to the brink and her pussy gripped his fingers so tightly, he thought she might break them, he broke away from her. Kneeling between her legs, he pushed her thighs further apart while working on the button and zipper of his jeans.

As soon as his cock escaped its confines, he lined up the head with her entrance and thrust into her.

Fuck, even with the orgasm she was tight.

Delia's legs tightened around his waist and Allard gripped her hips, lifting her up so the next thrust went deeper than before.

He moved inside her with slow sure strokes until they both fell over the edge together. Rolling onto his side, he took her with him. While he stroked her silk clad back and she petted his arms, they let sleep overtake them.

CHAPTER THIRTY-TWO

OVER time, Delia's body became habituated to Vixen's workouts. She still resented the fact that Maggie seemed to have more energy than the Energizer Bunny and could run circles around Delia while they ran through the forest on their daily runs that had turned into twice daily runs.

She also got used to the scents from the other shifters that lingered in the forest. Occasionally, Delia might glimpse one of the mountain lions who seemed to shadow them on their runs, but she hadn't met one of them yet. Even though she wanted to. She also wanted to see Vixen's griffin, but Allard, Maggie, and Finley assured her that waiting to see the legendary beast was a good thing and not because Vixen didn't trust her.

The best part about the workouts though, was that Delia let her wolf run afterwards. She didn't trust her wolf to get close to Allard's and hadn't participated in any of the pack outings, but that didn't mean she had to keep her wolf locked inside.

During one of these runs with Maggie's raccoon, who was even more hyper than Maggie, Delia's wolf came across a scent she didn't recognize. Her wolf growled.

Wolf.

Maggie scampered up a tree, chittering out a warning. From above them, in the sky, came a screech that nearly shattered her wolf's eardrums. And from her left and right, the eerie screams of mountain lions echoed through the woods.

Her wolf wanted to follow the strange scent, and it was all Delia could do to hold her back. Yeah, she had a small army surrounding her, but it didn't mean Delia was safe. Vixen's training had taught her that. No matter how strong Delia thought she was, there was always someone stronger. She learned it was usually Vixen, but Delia wasn't about to take a chance.

She urged her wolf to circle around and head back to the Lodge. The mountain lions patrolling the territory would take care of the intruder if he didn't heed the warnings.

Once back at the edge of the yard, she shifted back and pulled on her clothes she left in a neat pile on a large rock. Maggie was close behind her.

"Oh, wow. Vixen's out." Maggie craned her neck back and scanned the sky. "She doesn't like whoever is here."

Delia followed Maggie's gaze and looked up, hoping to catch sight of the griffin. "I don't think anyone out there does."

Maggie hopped around the edge of the yard, as though she might see Vixen's griffin if she was a few inches taller.

"Um, Mags?"

Maggie paused mid jump and looked over her shoulder at Delia. "Mags? I like that. You can call me Mags. Best friends have nicknames, right? I'm calling you Del. Do you like that? Or Lia? No, Del is better."

Delia closed her eyes for a moment and channeled all the lessons on decorum from her mother to keep herself from laughing at the little raccoon shifter. "Del is fine. But the males are all on the porch and Finley looks about ready to kill everyone who can see you. You might want to get dressed."

"Oh." Maggie turned and waved at Finley with a giggle before grabbing her clothes and dressing.

Once dressed, the females headed towards the porch and the males waiting for them. Halfway there, Finley and Allard broke from the others and closed the distance between them at a full run.

Allard was full of tension, but it didn't detract from how hot he was. With his blue eyes scanning the horizon for any threat, and his muscles coiled and ready to pounce beneath the tight fitting henley he wore, Delia wanted to climb up his body and urge him to his room.

"You good?" He asked as soon as he got close enough to pull her into a tight embrace.

"We're fine." Delia wrapped her arms around his waist and rubbed her cheek across his chest. Soothing both male and wolf. "Whoever was out there never got close and ran off when everyone announced their presence."

"Vixen took off and shifted so fast, we weren't sure what was happening." Finley explained the males' presence on the porch.

The Alpha female had scented the intruder before Delia's wolf noticed? No wonder Vixen was so convinced the Broken Peak Pack's size wouldn't matter in a war between packs. An alarm system like that would make it impossible for anyone to sneak up on them.

"You didn't shift." Delia lifted her face and looked up at Allard. "None of you did. Why?"

"We have humans here and a pup. Between Gareth's clan, Roose, and Vixen, we have enough time to wait and see what's going on before we react." Allard's hands roamed along her back and hips and ass, needing the touch to keep his wolf in check.

Finley snorted. "That and Bray forbade it. Allard's wolf running through the woods after you would have gotten Vixen's griffin riled up. And the last thing we need to do is explain to the Council why there's a shifter on our land with his head ripped off."

Delia's eyes widened at the admission before she carefully schooled her expression. Shifters trespassing on a pack's territory usually ended up near dead or dead, but never without their heads.

"Bray, Mac, and I are going to town to meet with the Council and show them the mating ceremony documents." Allard tucked Delia against his side and drew back to the porch. "You're going to stay here with the others. And not leave the Lodge."

She should really be at the meeting with them, since her name was scribbled all over those documents. It was on the tip of Delia's tongue to protest, but then reason kicked in. If she was right and some packs wanted her because of who she was supposed to be, Broken Peak was safer. Yeah, it grated on her that she couldn't be there to see Spencer Pearce's face when she kicked him out of the room because he had no right to demand to see the documents, but she couldn't put the rest of the pack in danger.

And she would if she demanded on accompanying Allard. Either the entire pack would have to follow them into town or they would have to split in half and leave the territory less protected. Even with help from Broken Peak's allies, it would put the entire pack at risk.

"When are you leaving?"

"As soon as Vixen gets back."

"How long will you be gone?" Yeah, Delia knew she teetered on the edge of nagging, but her wolf's anxiety pushed its way into her thoughts.

What if something happened while he was away? What if it ended up being a trap? Had they given Spencer Pearce too much time between the visit from the Council members and showing them the documents? What if he called in reinforcements?

It wasn't just Delia who was in danger, so was Allard. If Allard was removed, then Delia would once again be available.

"A few hours at most. We'll show them the ceremony document, and Mac and Bray will probably sign something. Once the Council members are satisficd, wc'll come back."

"You'll call when you get there and when you're coming back?" Full-on nagging mode had been engaged. Try as she might to avoid it, Delia had turned into the type of female she despised. The ones who hounded their mates about the tiniest details.

"Yeah, Red, I will." Allard kissed the top of her head and squeezed her shoulder as they mounted the steps of the porch. "Come on, lets get inside. Jackson and Leighton are about to lose their shit that they can't see their mates, but they won't go inside until we do."

They all traipsed inside. Allard kept his arm around Delia so they had to squeeze through the door together. Finley did the same with Maggie. Once the door was closed and locked behind them, Jackson and Leighton took off down the hallway. Leighton to find his mate and Jackson to find his family.

Bray turned to Allard. "Once Vixen's back, we need to head out."

"Got it." Allard walked past Bray and led Delia down to the kitchen. "Keep the phone Danielle gave you on hand."

She reached into her back pocket and pulled out a phone that must still be in prototype stages since she hadn't seen it on the market yet. "I know. It's been drilled into me to never go anywhere without it."

"We'll have to make a harness for your wolf so she can carry it with her when you shift."

As soon as they stepped into the kitchen, Allard gently set Delia down in a chair then headed to the fridge where he proceeded to pull out half its contents.

"I'm not hungry."

"You will be. The adrenaline from the intruder will wear off in a bit and then you'll be starving. You'll also crash pretty hard." He fixed up a plate full of cold cuts and cheese. All foods high in fat and protein.

"I know how adrenaline works," she smiled at Allard's back when he picked through the container of fresh fruit to find the best pieces for her. "What happened out there didn't get my adrenaline going. There was no fight or flight instinct kicking in."

"You sure about that, Red?" He set the plate down in front of her and sat next to her, prepared to watch her eat.

"Fight might have kicked in, but I didn't let it take over." She humored him and wrapped a piece of salami around some cheese then popped it into her mouth.

Her brother did the same thing with Geneva whenever something big happened. The need to take care and nurture overwhelmed him until Geneva gave in. She swore she went up two sizes since mating Lennon.

The sound of the front door opening and closing carried down to the kitchen and Allard's head snapped up to watch the doorway.

A few seconds later Bray and Vixen appeared.

"Mac's meeting you by the garage and he's impatient as hell. He could give Maggie a run for her money." Vixen's eyes flickered between Allard and Delia. "You did good out there, Delia, turning around like that."

Delia smiled under Vixen's praise and her wolf's chest filled with pride, as if it was all her wolf's doing and Delia hadn't forced the beast to turn away from the strange scent.

When Allard hadn't stood right away, Bray cleared his throat. "C'mon let's get going unless you want to listen to Mac complaining during the entire drive."

Allard waited for Delia to take another bite before he finally pushed away from the table.

"Make sure you both are fully equipped before you leave."

"We will." Both Bray and Allard spoke at the same time. As though their response to Vixen had been repeated so often that it had turned into a routine.

"Come on, Delia, we'll walk them out."

Allard growled low, but said nothing. Instead of heading out the front door like Delia expected, they turned down the hallway that housed her makeshift closet and the smaller rooms that served as offices.

"We're going to have to do some expanding, Bray." Vixen mused as they followed the hallway to its end.

"We'll figure it out."

Bray opened the door and revealed a room filled with weapons and, was that body armor? Across the room was another door. This looked to be reinforced with steel and had no less than three locks and deadbolts that Delia could see.

While the males grabbed their weapons and pulled on the heavy clothing, Vixen began the process of unlocking the massive door. By the time she finished the males were ready to leave.

Before Allard left, he stepped in front of Delia. He reached for her head, tilting her back and, bending his head down until his lips met hers. Then, in front of Bray and Vixen, he kissed her. And not a light peck either, but one of his patented toe curling, spine tingling kisses that sent shock waves through her entire body.

When he stepped away from her, it was all Delia could do not to fall over.

"Don't leave Vixen's side." Allard growled low in her ear and his voice sent another wave of tingling through her body.

Bray and Allard left and Vixen locked the door behind them. Once she was satisfied the door was secure, she turned back to Delia with a knowing smirk.

"Don't say it." Delia held her palm up.

"Wasn't going to."

"Is that a rocket launcher?" Delia had never actually seen one outside of movies, but hanging on the wall was what looked like a small cannon.

"Yep." Vixen grinned. "And we even have a helicopter in the garage."

"So you have what amounts to a small armory?"

"No. It's a larger armory. We can easily hunker down here for over a year. Food will get kind of boring, but we have the supplies for that too." Vixen nodded to the open door that led back to the hallway they came down.

"Will you ever teach me how to fire that rocket launcher?"

Delia stepped out of the room and Vixen came out behind her, locking that door as well. Which made sense. Between Foster and Maggie, the pack needed to be careful about keeping curious hands away from the weapons inside that room.

"Someday, but you know, I'm not sure you're supposed to be an expert with weapons." Vixen strode down the hallway and Delia hurried to stay even with her.

"You mean, what Mac and I talked about?"

"Think about it from a pack's perspective. Would you rather deal with a general or a diplomat?"

"You're the general and I'm the diplomat. Or at least that's what you and Mac believe, right?"

"You didn't answer my question," Vixen led Delia back into the kitchen and gestured to the plate full of food.

Great, Vixen was going to pick up on Allard's eating thing.

Delia sat down and picked at the fruit. "I thought I did."

"No, you answered with another question. Which is definitely diplomatic." Vixen sat across from her.

"If you're so convinced I'm supposed to be a diplomat, why have you been killing me with the daily workouts?" Delia leaned back in her chair and nibbled on a piece of cheese.

"The last thing I want is for any of you to have to fight your way out of a corner. If I can drill it into your bodies to run to safety, then I don't have to worry about your well-being while taking care of the problem."

"And the` males here? Or Maggie?"

"Maggie has skills that none of the boys here at Broken Peak have, and I have no problem exploiting them." Vixen reached across the table and snatched one of the slices of meat. "And I have no problem exploiting your skills either."

"But my skills aren't physical." Delia narrowed her eyes at Vixen. "Mac said you were always several steps ahead of everyone else. I don't think I fully comprehended his words."

"Oh?" Vixen asked with a smile.

"When the Council members showed up."

Vixen nodded. "Go on."

"You knew no matter what you said, it wouldn't change Spencer's mind."

Another nod.

"You could have handled them with weapons or threat of violence, but you didn't. You waited for me to come out there."

The smile on Vixen's face grew even larger, and the nodding hadn't stopped.

"Were you waiting to see how they'd react to me?" Delia cocked her head to the side and studied Vixen. "No. You knew how they'd react. It wasn't about you or me, it was about them. You wanted Spencer Pearce to witness you deferring to me."

"Want something to drink?" Vixen winked at Delia as she stood and walked to the fridge.

A drink was the last thing on Delia's mind. She ignored the offer and even the bottle of water Vixen placed in front of her. Delia's thoughts ricocheted off of one another until they fell into place. It was like a giant game of chess had been played out and she was only now realizing where everyone fit. "You're the queen, but I'm the king."

"Very good, Delia." Vixen opened her bottle of water and took a sip. "And what is the queen's job?"

"To protect the king."

"And the king's job?"

"The endgame. His power doesn't appear until the endgame."

"You're the endgame, Delia. You and, to a lesser extent, your brother. If we lose either of you before then, the game is over. For all of us."

CHAPTER THIRTY-THREE

ALLARD wished he was the one behind the wheel and not Bray.

As they drove out of War and back to Broken Peak, the rundown houses faded into the dense forest. The towering pines bowed from the winds and leaned into the highway. Except Allard couldn't care less about the passing scenery.

The only thing he cared about was getting home. To Delia.

The meeting with the two Council members had progressed smoothly without questions or hints of doubt at the authenticity of the documentation for the ceremony. They didn't even glance twice at the document Mac provided.

Although Mac and Joseph had spoken quietly with one another, the female, Colleen, had sat with Bray and Allard around the small table and said nothing. She hadn't even tried to fill the silence with small talk.

Whatever happened next was in the hands of the Council. Leaving the small restaurant they had met at, Allard put the concerns about the other packs behind him and focused on the Broken Peak Pack's future and how his fake mate might fit into it.

When they finally reached the turnoff that would take them down a logging road and to the massive garage that housed the pack's vehicles, and Vixen's new toy, Allard nearly told Bray to stop there so he could shift and take a direct path to the Lodge. But that would mean leaving behind all the equipment he'd taken with him and Vixen would probably punish him for not taking care of it the way he should have.

As soon as Bray pulled into the garage, which seemed like four hours since they turned off the highway, Allard was out of the SUV and heading toward the back tunnel into the Lodge.

Hopefully his Alpha called ahead for Vixen to unlock the door or he'd be forced to take the longer way around to the front door. And then he'd still have to double back to the equipment room to drop off the weapons and body armor.

Bray caught up with him before he got to the tunnel entrance, but Mac wasn't with him. He must have gone back to his cabin.

"That went better than expected." Bray punched in some numbers on the keypad and pressed his thumb against the scanner. As soon as he was recognized, the locks released, and the door slid open.

"Pearce wasn't there to smell up the place." Allard stepped into the darkened tunnel, lit only by the flickering yellow light bulbs hanging from the ceiling. "You let Vixen know we're back?"

"Yeah. And you might want to check your phone. Don't think Delia's too happy with you. Something about you not calling her."

Allard pulled out his phone, and sure enough, a text message from Delia waited for him.

'Bray called Vixen, so I'm assuming you aren't dead.'

Shit. He'd completely forgotten he promised to call her and let her know they were on their way back. He might have also forgotten the call saying they arrived safely.

His thumb flicked across the screen and he pressed the small phone icon next to her name. It didn't even ring once before she answered.

"Now, you're calling? After I spent the entire time wondering whether you were lying in a ditch somewhere?" Her words might have been chastising, but her tone wasn't. In fact, he even detected a trace of laughter.

"My mind was preoccupied." Wasn't a great excuse, but it was a reason.

The massive door that blocked the tunnel from the interior of the equipment room swung open and Delia's red hair glowed in the golden light like a beacon, calling him home.

Allard hurried along the tunnel, unfastening the gear from his body to make stripping it and returning the weapons to their proper place — something Vixen had drilled into them since her arrival — less time consuming. If he could have stripped out of the armored shirt, he would have done that on the run too, but that would probably end up with him running into a wall and risking a concussion. Wouldn't that be perfect? Making it to War and back without a scratch, and getting hurt as soon as he got home. His packmates would never let him live it down.

Her slightly worried expression changed into a welcoming smile as she watched his approach.

When he got close enough, he pulled her into his arms and kissed her. Not a nice good to see you kiss either. His tongue swept between her lips, seeking entrance and his Red obliged. By the time he finished, they were both out of breath.

"Bedroom. Now." Delia's hungry gaze took him in, like she couldn't get enough of him.

"Too far." Allard already had his weapons back in their place, but was struggling with the snug fit of the shirt meant to dissipate the force of any bullets aimed at his chest and back.

Delia helped as best she could, but the carbon fibers in the fabric made it impossible to pull it off in a rush. Too bad the carbon fibers made it impossible to cut through, because Allard was certainly close to the point of grabbing one of the knives off the wall and using it on the shirt. Finally, his wrist popped free and the damn thing was off. Delia was busy hanging it back up while Allard straightened the clothing still on his body.

"C'mon." He grabbed her by the wrist and pulled her out of the weapons' room. The closest room, where he knew they wouldn't be interrupted, was the one they used for her closet. Not the most romantic of places, but Allard didn't care. He'd make it up to her later.

"Don't we need to lock the equipment room door?" Delia raced to keep up with his long strides.

"Bray's coming, he'll lock things up."

He pulled her into the room filled with her clothes and shut the door behind them. He didn't bother turning on the light and better yet, Delia didn't seem bothered by the location since she reached down between them to unfasten his jeans.

Her hand wrapped around his cock and he swore she whined.

"Red, I'm not gonna last long if you keep touching me like that." He nipped at her neck and worked his hands down to her jeans. "You know, a skirt wouldn't be a bad thing right about now. You should start wearing them more often."

While he considered all the benefits of skirts, the two of them got her jeans down far enough to take off one of the legs. And whad'ya know, her panites came down too. Good. He wouldn't have to worry about tearing the fancy lace.

Allard's hands slid back up her legs and around to her ass and lifted her up.

"Wait."

"What do you mean wait?" Allard bit back the curse that almost came out. "Why wait? I can't wait, Red. This is already too long for me."

"Watch the clothes."

"Red." He pressed his lips against her neck and nipped at the skin. "You're killing me."

However, he did turn them around so her back was against the door and then slid into her. They both groaned as his cock filled her.

Her legs wrapped around his waist and with her arms tight around his neck, she moved her hips back and forth.

"Please."

"Please what, Red?"

"Please more."

And of course he obliged. He could take his time later on, back in their bedroom, but right now he needed to be inside her and she needed it too. It didn't take long before both of them were balancing on the edge. Allard reached between them and pressed his fingertip against her clit.

Delia went over first, her pussy tightening around him and bringing him along with her.

She pressed her forehead against his shoulder and took a deep breath then smacked his shoulder. Hard.

"Ow. What was that for?" Allard would have reached over and rubbed his shoulder, but that would have meant letting her go and pulling out of her. Something he wasn't willing to do just yet.

"Next time. Call." She smacked his shoulder a second time. "Now, put me down before Maggie gets it into her head that she needs to come and check on my clothes again."

Allard chuckled and eased her down to her feet. "Again?"

"She's convinced they might get lonely if they don't have regular visitors." Delia hopped around while pulling her panties and jeans up.

He tucked himself away and quietly wished the lights were on so he could have a clear view of her dance.

"Okay," she patted his arm. "All set."

"She really comes and checks on the clothes?" Allard opened the door and peeked down the hallway, checking to see if anyone was out there to witness their escape.

"Yep. Sometimes three times a day. And gives me reports on how my clothes are doing. She thinks they might be feeling neglected and wants me to consider rotating them with the clothes in the closet in our bedroom."

Our.

She called his bedroom, our. As in theirs. As in not his alone.

"Come on, Red." Allard grinned at her and pulled her down the hallway. "We need to get you some food."

"I just ate, like right before you left."

"Yeah, and I plan on spending a long night keeping you up, so you need to load up on carbs."

ALLARD WOKE UP TO A gently snoring Delia and carefully rolled out of bed so as not to wake her. After the marathon sex the night before, she was worn out and his wolf was proud as hell.

Breakfast. He'd fix her a nice tray of food, bring it back, and then they could replay some of last night's more interesting events. Since he planned on coming back to the room, getting dressed for the day wasn't a concern. Instead, he pulled on a pair of flannel pajama pants and left Delia to her morning dreams.

It was early enough that he didn't expect anyone to be in the kitchen yet, but Finley was sitting at the table eating a big bowl of Frosted Flakes.

"How are you and Delia doing?" Finley asked between a giant mouthful of sugary goodness.

"Good." Allard studied the contents of the fridge.

"Just good? She's fitting in here real well. And Maggie can't stop talking about her." Finley smirked as he scooped up another giant spoonful. "If Delia wasn't a female, I'd be jealous."

"Well, don't worry. Once we get things settled with the packs, she'll probably be on her way."

"Even with the mumbo jumbo from Mac and Vixen?"

"Especially with that." Finding what he wanted, Allard pulled the food out and set it on the counter. "Besides, it's all just fake. Remember? None of it is real. Not the fated mates shit, not the ceremony, nothing."

"You two seem to be spending a lot of time together for it all to be fake."

"Well that's all it is. Fake." Allard turned with a tray full of food and found Delia standing in the doorway dressed in her workout gear. Which, by the way, was totally hot on her. It didn't hide any of her sweet curves or those legs of hers that drove him crazy just imagining them wrapped around his waist.

Fuuuuck.

He almost asked how much she heard. Almost. But he didn't need to. Her expression gave truth to whatever answer she might have said. Delia heard it all.

Sure, they hadn't really talked about it since they held the ceremony, and Allard had just been going along with the ride. Or at least that's what he tried to tell himself.

Except he couldn't fake his need to keep her safe or her worrying about him last night.

They needed to have a chat about their future and how he wasn't ready for it to all end in a few weeks. He planned on doing that right after he fed her, but then Finely had to play the investigative reporter and ask his questions. And Delia had to overhear Allard's answers.

Fuck. Fuck. Fuck. Fuck.

Delia said nothing for a moment, just looked between Finley and Allard. Finally, after an eternity, she uttered an excruciatingly fake 'good morning' then turned and jogged down the hallway to the front of the Lodge.

"Fuck."

"Fix it. Fix it before Vixen and Bray figure out you broke it."

Yeah, Allard planned on it, but it was easier said than done.

CHAPTER THIRTY-FOUR

DELIA did her best to avoid Allard the entire day and was mostly successful. Maggie didn't realize it, but she had been instrumental in running interference. Normally, Delia might have experienced a bit of guilt for using her new friend that way, but the hurt from Allard's words that morning erased all the guilt with a single clean swipe.

Since that first night, when they agreed to the fake mating and the fake ceremony, neither of them had really talked about what would happen after the Council members left town. That was entirely on her. She should have forced him to sit down and talk about their expectations after the first time they made love.

No. They didn't make love. They had sex.

It was just a friends with benefits kind of thing and that's all Allard wanted. So that's all she wanted too.

That left only two obstacles in her Avoiding Allard All Day plan. Where she was going to sleep for the night and the barbecue Vixen declared the pack would have that night with all their allies. Who had a barbecue outside in January? It wasn't like West Virginia was far enough south to be warm in January. It might not be as cold as Chicago in winter, but War wasn't the tropics either.

"And so, you need a good hidey-hole. Without a hidey-hole all your treasures can be found." Maggie was currently explaining the benefits of what she termed a hidey-hole, but was really more of a stash where she and her raccoon stashed all the things they pilfered. "And Vixen's getting better at finding them, so I was thinking, I could borrow a corner of the apartment you have for your clothes?"

"Hm? Sure, that's fine." Delia hadn't really been listening, she was too busy not getting caught watching Allard, who was coming out of the woods and heading right towards them. Evasive maneuvers were required, and that's where Maggie came in again. "Why don't we head there now and we can pick something out to wear tonight."

Delia was getting tired of jeans or the running pants she had been wearing. Why not change things up for the barbecue? Besides, it wasn't like she had to worry about Allard thinking she was too snobby for Broken Peak, being that he was just her fake mate.

"Oh, and you know what we should do? We should bring some of your clothes from the closet to the apartment so they can visit with their friends." Maggie suddenly stopped hopping around and planted herself in front of Delia with her hands on her hips. "Did you say we? Like, as in me and you, we? Or Danielle and Eleanor and me, we?"

"Um, you?" Delia brushed past Maggie, not wanting to give Allard the chance to catch up.

"Oh, you really are my best friend, Del. Best friends share clothes. I read that in a book I heard." Maggie hurried after her and beat her to the makeshift closet. "Okay, you go in and I'm going to your room to pick some clothes to visit. I swear I won't touch anything else."

"That's fine." Delia stood in the center of the small room and stared at the clothes, pointedly ignoring the door where, just the night before she'd been pushed up against while Allard filled her so completely it was almost as though they fit perfectly together. Like they were made for each other.

DELIA SMOOTHED THE FABRIC OF the thin wool skirt down over her hips and wondered who came up with the great idea of wearing it to a barbecue. Oh, that's right. She did. With a little help from Maggie.

At least a little common sense prevailed, and she wore a pair of boots that went up to her knees, so at least her legs weren't completely bare. A heavy wool sweater complemented the look and did double duty in keeping her warm.

Maggie, though, had taken a different approach. She claimed it was so none of the clothes felt left out, and in Maggie's world, it probably made perfect sense. To the rest of the world, the little female was layered in clothes. Jeans under a skirt and blouse under a dress all topped off with not one, but two sweaters. She'd been contemplating how to wear two pairs of shoes before Delia finally stepped in and explained shoes preferred a solitary life and were the loners of the fashion world.

The sad thing was that Maggie didn't look out of place surrounded by the entirety of the Broken Peak Pack and all their friends. Five of whom could have all been on the covers on the Sports Illustrated bathing suit edition in the 90s. Those blond females, who could have doubled for the Swedish Bikini team from that beer ad during the same time, turned out to be the mountain lion shifters.

Delia, on the other hand, stuck out like a sore thumb.

But all that was okay, because sitting in front of her, along with the stack of burgers Bray had grilled up, was a big glass of Mac's moonshine.

Her fourth, assuming her brain functioned enough to still count right.

Might as well not let it go to waste. Just as she reached out for it, another hand came from the side and pushed it away. A large hand belonging to a male. A hand she'd recognize anywhere. How the hell could someone recognize hands? Was that even possible?

"Hey, that was mine."

"Yeah, and you've already had more than you should. Eat a burger." Allard growled low in her ear.

When had he sat next to her? She had been very careful to sit between Danielle and Mag-

Hey, where had Maggie gone? Traitor.

"I'm foon. I mean feen. I'm feen, see?"

Except she wasn't fine, and she knew it since the world had slowly tilted to the side. How everyone else managed to stay upright was a mystery to her, but she didn't have time to worry about that. She was more concerned about how a wall suddenly appeared in the middle of the yard, right when she needed it most.

"Magic." Except it didn't come out as the word magic, it was more of a slurry of consonants.

Shit on a brick. The moonshine was stronger than she remembered.

Delia giggled and then she was moving. Floating away from the table and back to the Lodge.

"Hey!"

"It's time for bed, Red."

"No. There's more moonshine left. And friends to talk with." Or at least that's what she thought she said. She wasn't sure about the order of the words as they came out of her mouth. "And burgers."

Maybe she'd close her eyes though. Just for a second. Or a minute.

Approximately 720 minutes later, Delia opened her eyes. And then closed them again. The room was dark, but it didn't matter. The sliver of light that slipped in through the bottom of the door was enough to send her head into a throbbing mess.

Shit.

What had she done last night? A quick survey of her body showed no signs of bruises or scratches. That was good.

But crap, what had she said? And in front of everyone? Oh, this was bad. This was bad on so many levels there was only one possible remedy. Pull the covers over her head and go back to sleep. If she was lucky, the world would come to a crashing end and she wouldn't have to face anyone.

The worst part about the whole thing though wasn't the headache or the fear that she might have said something horrible enough that she couldn't take back, but that she woke up alone in bed. Allard must have put her in bed and then left. His side hadn't even been slept in.

Fuckity fuck fuck.

What now?

What now, was that she got up, pulled on her big girl pants, and faced the music. Or took a shower before facing the music. There was no way she made for a pretty sight if her aching head and dry mouth and gritty eyes were anything to go by.

Stumbling across the hallway with her robe in one hand and a towel in the other, she went straight for the shower, completely bypassing the mirror. No need to confirm what she already knew, that she looked like a freight train ran over her then backed up to run over her a second time.

She didn't get out until the water shifted from burning hot to slightly tepid. And then it was a quick dry off before wrapping the robe around her and racing back to the room.

Broken Peak might be the breadth of where Delia could roam, but she didn't need to stay inside. Warm clothes, jeans and sturdy ankle boots with a heavy sweater, would be fine for the weather, even if she spent the entire day outside. The last thing she wanted though, was to run back to the bathroom to dry her hair. Or stay around in the room long enough for Allard to come back. A braid would have to do instead of a ponytail or letting it fall loose.

No muss, no fuss. Just like she wished her life was like at that moment.

By the time she was ready to face the rest of the pack and headed down to the kitchen, no one was around. Not even Eleanor working on sight words with Foster. Maggie wasn't even loitering in some corner waiting to pounce.

This was good though. It meant Delia could grab a cup of coffee and then head out and spend some time in the woods to let her wolf out for a run. After opening four cabinets, Delia found a giant insulated cup to hold half a pot of coffee. She added some cream and sugar, then headed out the front door.

With each step closer to the front room, she expected to find the pack either camped out on the couches and chairs or doing something outside, but even the porch was empty.

Where was everyone?

Not that she wondered where they were all hiding out for long since it made her escape into the woods easier.

What was just supposed to be a long walk through the woods turned into an all day outing. She found a small clearing close to the river and far enough away from the Lodge and edge of the territory to not be accidentally found. The perfect spot to think about everything that had happened since she arrived at Broken Peak and what would happen if she stayed.

When the sun hit the top of the sky, letting her know it was close to noon, she still hadn't worked through the jumbled thoughts.

On one hand, there was the whole thing with Vixen and Mac and the writings in the journals that were likely to be apocryphal. On the other, there was Allard and how he was supposed to be her mate by arrangement then turned into her fake mate, then the male she may or may not, but definitely did, have feelings for. Feelings that weren't reciprocated.

By the time the sun began its descent below the horizon, Delia came to a conclusion and one she had to share with Vixen and Bray at the very least.

Except when she stood to head back to the Lodge, her feet froze in place and refused to budge. The whole feet not moving thing was her wolf's doing. Her wolf wasn't happy with the decision and was more than a bit miffed at being left out of Delia's thought process.

What her wolf didn't understand was whether Delia faced the Alpha pair now or later, the conversation would be the same. Thanks for everything, but Vixen could handle the endgame just fine and Delia really needed to get back to Chicago. After avoiding Allard at all costs the day before, and spending today alone, Delia realized she couldn't stay at Broken Peak. Not if Allard was around.

Their mating might have been fake, but her feelings for him were very real. It was him or her and Delia would never ask the Alphas to make a choice. She'd do it for them.

It was dark when she finally convinced her wolf that sticking around Broken Peak was not in either of their best interests. What would happen when Allard eventually found a mate and brought her to live with him? That bitter pill wouldn't be easy for either of them to swallow, and her wolf reluctantly accepted Delia's decision.

By the time she approached the Lodge, she figured the rest of the pack had eaten dinner and was busy enough that she could sneak past them with no confrontation.

They weren't. Well, maybe they were, but Allard was sitting in the front room. As soon as she walked in, his stare pinned her in place.

"Are you okay?"

Well, now, that was a loaded question. Hell no, she wasn't okay. No one would be okay after overhearing what she had. Except she didn't think he was actually asking her about her emotional state. The question was probably aimed at her general well-being.

"Yeah, I'm fine." It wasn't a lie, exactly, but it also wasn't the truth. Physically, she was fine. Mentally though, so not okay.

"You realize you've been gone for the entire day?" Allard stood and crossed his arms over his chest. "And you didn't have your phone with you either."

Her body went into traitor mode, going all warm and tingly at the sight of his muscles flexing beneath the thin sleeves of his shirt. Thankfully her brain and mouth remained loyal.

She mirrored his pose and lifted her chin up and towards him. "I was within the borders of the pack's territory. And it wasn't as though I was hiding. I'm sure, if anyone looked hard enough, they could have found me."

The growl that came from Allard nearly caused her to turn tail and run down the hallway. And she very well might have, had she never heard his claims that she didn't mean anything to him. Instead, she returned his growl with one of her own.

The sound coming from her didn't have any of his protective low timbre that rumbled through her body with its sweet vibrations. However, her growl held all the frustration and anger that had been brewing over since she skulked out of the Lodge earlier that morning.

"That's all you've gotta say to me? That any of us could have found you?"

"Did you expect more?"

"Red-"

She held her hand out, palm facing him, stopping the next words from coming out. Whatever else he had to say, she didn't want to hear it.

"Nope. Not interested, Allard. So just don't. Okay?"

Allard scowled at her. "You know what, fine, I'm really not interested in arguing with you."

"Good. That's something else we can agree on." Delia turned and walked away before he could say anything more. She wasn't certain enough of her resolve in the decision she had made about her future with Broken Peak, but she was sure that Allard could wiggle his way past all her defenses if she wasn't careful.

CHAPTER THIRTY-FIVE

DELIA chickened out. She knew she had to speak with Vixen and Bray, but the timing was never right. Someone was always around and explaining that she needed to talk with them alone would just add gossip to the current rumor mill.

She still hadn't talked with either of the Alphas after a week. Quite possibly the longest week in her entire life. It was also pure torture. Another arduously long week came and went and still no conversation. The second week was even more difficult than the first.

Allard and she didn't speak, except for civil pleasantries in front of the other pack members. Delia slept alone in Allard's room and Allard slept wherever. She didn't ask and did her best to convince herself she didn't care.

The one time he actually said something to her before she walked away from him, was to remind her to be safe when she let her wolf run in the woods.

She filled her days training with Vixen, letting her wolf run, and reading through a journal Mac had conveniently left behind during one of his visits. Maggie tried to spend time with her, but Delia's heart wasn't in it. She never turned her back on the female or completely ignored her, but Delia struggled to spend time with someone who was always so happy when she was anything but.

Every few days, Allard attempted to approach her. usually she escaped before he could get close enough to say anything. The few times he got a sentence out, she found an excuse to walk away.

In the middle of the third week of giving Allard the silent treatment, he found her sitting on the bed in her room reading the journal. Well, his room, but she considered it her room now.

He closed and locked the door behind him then leaned back against it, as if he was worried she'd head right for it at the first opportunity. He wasn't wrong.

Delia slid a marker in the journal and set it on the bed next to her. If she wasn't careful, she'd likely throw it at his head. Anything that might cause him the same hurt he caused her.

"You and I are going to have a conversation, Red. Whether you want to or not, it's happening." His booted foot kicked back against the door and he dug his hands into his pockets. "Maggie's a mess because she thinks she's the cause of whatever funk you're in and Foster's been asking questions too."

Shit. She didn't want to hurt Maggie. Allard, definitely. Finley, a little, because ultimately he was the cause of what she overheard, but not Maggie.

"I'll talk with her."

"Not tonight you aren't."

"Fine then tomorrow."

"Nope. Not happening tomorrow either. Tonight you're gonna get a good night's sleep and tomorrow, we're having our chat."

"Well, I have things I need to do tomorrow."

"No you don't, Red. Vixen's giving you the day off from training. Shit, not even Leighton, who became obsessed with training, spent as much time working out as you have."

"That's not your decision to make."

"The hell it isn't." Allard crossed the space from the door to the bed in two steps. He picked her up by her forearms and carried her to the dresser so they both faced the mirror. "Look at yourself, Red. The female I'm looking at isn't the same female who showed up at Broken Peak all those weeks ago."

Again, he wasn't wrong. She'd lost enough weight for her clothes to hang loosely and even though she spent her days outside, her normally pale skin had become sallow. The dark circles under her eyes didn't help any either.

"So, yeah, this is my decision to make. Because if you so much as step out of this room tomorrow for anything except the bathroom or food, I will make it Vixen and Bray's decision to make."

"Fine." She pulled away from him, even though she really wanted to turn around and wrap her arms around his waist and hold him close. She couldn't do that anymore. The touching thing with him. It was too difficult.

"Gonna have to come up with a better word than that, Red. Fine doesn't cut it anymore."

"All right."

"All right, you'll come up with a better word?" The corners of his lips lifted, as though fighting against the urge to smile.

"No. All right, as in that's the better word." She sat back on the bed and tucked her legs up underneath her.

"Good then." He returned to the door and opened it. "I'm gonna fix you some food, bring it back here, and you're going to eat it."

"But I don't have to enjoy it." She muttered under her breath.

"No, you don't, Red." He laughed all the way down the hall.

Delia hated that the sound of his laughter warmed her. She despised her reaction, not because she didn't want those feelings, but because she couldn't separate the fake from the real with Allard.

She thought she could. Or at least she had convinced herself she could, but that had just been a pipe dream.

She'd been fooling herself thinking somehow it would all work itself out. That's what she'd been doing for the past weeks. Hoping something would happen and Allard would announce that it wasn't fake. That it was all real.

The conversation with Bray and Vixen would happen tomorrow. And then she'd go home and wait for the hurt to fade and her life to get back to some semblance of normal.

Tomorrow, she promised herself. She'd take care of it all tomorrow. Just like she promised herself every night since that fateful morning.

CHAPTER THIRTY-SIX

DELIA slept in, not waking until it was closer to lunch than breakfast. Without a window in the room, there was no sun to bring light to the dark room, and no one had made any noise outside her door causing her to wake up.

She'd picked at the food Allard brought her the night before. Then, when he finally left after he was satisfied with her caloric intake, she put her head down on the pillow and immediately fell asleep. Not waking until, holy crap, it was 11:00. She'd slept for over twelve hours assuming Allard hadn't changed the time on the clock. Which she wouldn't put past him if he thought turning back the clock would give her a few extra hours of sleep.

Resolved to finally talk with Vixen and Bray, Delia rolled out of bed and grabbed what she needed to take a quick shower. As soon she opened the bedroom door, she learned why no sounds interrupted her sleep.

A massive chocolate brown wolf was curled up in front of her door. Allard's wolf.

She'd never met him, but she'd seen him from a distance when she feigned disinterest in participating with the pack during their runs.

He was even more magnificent close up as he was from a distance.

All signs pointed in the direction that it would be in her best interest to step over the wolf and head to the shower, but when had she ever paid attention to the signs? Delia crouched down, and he lifted his head towards her. She couldn't resist scratching at the spot between his ears and his soft fur tickled her skin.

The wolf inside her itched to break free and finally meet Allard's wolf, but Delia held her back. Their wolves coming face to face with one another would have been catastrophically bad. Like worse than Armageddon bad.

Delia patted the wolf's head and stood. She might be pissed at Allard, but it didn't mean his wolf deserved her ire. For all she knew, his wolf had been making Allard's life as miserable as Delia's wolf was making hers.

She stepped over the wolf, who hadn't so much as moved but just stretched and shifted positions, and headed toward the bathroom. A shadow followed behind her. Apparently Allard's wolf didn't plan on leaving her alone. Great. He was just as dominant as Allard. Delia should have guessed as much.

When the wolf walked into the bathroom with her, she drew the line.

"Oh, no you don't. You can do your watchdog thing outside." She pushed him out, but didn't think for a minute she actually moved him. The wolf left because the wolf was allowing her to make him leave.

She took her time in the shower. Without having to worry about leaving enough hot water for the others, she let the water pound down on her shoulders and back. She even took the time to use a body scrub and to shave. It'd been weeks since she'd last taken care of things and she might have been giving sasquatch a run for his money in the winter woolies department.

Once her body and hair had been cleaned and scrubbed and conditioned, she stepped out of the shower and lathered lotion all over her body. It felt nice to spoil herself and wondered why she put aside the little niceties.

Punishment.

Of course her wolf would answer the rhetorical question. Delia disagreed with her wolf's sentiment, but didn't bother arguing. It had been all they did since Delia decided to leave and she really didn't have an interest in having the same argument with the stubborn beast.

She wrapped the towel around her hair, pulled on the robe, and opened the bathroom door. And whad'ya know, Allard's wolf was right where she left him. This time she didn't pet him or give him attention. He didn't need any encouragement. She stepped over him, walked back to the room, and closed the door on his snout.

"Okay then. Dress, then food, then Bray and Vixen." She might have said the words for her own benefit, but Allard's wolf definitely heard them as well since he replied with a low growl.

As she eyed the clothes in her closet, she wondered just what was the proper attire for announcing one was leaving. Comfortable, but professional. At least that's what her mother would say. Delia went with straight comfort. She pulled on a pair of khaki pants with their cuffs rolled up above her ankles, an oversized cashmere v-neck sweater that almost matched the color of her eyes, and slipped on a pair of leather loafers she hadn't worn since before arriving at Broken Peak.

She brushed out her wet hair then twisted it into a knot she fastened in place with two short sticks.

Dressed in an armor of comfort, she was finally prepared to have a conversation she'd been dreading. It wasn't leaving Broken Peak or even her friends behind, although that certainly didn't help matters. Delia didn't want to disappoint Vixen. But it was that or slowly fading away to nothing.

Her come to Jesus conversation with Allard the night before, when he forced Delia to look at herself, opened Delia's eyes to what was happening. She was slowly dying. Their mating might have been fake, but the bond she'd formed with Allard hadn't been and his confession was killing her.

Allard's wolf greeted her as soon as she opened the door. He stood there with his tail wagging and his tongue hanging out the side of his mouth.

"I'm going to get some food, is that okay with you?"

The wolf's tail wagged hard enough to cause his butt to wiggle from side to side with the movement.

"Come on then."

Maybe it was that she finally accepted what was happening, or it was the good night's sleep, but Delia was starving. Inside the fridge resided all the makings for a giant sandwich.

Over an inch of alternating layers of meat and cheese surrounded by lettuce between two thick slices of bread and some potato chips stuck between the lettuce and bread to keep the bread from going soggy, and Delia had the perfect sandwich. Instead of sitting in the kitchen, she took the sandwich with her to the front room.

Allard's wolf wasn't far behind, cleaning up the loose crumbs that left a trail back to the kitchen. Or would have if the wolf wasn't so efficient.

She sat down in one of the chairs closest to the window that looked out across the yard and watched as Foster ran from one new discovery to the next. Pointing out each new find to Maggie, who appeared just as enthusiastic about a stick or rock as the pup. Eleanor sat on the porch steps, cradling a mug between her palms and cheering them on.

Jackson and Finley hovered on the edge of the woods, heads bowed together in conversation. Even Tevin was out with the others.

Why did the scene in front of her feel like deja vu? She would have sworn she'd never seen the pack like this before, but it had all the markings of a day-to-day routine. Had she been so preoccupied with avoiding Allard that she'd ignored everything around her?

The camaraderie of Broken Peak was something missing from her father's pack. Families were close, but unless it was a pack event, no one really spent time with one another. She'd miss that part of Broken Peak. She'd also miss the pack members. Especially Maggie. Yeah, she was a lot crazy, but her antics never ceased to make Delia laugh.

Maybe she'd invite Maggie to come and visit Chicago. Sure, having a raccoon shifter visit a wolf shifter pack might raise some eyebrows. It wasn't like they wouldn't already be raised when Delia went back to Chicago with no mate by her side.

The thought of heading home alone chilled Delia. The gossip wouldn't bother her, neither would the pitying looks. It was the alone part that frightened her. The sandwich turned to cement in her mouth and it was all she could to finish the bite and keep it down. Instead of throwing the rest of her early lunch away, she shared it with Allard's wolf.

The time had come. She needed to find Bray and Vixen before she chickened out again. And it didn't look like Allard was shifting back soon, so it wasn't as though the conversation he insisted they have would take precedence.

She stood and walked to the door. Vixen tended to spend most of the day outside, so it would be the first place Delia looked for her. As soon as she opened the door, Allard's wolf pushed his way between her legs and the door, nearly knocking Delia over in his rush to get outside.

What the-

Shouts greeted her, but they weren't the welcoming sounds she expected.

"Get down!"

"Why didn't the alarms go off?"

"El, inside. Now!"

Chaos reigned. Or at least it looked like chaos. What actually played out in front of her was a carefully choreographed defensive movement, straight out of Vixen's play book. Tevin scooped Foster up and ran him back to the porch, dropping him by Eleanor's feet before returning to his position in the middle of the yard. Jackson had already shifted and partnered with Allard's wolf.

Eleanor, with a tight grip on Foster's hand rushed to the front door. "Come on, Delia, we need to get inside."

What? Get inside? No. Delia might not plan on staying at Broken Peak, but she was still a part of the pack until she had her conversation with the Alphas. That meant she protected the pack, just as the others were doing.

"You go." She was already pulling off her clothes, preparing to let her wolf spring free. It was fight-or-flight time, and Delia was going to fight. "Get Danielle as well and get to the equipment room."

Eleanor stared at Delia, eyes wide in shock.

"Now, Eleanor. Jackson can't do what he has to if he's worried about you and his pup."

The command in Delia's voice knocked Eleanor back into gear. She nodded once, then hurried into the Lodge. The sound of a lock closing into place eased the worry in Delia's chest she hadn't even realized was there.

Turning back to the yard, Delia scanned the forest. "Where are you?"

Nose in the air, she sniffed at the slight breeze, hoping to catch the scent of whatever caused the alarm.

"There you are…"

Yes, there. Go. Now.

Her wolf demanded freedom and Delia gave it to her. Fully and completely. The shift was painless, it always had been for her, but the brief moment where she and her wolf shared the same space and not just a consciousness, caused a wave of vertigo. Almost like being drunk, but no hangover the next morning.

As Delia pulled back, ceding control of both her body and mind to the animal inside her, the wolf stopped her.

No. Together.

The unusual request stopped Delia for a moment, but she didn't have time to consider her wolf's decision. She just obeyed and settled in for the ride. Her wolf took off, darting straight for the spot in the trees where Delia scented the intruders. The faintness of the scent put them at a safe distance from the Lodge, but it also made it impossible to determine the number and whether she recognized them.

A yipping and bark almost had her pivoting, but she resisted the tug pulling her back to the middle of the yard.

The uninvited guests came to Broken Peak for her and she was going to show them exactly who they would be dealing with. Even if her decision didn't qualify as the brightest idea.

Her wolf cut a path through the forest, weaving through the trees with the comfortable ease of someone who'd spent their lifetime exploring the forest and not a few weeks.

There! She shouted to her wolf, but didn't need to. The animal had already veered sharply to the left, closer to her target. Anger fueled her wolf, driving her faster and therefore closer to her target.

The dirt and dead leaves sprayed around her as her wolf skidded to a stop.

The three gray wolves from the bar stood at the perimeter of a small clearing.

Stupid.

Delia agreed.

The larger of the three males stepped closer. His dark gray fur was made darker from mud and broken twigs. Did he really think the wolves of Broken Peak would be fooled by his silly attempts to camouflage his scent? City wolves, sure. But not the wolves who spent their time in these woods.

Delia's wolf growled low. A warning. Or maybe an invitation.

The wolf shifted his weight to his back legs and leaped at her.

The sounds of the forest disappeared as Delia focused only on what was in front of her.

He was fast.

Delia was faster.

Her wolf crashed into him midair. They fell to the ground in a tangle of legs and teeth. Snarls and growls filled the silence.

The red wolf had an advantage. She was going for the kill.

The gray wolves were likely under orders not to kill her. It was why the two stayed back, biding their time.

Delia could use their hesitance against them.

The dark gray wolf bit down on her shoulder and ripped out a chunk of flesh. The red wolf didn't flinch, just fought back harder than before.

Delia re-calibrated her odds. Killing her might have been off the table, but causing her harm wouldn't be a problem. The two gray wolves paced along the edge of the clearing, the scent of blood driving the predators within them to seek the weakness and pounce on the vulnerability. She couldn't watch them and fight at the same time.

Or could she?

There was a reason her wolf wanted her present and sharing the same space.

The endgame. What was the endgame here?

Delia played out all the eventualities in her mind while her wolf fought back against the dark gray wolf, biting and clawing until he was the bloodier of the two wolves.

The king grew stronger in the endgame because he had powers the other pieces didn't. Edging her way deeper into her wolf's consciousness, she watched the surrounding area. Not through her wolf's eyes, but through her own.

Delia didn't need to fight, her wolf did. If her wolf focused on the dark gray wolf, and Delia focused on the other two, she could win.

The taste of iron coated her tongue, but Delia didn't know if it was her blood or the male's. It didn't matter, she reminded herself, and focused on one of the lighter males who was circling around to her back.

Delia nudged her wolf, and she adjusted, turning her body to keep her back protected and forcing the dark gray male to move with her or risk a snapped leg.

The dark gray wolf snapped at her, but only caught air as the wolf hopped backward.

More growls. More bites. More blood.

Once more the two wolves slammed into each other, but this time the red wolf was more than ready.

Delia was a born Alpha, she didn't need a bond with packmates to use her power on the dark gray wolf. It wouldn't last long, the gray wolf would be able to shake it off, but it would give her enough time to end the fight.

Wolf and female combined their will and pushed against the gray wolf. He stumbled and his grip slackened. As soon as he began to shake off the compulsion, the red wolf lunged.

Her jaws closed around his vulnerable jugular, teeth sinking into his flesh. With a violent shake of her head, she tore open his throat.

Dropping the chunk of flesh she gouged from his body, the red wolf stepped away from the dying male. She lifted her head and stared at the two males. A challenge.

A scream ripped through the air above them and the howling and barking returned.

Before either of the remaining two wolves could act, a dark brown wolf barreled into the clearing and slammed into one of the wolves. A massive black wolf came from the other side and took out the second.

It was the red wolf's turn to pace the perimeter, waiting for the opportunity to go in for another kill.

It never came. The brown and black wolves made quick work of the remaining intruders and soon their lifeless bodies laid next to their packmate's.

Delia's wolf pushed her way back inside and forced Delia to shift.

Well, now, that was a first. She'd have to have a conversation with her wolf about that. Later though. They needed to clean things up and figure out where the intruders came from before she did anything else.

The black wolf shifted first. Bray stood in his place, surveying the mess at his feet. "Vi's gonna be pissed."

Delia looked up at him. "Because I ran off?"

"No. Because she missed out on all the fun." He kicked at the corpse of the dark gray wolf. "You did this yourself?"

"My wolf, yes."

No. Not me. We. We did it together.

Bray nodded in approval. "C'mon, Allard, shift back already." He turned to look at the dark brown wolf, who had refused to release his grip on the wolf's throat. Like he might actually come back from the dead.

From behind, Delia heard a shot fire.

A gun? Who had a gun and who were they shooting at?

Burning. Why was Delia's chest burning?

A scream came from above and behind. Immediately followed by another scream, from a male. Or man. Delia couldn't tell. A pain in her chest, where she felt burning, exploded, and she fell forward.

Good thing she was already on her knees or she would have fallen on her face. Wait. Why had she been on her knees? Hadn't she been standing?

"Delia?"

Was that Allard? He shifted back? When? She was sorry she missed it. Allard might still be on her shit list, but it didn't mean she couldn't appreciate his body.

She pressed her hand against her chest. Maybe she could stop the burning.

Why was her hand wet?

"Don't touch it, baby." Allard wrapped his fingers around her wrist and pulled her hand away. "Come on, Red, stay with me."

Stay with him? She wasn't going anywhere. Her legs felt like lead and the idea of walking seemed worse than challenging those three wolves had been.

Shit, her chest hurt. Like really hurt, and the burning hadn't faded, instead it felt like her insides were on fire.

"Bray, do something." Allard's worried voice sent Delia and her wolf into a panic. Worried didn't bode well.

"What happened?" Another voice, male. Delia recognized it, but couldn't place a name with it.

"Here, press this down on the wound." That was Bray. She knew that. "She's been shot."

Shot? Holy shit. No wonder everything hurt.

Allard knelt over her, his face so close to hers their noses brushed against one another. "Come on, Red, keep your eyes open, okay?"

He pressed whatever Bray had given him down on her chest and it hurt more than the fucking bullet had.

Another scream echoed through her ears.

"I'm sorry, baby, I know it hurts, but we need to slow the bleeding."

Oh. That had been her scream.

"Is the bullet still in her?" The male she recognized but couldn't place asked.

"I don't know, I don't want to move her."

Another scream. The sound hadn't come from her, but only because she couldn't get enough air in her lungs to force out such a loud noise.

"Vixen must've found the shooter."

"Who the fuck cares? Do something, Mac. Fix her."

Mac. That's who was there with them.

"We need to see if the bullet went through. All the pressure in the world won't help her if she's bleeding out the back."

Strong hands lifted Delia's shoulder, and she might have screamed again. Or maybe she just groaned.

She didn't care about the noises anymore. The less she cared, the more the pain in her chest dulled. And when she closed her eyes, it hurt even less.

"Delia, open your eyes, baby. I need you to look at me."

"It went through her."

So many voices now, and they all blurred together.

"Bray, give me that. Here, okay, lay her back down. Gently. Good. Put pressure back on her wound."

"How bad?"

"Guessing lung, so we've got to worry about two holes, not just one."

Two holes definitely sounded worse than one.

"Delia, baby, it's all good. We got you."

She opened her eyes and looked up into Allard's blue ones. Beautiful blue eyes that reminded her of the water she swam in when visiting the Caribbean. "Don't lie."

"I'm not, baby. You're gonna be okay. I promise. Tell me you're gonna be okay."

"Can't lie."

"Then don't. Tell me you're gonna be okay." Allard pleaded with her.

What would the lie hurt? They weren't even mates. It wasn't like her dying would doom Allard to the same fate. If it made him feel better.

"I'm good." She closed her eyes, too tired to keep them open.

"Red, come on, look at me, baby."

"Wanna sleep."

"You can sleep later, baby, I promise. But right now, I need you to keep your eyes open."

She fought against the want to keep her eyes closed and obeyed Allard. Silly wolf, making demands when he wasn't even her mate.

"We gotta git her back to the Lodge."

"What about Vi?"

"She can't help with this. Hell, I'm not sure any of us can."

The males continued to talk, but their words garbled together and she didn't have the strength to listen and keep her eyes open.

"This is gonna hurt, Red, okay? But I promise it will be fast."

He was right. It did hurt. Whatever they were doing sent out a wave of excruciating pain from her chest to her body.

And then she was floating.

No. Not floating. Allard's arms were under her, carrying her. She supposed being carried was better than floating. Floating meant she was dead.

Or probably dead.

And Delia didn't want to die yet. She needed to yell at Allard. Tell him he was stupid for ignoring what was in front him. Make him see her feelings weren't fake.

She could die later. After she yelled at him.

"You aren't gonna die, Delia. And yes, you can yell at me all you want for as long as you want."

Delia lost track of time. Or maybe she faded in and out of consciousness. She couldn't tell anymore.

"Put her down here."

Allard set her down on a hard surface. A table maybe. Hey, was she in the kitchen?

"No, not in the kitchen, this is Bray and Vixen's room." One of the blond females from the barbecue appeared in Delia's line of sight. "Hi, I'm Maddie, we met already, but I'm going to do what I can to help you out."

Oh. How was a Sports Illustrated model going to help her?

"Not a Sports Illustrated model, but thank you." Maddie chuckled. "Before I came to Broken Peak, I was an attending physician in an ER."

"You were?"

"Yes, Allard, I was." Maddie came back into Delia's line of sight. "I'm going to examine you now. Mac filled me in with what he suspects, but I want to make sure, okay?"

Delia nodded or maybe she said okay, she couldn't tell. Whatever she did was enough for Maddie to jump into action.

"Allard, unless you're a trained nurse, you need to get the hell out of here. Same with you, Bray, if you're just gonna sit there and glare at Mac." Her hands moved over Delia's body, checking the wounds with a comforting efficiency. "We can all agree he's an asshole now and then argue about the details later."

That was the last thing Delia heard before she faded into the heavy dark mist that had been trying to pull her under since she had been shot.

CHAPTER THIRTY-SEVEN

ALLARD leaned back against the wall and slid down to the floor, pulling his knees up to his chest.

What the fuck had just happened?

When Delia's beautiful red wolf charged past him into the woods, he thought for sure he was going to lose her. But when he and Bray found her, she had already ripped out the throat of one large male and was looking to take on another.

He had been fully prepared to light into her for scaring the shit out of him once he convinced his wolf to let go of his new chew toy, and then she was shot.

Fucking shot.

How the fuck...

Bray stepped out of his bedroom and the door closed behind him with a loud snick. He sat down next to Allard, mirroring his pose.

"What the hell, Bray?"

"Maddie being a doctor? Yeah, surprised the hell out of me too. And why Mac hadn't brought her over when I first found Vi is something that old fucker's gonna answer for."

"No. What? No. I mean who the fuck shot Delia? How did we miss them?"

"I'm not sure, but from the sounds of things when we left, Vi was getting answers for us." Bray bumped his shoulder against Allard's. "She's strong. She'll be fine."

"Vi? Yeah, I've seen her rip out spines before."

"No, Delia, you idiot. As bad as that wound is, she's gonna make it."

"You don't know that." Allard stared up at the closed door. There was so much he wanted to say to Delia, so much he should have said to her and didn't.

He'd planned to talk to her today, to finally put into words everything he'd been thinking and feeling. But then those males showed up and his plans got shot to hell.

"Who were the males? Do you think they had anything to do with the shooter?"

"I'm assuming the same three you saw at the bar." Bray shrugged. "Her wolf took down that large male, even with the other two not in the fight, she shouldn't have been able to. Delia's wolf is strong and so is she. She's going to be fine."

"But why show up now? And why go after Delia?"

"Maybe she came across them before they could get to who they wanted?"

"They showed up when she showed up. It's not a coincidence."

"We'll figure it out. Once Vi gets back, we'll have more information to go on." Bray slapped his palm down on Allard's knee. "And you need to fix whatever shit went down with Delia. Bad enough that the rest of us have had to deal with her pretending not to mope and you pretending not to sulk, I can't imagine the hell it would be if you hadn't fixed things and she died out there."

"You're shit at comforting, Bray."

"Yeah, but I'm better than Vi." His Alpha grinned and leaned his head back against the wall. "It's gonna be okay, Allard. Vi's been shot multiple times, and she's still alive."

"She also has a fucking griffin inside her."

"And Delia has a fucking wolf inside her. What's your point?"

"You really do suck at this."

"Well, I'm not leaving you alone, so you get to spend more time with me sucking at comforting you. And for the record, I'm not trying to comfort."

"I marked her."

"We all saw it."

"No, I mean, I marked her. She didn't mark me yet, but that mark, that's enough for my wolf right?"

"What the fuck are you going on about?"

"What you did with Vixen when you claimed her. She hadn't claimed you, but you claimed her and it couldn't have just been her griffin, you had to have helped too."

"That was all her griffin. Only thing I did was flip the switch, the griffin did the rest."

Allard didn't believe him. He didn't think Bray was lying to him, but he'd heard about bonded mates sharing their strength with each other. She might not have claimed him, but his wolf had sure as fuck started some kind of bonding process with her.

"Out there, in the woods, when she was shot-"

"We don't have to talk about it."

"Just shut up for a sec. When Delia was shot, I felt it. I felt it like I had been shot. And when we moved her, I felt that too." He rubbed his chest where Delia had been shot. "I thought I was the one who got shot, Bray, that's how real it felt."

Bray's head pivoted around until he completely faced Allard. Blinked once, then twice, then a third time. Real slow. Like Allard had turned into a giant purple unicorn and Bray was just now seeing it.

"Is that what it's like with you and Vixen?"

"No. I mean, I can tell when she's pissed or angry, and I sort of know when she's hurt, but I sure as hell don't feel it."

"Well, I did, so explain that to me."

"You don't believe in the mumbo jumbo crap, remember?"

"This isn't mumbo jumbo crap, Bray. And it fits with the bonded mates thing, where if one dies the other one usually will as well."

"Yeah, but when my mate stubs her toe, my toe doesn't hurt in sympathy. And you aren't bonded." Bray smirked. The asshole actually smirked at him. "The whole thing is one big farce, remember?"

"It might work though and I don't have the same faith in Maddie fixing that hole in her lung as you do."

"We don't know that the bullet went through her lung, but yeah, no harm in trying, I guess."

Allard hadn't ever bonded with a female before so he didn't know what it felt like, but when he'd been chasing Delia's wolf through the woods, something pulled at his wolf, guiding him along her path. It was the only reason they found her as soon as they had. He wasn't willing to shift, they didn't need his wolf pacing the hallway and snapping at anyone who came within fifty feet of the room, but would allow his wolf closer to the surface.

His wolf didn't hesitate or even wonder what Allard had planned. The wolf leaped into Allard's thoughts and showed him exactly what he was looking for. A rope of light fed from Allard's chest and disappeared right through the door. Allard didn't need to see it to know where it went. Straight to Delia.

What to do with the bond that he could suddenly now see, posed a problem. He hadn't thought that far ahead when he brought up the idea to Bray. He shouldn't have worried. His wolf pushed his strength through the bond. At one point, the connection between them frayed and nearly snapped, but his wolf sent another surge and reinforced the bond.

Seconds turned to minutes and minutes turned to hours. Allard lost track of all sense of time. Strong hands pressed down on his shoulders, gently shaking him.

"Allard, come on back to me." Bray's sharp voice yanked Allard out of his daze. His Alpha crouched in front of him, staring down at Allard with a concerned expression. "You've been out for a while."

"How's Delia?"

"Not sure, but Mac hasn't come out to give us any news yet, so she must be doing okay."

Allard pressed his palm against his forehead and rubbed. "Bray, I'm not sure the no news is good news idiom is appropriate here."

"Allard?" The door to Bray and Vixen's room opened and Mac poked his head out. "Why don't you come in."

He leaned to the left, looking around Bray to get an unrestricted view of Mac. The old shifter didn't have the look of someone who was about to share bad news, but Allard wouldn't put anything past Mac.

Bray stood and nodded, then reached down to help Allard to his feet. "Go on."

Allard took a deep breath. He pushed his way past Mac and into the room.

Delia was lying on the table, covered with a sheet. She barely had any color in her cheeks, and her lips were dry and cracked, but her eyes were open. She looked so fragile, Allard was scared she'd break if he touched her.

Maddie looked up while cleaning the detritus from Delia's makeshift surgery. "She's awake, but still a little out of it."

"She'll be okay?"

"Okay is relative. She'll be sore until her body heals, and I'm prescribing bed rest until those wounds close, but yeah, Delia will be just fine."

"Can I move her?" Allard hovered over Delia, not sure how to touch her without causing more pain. "Bring her back to our room instead of staying here?"

"I'm awake." Delia's voice was rough, like she'd swallowed a bucket full of glass. "You can ask me."

Her vulnerability drove him to act before Maddie answered. He scooped her up in his arms and held her close.

Maddie glanced over her shoulder at them and smiled. "Let's have her stay here for a bit. Things look good, but just in case something happens, it will be easier to handle it here."

Allard bobbed his head up and down like her words made complete sense. For all he knew, she was telling him he had to stand on his head for the entire night. Taking Delia to Bray and Vixen's bed felt wrong, so instead he carried her to the chairs Vixen placed in front of the window that looked out to the side yard.

As soon as his ass hit the cushion, he pulled her tight against his chest. Allard pressed his lips against the top of her head and breathed in her scent. Wildflowers in full bloom.

Delia rubbed her cheek against his chest and it eased both his wolf and him, but he still wasn't convinced she was going to be okay. It would be days before he wouldn't need to press his ear against her heart to check that she was still alive.

CHAPTER THIRTY-EIGHT

BRAY opened the door to Allard and Delia's room and cleared his throat until Allard looked up from his position by the side of the bed.

He hadn't slept since bringing her back to their room and was exhausted, but Allard wanted to be awake and there when Delia finally woke up. Maddie assured him that Delia would be fine and her wolf would speed up Maddie's handy work. But neither he nor his wolf would be satisfied until Delia woke up.

Bray jerked his head toward the hallway and Allard nodded. He glanced over at Maggie, who was comforting Delia's clothes hanging in the closet.

"Will you watch her while I step out for a few?"

Maggie's head bobbed up and down and she scurried over to the chair Allard vacated.

Allard stepped out of the room and closed it behind him. Whatever Bray had to say, he didn't want Delia hearing if she suddenly woke up.

"What's up?"

"Come and talk with Vixen and me for a minute." An order, not a request.

"Yeah. Sure." Allard looked over his shoulder at the closed door. What he had wanted to say was that they could talk there, steps away from Delia if she woke up. Instead, he followed Bray down the hallway to the small room he used as an office.

Vixen was already waiting for them, studying something on the screen of a tablet. She didn't even look up when they stepped into the office and Bray closed the door behind them.

"Mind telling me why I'm here?" Allard sat down in one of the chairs not used by Bray at his desk.

"Spencer Pearce." Vixen cut to the chase.

"What about him?"

"He was the shooter."

Allard was going to kill him. Rip out his throat and disembowel him and then put it all back together so he could do it again. "Where is he?"

"I have him in the shed. Figured you'd want to take care of him. But there's something you need to know." Vixen looked over at Bray, but didn't continue.

Bray shook his head and lifted his hands up, as if asking what she wanted from him. She rolled her eyes at Bray's lack of participation.

"Will one of you say something?"

"Delia wasn't the target. You were. He's a bad shot and hit her instead."

"What? Why?" He was nothing in the scheme of things.

"Turns out that the Northwest Pack has their own Mac who keeps track of the legends that have been passed down. They wanted Delia, which both she and I suspected, and figured the easiest way to get to her was to get rid of you."

"And those three males? Were they part of the Northwest Pack too? How come Delia didn't recognize them."

"This is where things get interesting." Bray muttered under his breath. "Like they weren't interesting enough already."

"Nope, they belonged to a small bachelor pack in the Black Hills."

"What the hell, Vixen? How would they even know about Delia?"

"Apparently, wolf shifters have a phone tree in place for the latest rumors." Bray added. "From what Spencer said, he didn't even know they were here until Spencer ran into them and then it was a matter of taking advantage of the opportunity."

"How small are they if they can risk sending three wolves here?" Allard narrowed his eyes at Vixen. They were keeping something back, but he didn't know what.

"From what Danielle was able to dig up, maybe ten or twelve males. All bachelors and all younger sons of Alphas." Vixen and Bray shared a look.

"Oh for fuck's sake. Just tell me already."

"They work for hire. They don't care about Delia, or you really, they just had one job. Bring Delia back to the male who hired them."

"Why would the Northwest Pack hire them if they already sent Spencer out here?"

"They didn't." Bray looked down at his feet. "Your father did."

"Fuck." Allard pressed the heel of his palms to his eyes. "What was he thinking?"

"Bring her back to Denver and maybe you'd follow?" Vixen suggested. "But there is a bright side to all this."

"How is there a bright side to my father basically declaring war on Broken Peak?"

"Well, in all fairness, technically he declared war on the Chicago Pack because you're not really mated."

"That's gonna change as soon as Delia wakes up."

"Oh." Vixen's eyes widened. "Does she know about this? Or is this one of those things you've decided and expect her to go along with?"

Allard glared at his Alpha. It was on the tip of his tongue to tell her to shut up, but he thought better of it.

"If I've learned anything from Vixen, it's that it's better to ask. You'll still get what you want, but without all the foot stomping and eye rolling."

"I don't stomp my feet." However, she didn't deny the eye rolling. "Back to the bright side. I've reached out to the Black Hills Pack and they won't retaliate. In fact, the way your father presented it, they thought we were holding Delia, and by default you, against her will."

"Your father's gonna have a mess on his hands between Everest Lyall and the leader of the Black Hills Pack. He won't have time to bother us for a while."

"And the Northwest Pack?"

"They'll probably continue to be a problem."

"And Spencer Pearce? Are we sending him back to them?"

"After you've finished with him, sure. If you want. I figured we'd just throw him out with the rest of the trash." Vixen shrugged. "His fate is in your hands, Allard. I won't take that away from you."

"I'll take care of him later." Allard pushed up to his feet and left the small office.

He needed to get back to Delia. Worrying about the info bomb Vixen and Bray dropped in his lap could wait until after Delia finally woke up.

CHAPTER THIRTY-NINE

WARM lips pressing against the top of her hand was the perfect alarm clock. Delia would have to figure out how to market it. A fortune could be made from it.

She took a deep breath and nothing hurt. She took another deep breath, just to make sure. Yep, no pain.

Was she dead?

There went her money-making scheme. Unless they had Amazon Prime in Heaven. Was she even in Heaven?

She opened her eyes. Sitting next to her with her hand held between his, Allard kissed each of her fingers.

Shit. He looked more tired than Delia felt.

"Maddie worked on you, but your wolf did the heavy lifting, or at least that's what she told me."

"I'm alive?" She blinked several times at the male, not quite believing he was really there.

"Yeah. You're alive." Allard chuckled and kissed his way up her arm. "You were shot though."

"I remember." Delia ran her hand over her chest. "Is the scar bad?"

Allard laughed softly. "No, Red, it's not bad, or it won't be bad. It's still healing though."

He pulled the sheet down and lifted the bottom of her shirt then pressed his lips down over the wound. She lifted her head to see what Allard was talking about, but his head blocked her view.

Reaching down, she combed her fingers through his hair. "I'm really okay and this isn't some dream?"

"It's not a dream." Allard pressed the side of his cheek down on her stomach and his whiskers tickled her skin. "But you've been asleep for a while."

"How long?"

"You woke up for a little bit, after Maddie finished, but that was yesterday. You've been asleep for a little under twenty hours now."

"That long?"

"The longest day of my life."

She frowned as her memories of what had happened came back in a slow trickle. "Who shot me?"

"Spencer Pearce."

"What? Why did he do that?"

"He wasn't aiming at you, he was aiming at me."

"That makes no sense."

"Nothing about what happened yesterday makes any sense." He rubbed his nose along her chest, pushing her shirt up with him. "Delia, you scared me yesterday. Promise you won't do that again."

"Get shot? I don't plan on running in front of a gun in the near future."

"I thought I was going to lose you, Red, before I had a chance to tell you everything I needed to."

She thought she was going to die, in fact she was so close to giving up, but something pushed its way into her body and kept her from just floating away. Delia blinked back the tears forming behind her eyes. "I remember Maddie talking to me and I was fading in and out and then I was looking down. I saw me, lying on a table, but it wasn't me. And then something pulled me back. Was that you?"

Allard looked up and nodded at her. "You can't die, Delia. I can't live without you."

"Sure you can." She swallowed back the lump growing in her throat and tugged his head closer to her. "You've managed so far without any problems."

He kissed his way up her body, careful to keep his weight from pressing down on her. "About that."

"About what?"

"Managing without problems. That might have been true before you came here, but these past few weeks with you ignoring me, I've been miserable. What's between us isn't fake and you and I are getting mated. For real this time. And then you're gonna mark me and let your wolf claim me and we'll be bonded."

"Oh, is that so?"

"Yes."

And that was that. At least according to Allard. Delia's opinion on that matter wasn't important, apparently. "And what if I disagree?"

"Then you'd be a liar, because you know as well as I do that nothing about us is fake."

He didn't lie. But she wasn't ready to admit it just yet, she planned on making him suffer. Not too much and not for long, but his ego could stand a check. "I'll think about it."

Allard growled low and swept down, covering her mouth with his. "I'll give you thirty seconds."

"I'm still angry with you."

"That's fine. You can be angry with me and still mate me. For real this time." He nipped and kissed her lips.

"I love you, Allard." The words spilled from her mouth before she could stop them.

He pressed up on his arms and gazed down at her with a smug smile on his face. "Good. Because I love you too, Delia."

The small pit in her stomach, the one that hadn't gone away since she woke up the day before, God it felt like a lifetime ago, disappeared. A swarm of fluttering butterflies took its place, sending warm tingles throughout her body.

"Allard."

He paused his kissing. "Hm?"

"I need you."

"I'm right here and not going anywhere."

She wiggled her hips beneath him. "No, I need you."

It had been weeks since the last time he was inside her. She needed to feel alive right then, to know that all was right in the world, even if it wasn't.

"You're not a hundred percent yet, and Maddie made me promise we wouldn't do anything in case the stitches tore."

Yeah, Delia didn't much care about the doctor's orders. Plus, she hadn't been awake to hear them so they didn't count.

"Please, Allard? I need you. More than I need oxygen."

She didn't have to ask again. He reached between them and unfastened his jeans then slid into her slowly. It didn't take long before he was moving inside of her, groaning in time with her moans. His lips found hers again, and he kissed her, swallowing every noise she made and every breath she took.

It was like they were joined together, and not just because he was inside her. She felt everything he was feeling. Experiencing everything he experienced. And, somehow, she knew it was the same for him.

"I love you, Delia." He growled low as he came inside her, bringing her along with him.

"I know."

He rolled over, bringing her with him.

"Do you want anything? Food? A shower?"

"A shower sounds nice." Her stomach grumbled out its disagreement with her decision.

"Food first, then a shower, then Maggie."

"Why is Maggie on the list?"

"Because when she hasn't been in here waiting for you to wake up, she's been spending time with your clothes, trying to comfort them. She has a weird attachment to your clothes." Allard glanced at the closed door. "I'm surprised she isn't pacing the hallway."

Delia grinned at him. "I'm not sure who'd I'd miss more if I wasn't here. You or Maggie."

"Me. Always me." He pressed a kiss to her forehead "I'll get you some food."

"Already on it!" Maggie yelled through the door.

"See, I told you." Allard grumbled and rolled out of bed while keeping her in his arms. "Let's shower while the coast is clear."

One long hot shower later, after both of them were clean and getting dressed — Allard on his own, Delia, with a lot of help from Allard — someone knocked.

"I have, um, food." Maggie whispered through the door.

Allard opened the door and looked down at the little female standing in the doorway with a tray stacked high with all different kinds of food, including three flavors of Oreos — double stuffed, regular, and vanilla. "Why are you whispering?"

"I don't want anyone else to know Delia's awake yet." She explained, as though it made perfect sense.

"Okay?" Allard opened the door and let the little shifter in.

That the tray didn't tip her over as she crossed the room to the bed was a miracle. She put it on the bed, looked up at Delia, then burst into tears.

Delia looked over at Allard with a helpless expression. The only help he offered her was a shrug.

Delia patted the bed next to her. "What's wrong, Mags?"

At the use of the little raccoon shifter's nickname, a new wave of tears came, even worse than the first.

"I was so worried. What happened if you didn't get better or never woke up? Your clothes would miss you."

"Well, you don't have to worry because I'm here." Delia ignored the clothes comment. At some point she'd need to have a conversation with Maggie about clothes not being sentient, but now didn't seem like the right time.

"Come on up here with me and you can eat with us."

"I need to take care of something." Allard crossed the floor and was next to Delia in less than a second. He pressed his lips against the top of her head. "But I'll be back before you know it. I promise."

He left before she could ask more questions.

While Delia ate the food on the tray, Maggie filled her in on everything that had happened at Broken Peak since Delia had been asleep.

CHAPTER FORTY

ALLARD stood in front of the male hanging from the ceiling. Vixen lounged against the wall next to the door frame and Bray mirrored her pose on the other side of the door.

Vixen used the shed whenever any unwanted visitors to Broken Peak survived their first meeting with the pack. He had never actually witnessed how she utilized the small building, but from the scent of death and old blood lingering inside the building, he could guess.

So could Spencer Pearce, if the scent of fear oozing from him was anything to go by.

"You shot my mate." Allard stared at the male.

Whatever Spencer Pearce was, contrite wasn't one of them. Allard expected the male to plead for his life, beg forgiveness, or even try to explain he hadn't intended to shoot Delia. He did none of those things.

He just met Allard's stare.

Never faltering.

Not even when Allard pulled out his knife and sliced the male from his groin to his neck.

CHAPTER FORTY-ONE

DELIA stood in the middle of the large front yard, surrounded by her family. Her Broken Peak family, and her immediate family. Even Lennon and Geneva had made the trip out.

Talk about surreal.

If someone had sat Delia down and explained she would have not one, but two mating ceremonies during her life and both would include the male who'd been the second part of the arranged mating pact made between her father and his before they were even born, she would've laughed in their face.

If they had also included the bit about the first mating being fake and the second being genuine, Delia would have wondered if they were certifiably insane and needed to be committed.

And yet that was exactly what was happening.

Except this time there was white silk and bridesmaids in dresses that would never see the light of day again. That had been Maggie's doing. Convinced that she'd never have another opportunity to be a bridesmaid, Maggie convinced Vixen that she absolutely had to, under no circumstances could she not, wear a bridesmaid dress and Delia needed a real wedding dress.

Even though there were no bridesmaids participating in the actual ceremony and Danielle and Eleanor had demurred, Vixen relented. The chosen wedding dress wasn't as bad considering Delia didn't have a say in the matter. It was a simple white silk gown with spaghetti straps and skimmed the ground with each step.

The bridesmaid dresses didn't fare as well. Maggie, not wanting Delia's second best friend to feel left out, insisted Geneva wear the same pastel pink taffeta monstrosity that had shoulders so puffy they might have been wings. Geneva had put it on like the good sport she was and even maintained a straight face. Until Maggie, who led the way from the porch to the group of males standing around Allard who was waiting for Delia, paused and curtsied to both Mia and Everest Lyall.

At that point, all bets were off and Delia had to help her friend across the lawn.

Mac beamed a smile at her when she finally stood next to Allard, who reached for her hand and grabbed it, like he was scared she might bolt. He read from an old book again, but this time the words were different. He didn't recite the oaths or list the obligations and duties. Instead he read about a time long ago, when dragons and griffins ruled the skies and the shifters.

The same entry he made Delia read when she first arrived at Broken Peak. Then he read from another section, one she hadn't heard before.

"The Great Shifters understood the Sentinels would need support. That it would be impossible to fulfill their duties without the unconditional love and devoted protection of mates. And so they spent the next several months, planting the seeds for a group of males who would be strong enough to care for their mates without interfering in their mates' duties.

"And so, six pairs of Great Shifters, set off across the land in search of the perfect candidates. Each pair, a dragon and griffin shifter, spent months observing the lesser shifters from a distance, but had little success with their endeavor. When they were near the brink of giving up and returning home in defeat, one of the pairs came to a realization. The ideal mate wouldn't be found in the sons of fathers, but the sons of mothers.

"Word spread to all the pairs and instead of looking for the qualities they desired in the Alpha males of packs, they turned their attention to the Alpha females. Soon, each of the pairs found their ideal candidate. Strong in heart, iron in will, and fierce in thought.

"Within each of their bloodlines was planted a kernel of the Great Shifters magic. A blend of both dragons and griffins to enhance their innate traits.

"Under different circumstances these males could have been Alphas in their own right. Instead, they would be the Sentinels' Sentinels. Guardians, protectors, defenders, and lovers fated to stand next to the Sentinels for as long as they both lived."

Mac closed the book and raised his head, his gaze capturing all the witnesses to the ceremony.

From the shocked expressions plastered across everyone's face, they'd never heard those words before. Not Eleanor, who spent all her spare time with her nose in the journals. Not Delia's parents, who had their own version of the legends. Not Delia's brother, who would eventually become the leader of all the wolf shifters. Not even Vixen, who was finally ten steps behind, along with everyone else.

No one spoke for several minutes.

"Wait, that's not fair. I'm supposed to be the only one with dragon stuff inside them!" Maggie's protest broke through the silence and woke everyone from their shock.

They all began speaking at once, questioning Mac, questioning the words themselves. The cacophony of words made no sense, and Mac just leaned back on his heels and chuckled. Waiting for everyone to settle down. Which didn't happen for another ten minutes.

Delia glanced over at Allard, who hadn't stopped smiling since she'd stepped outside the Lodge's front door.

"Why are you grinning like that?"

He pressed his hands to her cheeks and bent his head down until his lips brushed against hers. "Remember what I said to you when you first stepped onto Broken Peak Pack territory?"

"You said a lot of things."

"I said I wouldn't mate you until it wasn't because of an agreement."

"Oh, that part." Delia's cheeks flushed at the memory of her body's response to those words and from the fluttering of the butterflies and the tingles running through her body, nothing had changed.

"Yeah, that part." Allard kissed her, keeping it chaste out of respect for the audience present. "I love you, Delia, whether it was arranged or fated, I love you."

"I love you too, Allard."

"I know."

This time, when he kissed her, he didn't care who might witness their intimacy. His soft lips pressed against hers and his nose rubbed hers as he tilted his head. The tip of his tongue brushed against her lips until she opened her mouth. Allard pulled her against him, holding her just where he wanted and deepened the kiss.

He didn't stop kissing her, not even when someone coughed.

An hour later they all gathered in the Lodge's kitchen, sitting around the table and sharing the food piled high on the island and drinking from Mac's never ending stash of moonshine.

The females talked about the reception the Lyalls planned on hosting in Chicago for the newly mated pair and the potential guest list. The males spoke about security measures and pack politics, doing their best to avoid being dragged into the decision tree surrounding what types of food should be served.

Allard looked over at Tevin, who'd been remarkably silent since the mating ceremony.

"What's up?"

Tevin lifted his drink to his mouth and finished half the glass of moonshine in two swallows. "I'm next."

"What?" Finley joined in. "You're next for what?"

"Mating. I'm next."

"Well, yeah, we figured eventually you'd find your mate, and with the way it's been working so far, she'd just show up someday and that would be that." Finley looked over Tevin's head at Allard. "Although, I don't think any of us expected Allard's mate to be arranged."

"It's not a bad thing when it happens." Allard ignored the silent condemnation that he hadn't shared the arranged mating or his reason for coming to Broken Peak with Finley. Instead, he looked around the room until his gaze settled on Delia. His no longer fake mate and very real mate. "You know when Eleanor pulls out one of her puzzles and we all pretend to hate doing it, but secretly hope we're the one who gets to put that last piece in?"

"We do?" Finley asked.

Allard ignored Finley's comment. Again. "It's like that final piece fitting into place and you realize just what it means to be content."

"It's like everything is right in the world." Leighton added.

"Like you found something you didn't even realize you were missing," said Jackson.

"When you find your mate, or she finds you, everything inside you settles into place." Finley finally got on board with the conversation.

"At the risk of sounding like a movie from the 90s, it's a feeling of completion." Lennon, who spent most of the night glaring at Allard for daring to kiss his sister, said it best.

"Yeah," Allard gazed across the room at Delia. "She completes me."

TURN THE PAGE FOR *BROKEN CROWN EXTRAS,* INCLUDING

The official, Jules Crisare-Sanctioned "What Kind of Shifter are You?" Quiz

An excerpt from the next Broken Peak novel, *BROKEN WITCH*

And More!

THE OFFICIAL "WHAT KIND OF SHIFTER ARE YOU?" QUIZ

You've read Broken Hero and laughed at the antics of the Broken Peak Pack and cheered when Bray claimed Vixen and accidentally on purpose released the Griffin lurking inside of her. Right? I mean maybe you didn't do all those things, but let's just pretend you have. Now, I bet you're wondering where you'd fit in the pack. Would you be a wolf shifter? Or a griffin shifter? Or maybe another kind of shifter entirely. Well, you no longer have to wonder. In the short time it takes you to answer the questions below, you'll find out what kind of shifter you are.

WHAT SHIFTER AM I?

(If you want to find out what kind of shifter your partner is, replace "you" with "he/she/they". Depending on the result, you might want to keep it to yourself.)

1. **When Vixen and Bray invite you to a barbecue at Broken Peak, you:**

   a. Hide in the woods and hope no one finds you

   b. Show up earlier and be the last to leave and drink the most moonshine

2. **Vixen asks you to steal a shifter artifact from a private collector who refuses to sell (there's no chance of getting caught), you:**

   a. Tell her no way

   b. Tell her sure, why not

3. **Vixen thinks you should find a mate, you:**

   a. Go out with whoever Mac recommends, and of course they're a perfect match, so you agree.

   b. Create profiles on shifter-r-us with the rest of Broken Peak Pack and go out on group dates so your friends can give you instant advice. Plus, if they don't like your friends, they aren't for you.

4. War passed a new ordinance, barring all concealed weapons, even daggers, you:

    a. Don't bring the dagger Vixen got for you into town and leave it at home instead

    b. Ignore the ordinance, besides it's not like you go to War all that often

5. After a long day chasing down false alarms that led no where followed by a double dose of training from Vixen, you just want to go home and fall into bed, but your best friend sends a text, asking if you want to go out for dinner in thirty minutes, you:

    a. Call them back right away, since you plan on venting and your best friend is a great listener

    b. Ignore the message and call your friend back the next morning, you plan on spending the night alone with your favorite book

6. While walking through the park late at night with no one around, you see a new "Keep Off Grass" sign, you:

    a. Complain to yourself, but avoid walking on the grass

    b. Yank the sign out, throw it into the trees, then gleefully hop around on the grass since there's no more sign to stop you

ANSWERS

1. a=1, b=0

3. a=0, b=1

4. a=1, b=0

5. a=0, b=1

6. a=1, b=0

Add up your points! Have the number? Great, now if you scored:

0-1 GRIFFIN
Always up for a group hunt or hanging out with the pack, even if it means exploring forbidden territory.

2 WOLF
You take every opportunity to spend time with your friend and pack and always obey your Alpha.

3-4 COYOTE
You don't mind occasionally hanging out with friends, but prefer to spend most of your time alone with your still and never let something like rules get in the way of doing something.

5-6 BEAR
You're the strong and silent type, always ready to help your few close friends you have as long as your aren't breaking any rules.

AN EXCERPT FROM THE NEXT BROKEN PEAK PACK NOVEL, *BROKEN WITCH*

Tevin is the only member of Broken Peak Pack without a mate and doesn't want one. He's fine with the one-night stands that lead nowhere. And then he finds Cassandra. She's not like any of the others - strong, independent, elegant, and sexy. Everything he and his wolf want, even if it's only for one night. With her life in jeopardy, fate and love face the danger. Will Broken Peak lose its witch and Tevin lose his mate. Or can Tevin keep the woman he loves safe?

Tevin strode into the Dirty Whistle and bit back the urge to groan. The couples surrounding him made the trip to the bar about as thrilling as a root canal. Not that Tevin had ever had a root canal, but he heard about them from others. At least they had gone to a bar, and he could spend the evening drinking.

A lot, if he was going to get through the evening without gagging.

When Allard handed back the beers to the rest of the pack, Tevin snatched two, then headed towards one of the few empty tables in the bar. Not that the Dirty Whistle was known as a sit-down establishment, but they only had a handful of high-tops. That a table was available was a fucking miracle.

Even better, it was in a corner and gave Tevin and the others a clear view of the room and the door.

It didn't take a rocket scientist to figure out something was up. Since Vixen's arrival at Broken Peak, none of the males had ventured to a bar for a relaxing evening in town. Tevin might have sneaked out on a few nights, but that was only after Danielle, Leighton's mate, arrived and added several layers of security to the pack.

"I. Love. Costco!" Maggie jumped around and Tevin looked away from her enthusiasm.

There was only so much of Maggie's unbridled joy that he could take, and no amount of beer in the world could help.

The others shared stories about the pack with Delia, and Tevin finished his first bottle of beer. Yeah, it was definitely going to be a multiple drink night. Maybe he could slip away to the bar and get a shot of something.

But then, alcohol didn't really have the same effect on shifters as it did on humans, and Tevin would need to drink a few bottles of bourbon in less than an hour to get as drunk as he needed to be.

Aw, crap, they were kissing now.

Tevin rubbed the heels of his hand against his eyes, sort of wishing that he could erase the image from his retinas.

Gratefully, Finley intervened. "We need more beer!"

And the new happy couple ventured back to the bar, leaving Tevin to consider how miserable life in the pack would be.

As far as Tevin could tell, he had two options. Stay at Broken Peak and be miserable, or leave and hopefully find a pack who was in need of an Alpha. That was the whole reason he came to Broken Peak to begin with. No Alpha wanted an Alpha in their pack that wasn't their own son.

That was why he was sent away in the first place. After his parents died in a car crash, the Alpha of his pack kicked him out. He wasn't even twelve years old and living on the street. For a year, Tevin did the best he could to survive. The only reason he was still alive and hadn't gone feral was because a female shifter found him and sent him to Mac, who promptly dropped Tevin off at Bray's front door.

As shitty as life was at Broken Peak with all the couples, it was a hell of a lot better than wandering in the world on his own.

Movement in Tevin's peripheral vision yanked him out of his melancholy, and he turned his attention to the man talking with Delia and Allard.

The man was unfamiliar, but he spoke with Allard as though they knew one another.

Tevin narrowed his eyes and took a deep breath. No unfamiliar scents from fur. However, there was a slightly odd scent of magic. And not like the not-human magic that Vixen had. This was old magic.

The last time he remembered smelling old magic in the air was right before the female came and picked him up off the street.

"What is it?" Finley asked.

"Nothing. Just thought I saw someone I recognized."

"Who?" Maggie's head spun around as she scanned the bar, but Finley wrapped his arm around her neck before she drew attention to the rest of the pack standing at the table.

"Don't worry about it, Pocket. This was Tevin's favorite hangout. I'd be surprised if he didn't see someone he knew here."

Tevin kept his gaze locked on the man as he turned away from Allard and Delia and melted into the crowd.

Unfortunately Tevin's excuse didn't prevent the litany of questions the rest of the pack shot out at Delia and Allard as soon as they returned.

When Allard didn't answer any questions about the man with the old Magic and Delia changed the subject, Tevin shifted around the table, so he had a better view of the bar. He wasn't certain why he expected it. Maybe it was his wolf who alerted him, but he wasn't surprised when the bell above the door rang. He was the last of his pack to look at the door.

Three males stood in front of the door and scented the air. Just as the five males from Broken Peak were doing.

"Five to three."

Of course, Leighton would be the one spoiling for a fight. And from the looks of the males, they could handle five males. They probably would lose, but not before inflicting a lot of damage. The best action was not to fight, but explaining that to Leighton would fall on deaf ears.

"Excuse me." The female's voice was deep and husky and sent a tingle down Tevin's spine.

Shit. He hadn't seen her naked body, and he wanted a taste of her.

"I said, excuse me."

The female pushed through the wall of males and emerged on the other side in full view of the entire room.

Fuck him. She looked as good as she sounded. Tall, like really tall, since the top of her head hit somewhere between the males' noses and chins. Her long blond hair fell down past her shoulders. And whad'ya know? Her body was rocking, too. All curves and swells. She looked like she came right out of one of those old movies.

"Didn't your mamas teach you boys any manners?" She didn't wait for a response before sashaying her way through the crowd to the bar. "Sheesh, you'd think you'd been born in a barn."

And just like that, the night turned from a boring love fest into a different kind of love fest. "Am I needed here? Or do you all think you can handle this. Because a woman is standing over at the bar who has my name written all over her."

"Yeah, go for it."

Allard gave Tevin the okay, and he grabbed both his beers then headed toward the delightful woman. "Don't wait for me, I'll make my own way home."

After he spent most of the night with the blond, because there was no way he wouldn't find a way to spend as much time as he could with her.

The way she waved to get the bartender's attention, all bent over the bar with her ass up in the air drove Tevin wild. And then the female had the audacity to kick up a leg, and every man within a ten-foot radius eyed her.

Nope. Wasn't happening. Not if Tevin had anything to do with it.

ACKNOWLEDGMENTS

Sitting down to write an acknowledgment page is much like making an acceptance speech at an award's show. It's more than likely that you will forget someone and then have to spend hours on the phone apologizing for the misstep. And God help you, if it's your mother. So, I should probably get that one out of the way first, right? I need to acknowledge my parents, especially my mother, who have supported me and define the phrase unconditional love.

I must thank the readers of Broken Peak Pack and the Sentinels of the Silver Orb for their patience and understanding during the delays while finding the best story for Delia and Allard.

I am ever grateful to Cassandra. If I was part of a team, she'd be the coach, GM, and manager. Without her, Broken Peak would never be the world it currently is.

Chan, she's a pillar of unconditional support and a reminder that I am not a complete and total hack when the insecurity hits and I spiral into the dreaded impostor syndrome.

Finally, and of course not least, the wonderful individuals who are responsible for the creation of the collector's edition of the Broken Peak Pack Omnibus: Kasey S., Sherry M., Meg M., Pyndan, Erin C., Rhel, Kieran, Rafael P., Sarah, and Melanie B. Little did they know that by supporting one little Kickstarter, they'd find a permanent spot on my acknowledgments page.

ABOUT THE AUTHOR

Jules Crisare loves writing sexy shifter romances. The growly and dominant males of Broken Peak and the Silver Sentinels are the ones bending to the strong wills of the smart heroines who cross their paths. Seriously, only strong heroines need apply to capture the hearts of these sexy alphas. Get your shifter loving fingers ready to turn those pages and explore the world of the Sentinels of the Silver Orb.

www.JCrisare.com